Alison Dye

Alison Dye was born and brought up in New York State, and worked in New York for several years before moving with her small daughter to Ireland in 1987, where she now teaches at Trinity College, Dublin. In 1989, her story 'On the Development of a Free Spirit' won the *Stand* International Short Story Competition, and in 1994 she had her first novel published, THE SENSE OF THINGS, which was shortlisted for the Whitbread First Novel Award.

To Auntie Cindy
I couldn't decide what
to get you until it hit me
that the best present would
be the one that I'd like
for myself! a Book!
I've been eying this for
quite a while and it
looks good.
Love Christy
xxoo

SCEPTRE

Also by Alison Dye

The Sense of Things

Memories of Snow

ALISON DYE

SCEPTRE

First published in 1995 by Hodder and Stoughton
A division of Hodder Headline PLC
A Sceptre Paperback

10 9 8 7 6 5 4 3 2 1

A CIP catalogue record for this book is available from the British Library

ISBN 0 340 64725 6

Typeset by Palimpsest Book Production Limited,
Polmont, Stirlingshire
Printed and bound in Great Britain by
Cox and Wyman Ltd, Reading, Berkshire

Hodder and Stoughton
A division of Hodder Headline PLC
338 Euston Road
London NW1 3BH

For my mother and father

1

Private Raymond Smith rolled onto his knees and swept the crusty snow to the edge of the tarpaulin lining the floor of his foxhole, four a.m., 15 December, 1944. He had been awake since the first sign of darkness, hours earlier. Bunched up beside him, his boyhood friend, Johnny Martin, was shuddering from the cold and crying in his sleep. Raymond could smell that Johnny had diarrhoea again.

Raymond pushed their rifles away and took off his gloves. Then he gripped a torch in his teeth and undid the straps of his canvas knapsack in the dim and wobbly light. He reached into the bag and removed a container made of two cooking pots sealed together at the rims with heavy tape, and bound with twine like a parcel. Raymond had shot off the pot handles and filed their jagged ends for packing, but he handled the invention carefully to avoid cutting himself or the knapsack.

His rigid fingers pulled at the rope with unexpected speed and dexterity. Raw and frozen, they were no longer attached to his body: he felt himself stand off to the side as they manipulated several neatly arranged knots like an efficient machine and pulled off the tape.

Using the back of one hand, Raymond then wound the twine and the tape into tight skeins which he placed in a pocket on the outside of the bag. The foxhole was small and he kept his elbows tucked into his sides as he worked.

He separated the halves of his makeshift shell and removed two thin, coarse blankets, a flannel shirt, and a pair of trousers, all tied together in a compact ball. He held each item against his face: everything was cold but still dry. He folded one of the blankets several times to make a cushion and patted the soft shirt around it. He dug into his knapsack again and took out a roll of waxed paper – traded in the mess tent for cigarettes – and ripped off a square.

His teeth had begun to chatter badly, so he spat the torch to the ground and switched it off.

Johnny was delirious now. Raymond removed his friend's helmet and his cold, damp blanket. He slipped his hand carefully under the boy's head. He laid the cushion on top of the waxed paper and lowered Johnny's face sideways onto the flannel.

As the first grey light of morning began to hover over the Schnee Eifel, Raymond finished cleaning Johnny. He dressed him in fresh trousers and covered him with the extra blanket as he slept quietly. He wrapped the soiled clothing in waxed paper for washing the next day.

Raymond jammed his hands into his armpits, pressing and massaging the deadened fingers before edging them back into his wet gloves.

He picked up one of the rifles and adjusted his helmet. His heart was pounding, his breathing clipped and pained from the cold. He was exhausted, and yet he could not stop his eyes darting along the Front, straining to penetrate the miserable daylight.

An ominous, pleading sorrow that seemed vaguely familiar had the strange effect of warming Raymond. Since the crossing from Southampton, he had been aware of nothing but a gnawing dread in his stomach, as if it were held in the grip of an inexorably tightening fate. In this dread, too, Raymond registered bereavements of another time, of another Godforsaken plain such as this, whose geography lay camouflaged beyond the horizon of his now-frozen consciousness. Apart from these unnameable sensations, Raymond had been aware of no physical or emotional existence for days.

In his sleep, Johnny began to kick: he was trying to run.

Completely alone, Raymond grew restless and confused, lost in a maze of dimly lit crossroads as one tremor in his body converged on another in a hopeless search for an unimpeded path.

He bolted to his feet, jumped up and down, slapped his thighs and arms, jogged in place.

In seconds he was tight and alert again, totally consumed in searching the fog for signs of the enemy.

Twenty-four hours later, in the early morning of Saturday, 16 December, 1944, a dense fog moved south from Arnhem and east from St Vith. By three a.m., Raymond Smith's position on the seven-mile-wide Losheim Gap in the Schnee Eifel, the snow plateau, was clogged with a thick grey mist.

Surrounding this high ground in the Ardennes forest were acres of stalwart, elderly spruce and Scots pines. Ribbons of wet snow draped over the wide, leafy branches, bending them into graceful arcs.

Below the plateau, in a deeply cut valley cradling the Our River, stands of oak-birch and beech trees sheltered rich fields near the river basin. Here, in peacetime, farmers cultivated oats, rye, trefoil and potatoes. Red and roe deer, wild boar and rabbits still inhabited the forests and grassy farmlands in small numbers; the dairy cows and sheep which normally grazed in the protected valleys were gone. The Rhine lay fifty miles to the east, across the Belgian-German border.

For weeks, visibility in the area had been poor. Raymond, Johnny Martin, and the other men of the American 108th Infantry Division – young troops recently arrived from New York – saw nothing of what lay below or beyond the Schnee Eifel. They retained little sense of the rugged terrain of the Ardennes – hills, uplands, ravines, dense woods, and twisting roads – which they had crossed in convoys from France on 12 December.

For days, torrential rain had poured down on the soldiers as they crouched in open trucks headed for the Schnee Eifel. By the time they reached their destination, many were sick.

At three a.m. on the 16th, the temperature suddenly dropped. Fresh snow began to fall on the soldiers' encampment, burying tents, tanks, and guns. Exhausted men, cramped in foxholes, nearly froze. To the west, the villages of St Vith, Malmedy, Vielselm, and Meyerode were obscured by snow and icy rain.

Lacking any previous experience of combat, the soldiers did not know that this hazardous topography and blinding weather would gradually cut them off from base camps and commanders. Much of the fighting would be reduced to the random actions of small groups of men, far from the support and guidance of their units at the front line.

Raymond and Johnny's regiment, and one other, were placed in forward positions in the Losheim Gap. A third held the rear. This assignment was calculated to pose little threat to the inexperienced troops, and would prepare them gently for the coming months: the Allies were about to push across the Rhine, link up with the Russian army, and end the war.

Germany was presumed crippled, on the verge of defeat, and incapable of mounting a counter-offensive.

2

Grandfather Willard Racket awoke, Tuesday, 30 August, 1949, Halfmoon, New York, Albany-Rennsalaer County.

He hurled himself from the wobbly metal bed and staggered to his oak bureau, head spinning around the shabby bedroom of his stone farmhouse.

The old man fumbled with his longjohns. He had lost more than ten pounds since his daughter's admission to the hospital in a coma on 19 August. He had dozed fitfully on plastic waiting room chairs with his small granddaughter Lucy and their neighbour, Hazel Martin, until, finally, on the 26th, Barbara Jean died.

He had eaten little and drunk only black coffee. Now the seat of the longjohns drooped and the cuffs spilled over his feet onto the floor. The top of the dingy underclothes gave scant comfort to his shoulders, which held the garment like a hanger.

Grasping the waist of the pants with one hand, Grandfather Racket yanked open the top drawer of his bureau with the other. He fumbled through socks, undershirts, and more longjohns. He flung these around the room until he found a bundle of papers and envelopes tied with burlap threads.

His bony chest heaved and flattened as he breathed. He sat down on the edge of the bed and pinched the corner of an envelope which he carefully extracted from the pile on his lap. He opened it. His heart pounded. He removed and unfolded a piece of paper.

The old man held it close to his face as if the bright sunlight flooding his room were a spreading darkness. He inspected every line, his eyes pulled left, right, and back again across the page as if drawn and guided by magnets. He smiled, folded the paper, and reinserted it into the envelope which he then placed carefully on his right thigh. He repeated his search eleven times until three more documents were balanced on his leg.

Clutching these, he sprang from the bed and stood to his full height, still five-foot-ten at seventy-eight. He combed his free hand through thick white hair that had once been black. His straight nose and high cheekbones were more prominent since his daughter's illness and death, and his head and face now had the look of a hawk.

His blue eyes darted around the room and confirmed he had overlooked nothing. He pulled his worn leather belt from the trousers at the end of his bed and bound this around the waist of the longjohns.

He opened the door. He surveyed the hall up and down and saw no sign of his son or daughter-in-law.

He ran stiff-legged like a wind-up soldier the length of this hall, barefoot, to the living room. He did not stop there, only turned his head for an instant and saw the open casket containing the body of his daughter at the far end of the room. He pushed through a door which would take him into the front hall of the house and out.

3

The old man shivered up the dirt road. The sun had not yet softened the sharp morning gusts, nor the stiff, unyielding ground beneath his feet.

Grandfather Racket was numb to the sticks and pebbles jabbing at his leathery soles. He hobbled as fast as he could away from the house towards the barn and its towering thirty-foot high silo. His farmhand, Raymond Smith, lived in a bungalow just below the barn, beside a cluster of oak and pine trees which did little to protect the ramshackle dwelling from Halfmoon's harsh winter winds and snow.

He banged on the frame of Raymond's screen door. There was no reply. He opened it. He dropped the bundle of papers on the ground and began slamming his hand against the inner door. He raced to the one window provided on the side of the house and pressed his face to it.

Raymond lay crumpled on his cot in a drunken sleep. He was fully clothed in denim overalls, tee shirt, and boots. He snored restlessly. The usually clean and ordered room, brightly painted and decorated in contrast to the sullen exterior, was a sea of garbage.

'Wake up!' screamed Grandfather Racket, pounding on the fragile pane of glass. He tore back to the door. It was stuck. He picked up his papers, pushed hard, and stumbled in.

'They're going to take her,' wept the old man. He hurled himself at Raymond's bed and clutched at the man's shoulders.

The tall, muscular young farmer rolled on to his back. He did not open his eyes. His thick auburn hair was matted, uncombed for days.

'That's right,' he slurred. He rolled his tongue around dry, swollen lips.

'Do you hear what I'm sayin', Raymond?' pleaded Grandfather Racket. 'You got to listen to me. They're going to take Lucy. But we can stop them, I've got papers, you've got papers, we'll get a lawyer. Wake up!'

'Okay,' replied Raymond, and fell asleep again.

Grandfather Racket struck the young man across the face.

'I'll do it myself, you good-for-nothing! What use are you?'

He reeled out of the cabin. The seat of his longjohns flapped at his behind. He repeatedly hauled up the belt at the frayed waistband and let go, bobbing up and down until he reached the house.

4

Howard Racket paced the lopsided floor of the guest room, 7:48 a.m. In three hours the minister and guests would arrive for his sister's funeral. He was smoking a Lucky Strike.

He wore a shiny blue ladies' kimono and matching slippers, a gift set from his wife Shirley. He tightened the sash of the kimono, then had to let it out again.

'I don't know why you bought me this thing. I'm too goddamn fat. I look like a pear.'

Shirley turned in the bed and looked at him.

'I bought it because you look very handsome in bright blue, How-How. I have eyes. And I love the way your squishy bottom hangs out the back. To me you're not fat.'

'I thought I heard Pops get up,' said Howard. 'I'm sure I heard something.'

'Howie, please. Let me sleep. We have a hectic day ahead. Why don't you lie down and relax?'

'I can't relax. There's a lot to figure out.' He puffed on his cigarette.

'All the little details will fall into place, honey,' mumbled Shirley. 'Your Shir-Shir will take care of everything.'

Her voice trailed off and she was asleep. Her sparkling blonde bouffant hairdo was held in place by a net and dozens of pins. As Shirley dozed, she kept shifting her head on the pillow as the pins prodded her scalp. Her white silk nightgown blended seamlessly with her alabaster skin.

'I'm the only person who doesn't lose weight when he smokes,' said Howard.

He sat down on the edge of the bed and held his head.

'Oh, God, Babs,' he said to his dead sister. 'You've really done it this time.'

Suddenly Shirley sat up.

'Wasn't that a refreshing sleep,' she said. She propped herself on an elbow and reached over to the bedside table for her lipstick. She applied it liberally, with her chin up, squinting into a small pocket mirror.

'You amaze me,' said Howard.

'Have you been crying again? What did I tell you?' She wagged a coy finger at Howard as she tipped her face from side to side in the mirror.

'I can't believe it,' said Howard. He buried his face in Shirley's lap.

'Be careful of my nightie, How-How. Don't stain it.'

She pushed his head off her legs and put an arm around him.

'Come up here, on my shoulder.'

She patted Howard's head.

'Look how that sister of yours is making you suffer. She brought it on herself and never once thought of how the rest of us would feel.'

Howard leapt from the bed.

'She *died*. She *died*. You think she wanted to? You think she felt like it? It's not a trip to the supermarket, Shirley. Have you lost your mind? She got an embolism.'

'What she had was a *stroke*, Howie. That's more or less the situation. All the activity, the jumping around, not cooperating. One thought after another. And having a child with no husband. The brain was under pressure, Howard, that's why I keep telling you to relax. You're her brother. It could be in the family and end me up a widow, that selfishness. She came and went as she pleased and the other day she just went, no regard for anyone else.'

'I hate you, Shirley. I hate you!' screamed Howard.

'That's it, get it out,' replied Shirley, applying powder to her nose. 'Don't let emotion build up.'

Howard cinched the bathrobe sadistically around his waist. He threw down the butt of his cigarette and ground it into the floor with his foot.

'I paid a dollar twenty-nine for that outfit. How could you? Those beautiful slippers . . .'

'You're a pain in the ass,' he yelled. 'You don't stop for a minute.'

'A dollar twenty-nine. I'm never buying you another present as long as I live, the thanks I get.'

'And last week you tell me we're going to take the child. Ha! A four-year-old girl. I don't know the first goddamn thing about children. And I don't want to. I hate them.'

'Howard Racket, I am shocked at you. Are you telling me you would turn away your own sister's child? After we bought all those nice toys and had the room painted.'

'That's exactly what I'm telling you,' he said. '*You* bought all that crap, Shirley. *You*. Not *we*. The only "we" in it was the goddamn money. And for what? A pain in the ass, that's what. I'm leaving you, Shirley, this time I really mean it, you've gone too far. I've had enough of your big ideas.'

He wrenched open the bedroom door and stormed out. The walls shook. He opened the door from the outside and slammed it again.

'There! Now you know how it feels.'

'I do not,' Shirley shouted back.

Howard took a deep breath. His legs were shaking. He closed his eyes and tipped his head back against the wall. He clenched and unclenched his fists, took another breath, and opened his eyes. He stared at the ceiling. Then he turned and opened the door.

Shirley was sitting on the bed, hands folded on her lap. Tears glistened in her eyes.

'Howard, I am truly sorry I insulted your dead sister. I couldn't stand her.' She held out her arms. 'But I love *you*.'

Howard went to the bed and pulled her up.

'We'll take Lucy. It's what you've always wanted. I shouldn't have yelled.'

'Howard, I firmly and completely believe it is my fault I never got pregnant.'

'You don't have to say that,' he replied.

'I mean it. You always felt bad about your sperm and you shouldn't have. I know that's why you got upset just then.'

Howard's face turned red.

'I hear you in the bathroom, How-How. You do that so you can look at them, don't you?'

'Shirley. Please.'

'I thought so.'

She slowly undid the sash around Howard's waist, and opened the kimono. She eased her hand between his thick, soft thighs.

'Do you like that, Howie?'

He nodded.

'I'm sorry for all those things I said about Babs. It's been so sudden and upsetting. Especially for you.'

She massaged, standing. Then she drew him to the bed, lifted her nightgown, and pulled him down.

'Now, How, now!'

'Get ready, Shir-Shir. I'm going to do it to you.'

The sequins he had put on her hair at bedtime flew out from under her hairnet as Howard flopped up and down on his wife.

'How about *this*.'

'Oh, Howard, you are great!'

'Damn right, Shirley, damn right. I bet the old man can't do *this*.'

5

Grandfather Racket took a breath that pained his ribs. He opened the front door of the farmhouse, crouched, and stepped silently inside. He heard nothing, he felt no movement. He crept into the living room.

There he became aware of the voices of his son and daughter-in-law in the kitchen.

Clutching his packet, he tiptoed the length of the living room. He did not recall that his daughter's body was laid out in front of him as he stole past the coffin. He placed his ear against the kitchen door.

'We'll never convince him,' said Howard. 'Pops will never agree and we can't say anything to Lucy until he does. She'll just get confused. Maybe we should give it a little more time, Shirley, not take her tonight after all. What if he makes trouble?'

'I'm ashamed of you, Howard,' said Shirley. 'You sound like a frightened old man.'

'I'm telling you, Shirley, this is a nightmare. It's not going to be simple.'

'And I am telling *you* the last thing that girl needs is nervous leadership. We must display confidence at all times. Your poor father doesn't know what he's talking about. He's just upset and reacting every which way.'

'But we haven't been able to find a will, Shirley. Don't

you see what I'm saying? If Babsie left no will, maybe he's entitled. They've been living with him since Lucy was born.'

'Oh, poo. The man can't think straight for two minutes, How-How. We'll get a doctor to sign something. Anyway, it won't be necessary. He'll back down.'

'He never backed down in his life. And who the hell is Lucy's father, Shirley? What if some guy comes along? What about that? That's been on my mind all week.'

'Nobody's coming along, Howard, forget it. Whoever it might have been is long gone, a one-night stand. That was the extent of any commitment your sister ever made. She told us at the time she had no idea who it was. Somebody in Akron where she worked at that rubber factory during the war.'

'Yeah? Well, you know what I think?'

'There is nothing to think about, Howard. I don't want to hear another word.'

'I think it's Raymond.'

'You do not.'

'I've always thought that.'

'Don't be ridiculous, you never mentioned one word to me. Pull yourself together and face your responsibilities. I won't have you running away like a big baby. Raymond Smith indeed.'

'Come on, Shirley. Quit lying to yourself. My father has more secrets than the FBI. And Babs was just like him. What they didn't want people to know, no one knew.'

'Not around here, Howard. Don't flatter them. People in these towns know everything and tell everything, and no one has ever mentioned one word about Raymond Smith being the father. I would have heard. In fact, you will recall that what I *did* hear was it was some soldier in Akron home on leave. So that's that.'

'No,' replied Howard, 'that isn't that. I'm telling you.'

'He was in France or someplace,' said Shirley, 'wherever the war was that year. He wasn't home in bed with *her*. For God's sake, Howard, she was in Akron for over two years.'

Howard paused.

'Listen to me, Shirley. Because we'd better face it now. Raymond was drafted around September 1944. Right? Babsie came back just before he went overseas. Pops went wild. He and Hazel had persuaded the authorities to stay away from Raymond after Pearl Harbor, but then they insisted. A big call-up, everybody taken. The last push to beat the Krauts, etc. etc., so Babsie came home to work the farm. They were here together October-November, something like that, before he was shipped out.'

'Howard, it's not Raymond. Everybody said she went to Akron to get away from him. And no doubt had herself quite a time in the bargain. She could have been pregnant when she got back here from Ohio. They were all doing it in those places.'

'Think about it, Shirley. Think exactly when Babs came home, when he left, and when Lucy was born.'

'I don't want to,' replied Shirley.

'All I'm saying is what if. Because if I'm right, this will be a bigger mess than you think.'

'What if nothing. I'm not going to think about it.'

'But you *are* thinking about it. I can see it in your eyes. Why do you keep turning away from me like that? Because you don't want to face the fact that Lucy's father has been right under our noses all the time, and now, as usual, when you want something, you're determined to have it no matter what. Well, I say we give up before we get in any deeper. It's none of our business, let him have her.'

'No! Typical. We've already told Tyler Hughes to prepare the papers, and now you want to back down, slink away. You never stand up for anything. You don't think we can raise that beautiful child better than him? What rights has he got? And anyway, it's not him. You're making it up, it's what you always do, twist things around so you can avoid reality. Since 1944 she kept him on a string? Five years? Come on, Howard. Five years and he says nothing, demands nothing? Does all the work on this godforsaken farm just for a place to live?'

'Exactly,' replied Howard. 'A place to live near Babs and the child, provided he keeps quiet. He never had a home in his life, Shirley. And now Babsie's gone, maybe he starts talking. Admits he's the father and tries to claim Lucy. Maybe even tries to take over the farm.'

They looked at each other.

'No,' said Shirley. 'And that's final. When Pops gets up, you are going to tell him again that Lucy will be living in Little Hoosick with us.'

Howard looked up at the ceiling, shook his head, and laughed.

'It's Raymond, Babs, isn't it?' he called out. 'You never lost your touch, right to the end.'

'I don't want to hear any more, Howard. This is not a laughing matter. We've been through this type of thing for years and you are not going to succeed, you will not wear me down.'

'When was the last time I wore you down?' said Howard.

'That's not funny,' snapped Shirley. 'I am ending this discussion. You have your instructions and I expect them to be carried out. That girl needs us. And now I am going to re-arrange these cupboards. That sister of yours had everything in the wrong place.'

'Jesus Christ, Shirley, who cares about goddamn cupboards?'

'And by the way, while we're on the subject, I don't see why the business should pick up the tab for solid mahogany. Your sister wouldn't know quality if it walked in front of her. Anyway, I thought we agreed, display her in the mahogany, bury her in the pine. Then last night when we laid her out you tell me we're going all the way with mahogany. The Racket Funeral Home is not just you, Howard. It's me. And it was my father's before me, my father who said you could change the name after he died. If you recall.'

'How could I forget,' sighed Howard.

'So I want everything to be joint, just like we always do. Joint decisions right down the line. Therefore we bury her in the pine.'

'She's my sister, Shirley, for God's sake. You want me to stand up for something, I'll stand up for something. Mahogany. Mahogany!' shouted Howard. 'Are you goddamn deaf?'

Shirley leaned over and slapped him across the face. 'She *was* your sister. Then and now are two different things. You'll confuse the child's thinking.'

'Shut up,' cried Howard. 'Just shut up. Babs *is* my sister. *Is*.'

'Howard Racket, you leave the room this minute if you have to bawl. You're just overtired. And keep your voice down, you'll wake the child. I only gave her one phenobarbital last night.'

Grandfather Racket straightened himself, shoved open the door, and stepped into the kitchen.

6

'What is it you vultures don't want that child to hear?'

Howard and Shirley stared.

'Why, hello, Pops,' said Shirley. 'We didn't know you were up.'

'Of course not,' he replied. 'I don't make noise like some people. And while we're at it, cut out that calling me Pops.'

He pulled up a chair and sat at the table. He placed his papers on his lap.

'Get me a cup of coffee,' he said.

Howard moved carefully toward the counter, watching his father from the corner of his eye.

'I don't want any,' said Shirley. 'And Pops has had enough. I don't know what it is with all this coffee lately. Pops needs to eat. How about a peanut butter sandwich?' she shouted.

'I'm not deaf, you bitch!'

Howard came to the table with two cups of coffee. He sat down beside his father.

'She's only thinking of your health, Dad,' he said.

'She is not,' said Grandfather Racket.

'If he has a heart attack, Howie, it will be on your conscience, not mine. Pops has been told, especially this week he was told, go easy on the coffee, and what does he do? Drinks it day and night. He looks terrible.'

'Look at yourself,' said the old man, gulping the hot drink. 'Give me another cup, Howard. You make it nice. And I want a saltine.'

'You see, How-How, he's hungry.'

'I'm not hungry. Get me a goddamn saltine.'

'Pops, honey,' said Shirley, taking his arm, 'that coffee will rot your insides.'

'You'd like that, wouldn't you?' he replied.

'How-How, listen to him. He's not functioning, he's over-tired. We should talk now before he conks out.'

'There's nothing wrong with *me*,' said Grandfather Racket.

Howard planted his elbows on the table and massaged his forehead with jumpy fingertips. Shirley looked at him sternly.

'Howard,' she said, 'you know what you have to do.'

'Oh, for Christ sake, Shirley,' he replied.

'Nice marriage you got there, Howard,' said Grandfather Racket.

'Oh, shut up. The only thing we have to talk about is this question of what happens to Lucy.'

'You two made your position clear last night. Only I don't agree. So now I'm the problem, is that it?'

'Lucy needs a woman to mould her, Pops,' said Shirley. 'A mother. Me. Not that I'm bragging, but you can understand what I'm saying, can't you?'

'She doesn't need you for anything,' replied Grandfather Racket. 'And neither do I.'

'Dad,' said Howard, 'we have to pull together. For Lucy's sake. Listen to me. Please. Babsie is dead. I can't believe it, you can't believe it. But it's true. Lucy has got to have parents. She's got to have a normal life.'

'I believe it,' said Shirley. 'It was bound to happen.'

'Every time she saw *you* she got blood pressure,' shouted Grandfather Racket. 'When she didn't see *you* she was fine.'

'He's getting upset, Howard.'

'I'm not upset!'

'Get him a Kleenex, How-How.'

'Hold on, Dad,' said Howard.

Howard brought a box of tissues to the table. He pulled a chair close to his father and dabbed his eyes. Grandfather Racket sat as rigid as the cold cup in his hands. He stopped crying.

'That's my daughter you're talking about,' he said. 'And *her* daughter. They're mine. Get your mitts off them.'

'He's going to make himself sick, Howard. He's getting all red.'

'You're the ones making me sick.' Grandfather Racket spat back. 'Lucy lives with me and that's final. This is her house, any fool can see where she lives.'

'Pops,' said Shirley, 'don't be so selfish. We've always wanted children and unfortunately we have not been blessed in the normal way. You wouldn't want to take this chance away from us, would you? It's probably our last. Think of somebody else for once.'

'I knew when you married her,' said Grandfather Racket. 'I knew when you went off with this bitch.'

'What did you know?' roared Howard. He pushed his chair away from the table and rocketed to his feet.

'You'd amount to nothing, that's what I knew,' retorted Grandfather Racket. 'Mr Bigshot College Degree. You wouldn't work the farm when you should have. Oh, no. No real work for you. But then this bitch sees dollar signs on every acre and suddenly you want it. Didn't you just slobber, the two of you, at the thought of me in one of your cheap little caskets, a delectable little corpse. Well, there'll be nothing for you, so there. I'm still alive.'

Grandfather Racket jumped up and thumped his chest with his fist.

'See? The ticker is fine, the bones is fine. Pick at your

own carcass. And this farm belongs to *me*. *Me, me, me*. And so does Lucy!'

'All talk, old man,' sneered Howard. 'That's all you ever were, a big bag of wind, you never stopped. At me and at me and at me. I'm lucky I got through high school the way you worked me and cut me down, one stupid job after another on your precious stupid farm, just to remind me I was nobody and you were Big Mr Somebody. And you wonder why I left! Well, you're not the boss now, Dad. I'm in charge. And there'll be no more calling Shirley a bitch.'

'Bitch, bitch, bitch.'

'Oh, Howard,' sobbed Shirley, 'that word really hurts my feelings.'

'You think you can insult anybody you want!' screamed Howard. 'Don't you? And you think nobody will stand up to you.'

'So do it, Howard,' said Grandfather Racket. 'Stand up to me. What are you waiting for?'

'Oh, Pops,' sniffled Shirley. 'Howard is trying so hard not to take advantage of you. You're a weak old man.'

'What did I tell that bitch about calling me Pops?'

Howard collapsed into his chair. Grandfather Racket remained standing.

'If you try to take Lucy,' he said, 'I'll call the police and have you both arrested.'

'For Christ sake,' sighed Howard. 'We're trying to be reasonable. She can't live here. How will you manage? Think about it. The police will laugh at you.'

'Don't push me,' replied Grandfather Racket. 'I'll exercise my rights. You won't get away with it.'

'Rights, schmights,' said Shirley. 'You're not fit. She'll turn out like Babs.'

'Jealous, aren't you? She's the smartest girl in the school, just like her mother. And you think you're so great because your old man taught you how to pickle stiffs.'

'Jesus, Dad,' said Howard.

'It's all right,' replied Shirley. 'I am proud of my heritage, you mean old man. I can hold my head high. My father was the finest trade embalmer in Albany-Rennsalaer. Everyone knows it. He did all the best Presbyterians, and I was blessed that even though I had the handicap of being a girl he taught me the trade. He said I had the fingers for it, a real good feel. And I'll tell you, Pops, it's a big step up from farming. A *skill.* If you'd had your way, How-How would have amounted to nothing on this place. Mortuary science has stretched his mind.'

'Money has stretched his mind,' said Grandfather Racket. 'Preying on upset people. He hadn't got much of a mind to begin with.'

Howard groaned.

'So that's the end of it,' said Grandfather Racket. 'My little Lucy stays where she is, where she's happy.'

'Say something, Howard,' ordered Shirley.

'Look, Dad,' he said. 'It's not going to be like that any more. Don't you understand? Let's get it straight now so Lucy isn't confused later. I'm sorry. But I have as much right to her as you, and I'm married. I can give her a proper home.'

'You call a house full of dead bodies a proper home? Don't force my hand, Howard. I am trying to reason with you. Lucy has lived her whole life with me. Right here in this house. It's as simple as that.'

'What hand?' said Howard.

He looked at Shirley who quickly looked away.

'All right,' said Grandfather Racket. 'If that's the way you want it.'

He plunked his packet of papers into the centre of the table.

'These papers prove Lucy stays with me. You two nuts

got no rights and privileges. She don't go down to Little Hoosick to your graveyard business. End of discussion.'

Shirley stuck her tongue out at Grandfather Racket.

'Let me tell you I don't like the way you speak about my father's lifetime of hard work. Not one bit. And what about the *child's* feelings? Did you ever think about that? Do you ever put anyone else first? No. It's so obvious I can answer it myself. You're only thinking of what *you* want, as usual.'

She jabbed the table three times.

'Selfish, selfish, selfish. That's all you are.'

'It's not polite to poke the table,' yelled Grandfather Racket. 'That's my table you're poking.'

'You and your stupid table. Quit hurting my feelings!'

'Shirley, that's enough,' said Howard. 'Let's just talk about the thing.'

'Suits me fine,' said Grandfather Racket. 'First you two can cast your eyes on them papers. Then we'll talk.'

He separated four items from his packet and laid them out on the table. He remained standing.

'I hope you are prepared to discuss this rationally,' Howard said to his father. 'Because if not, there will be no discussion at all. Do I make myself clear?'

'This isn't a discussion,' replied the old man. 'I am presenting my evidence. These papers is my case against you.'

'Good Lord, Pops,' said Shirley, 'this isn't the United Nations, now is it?'

'And you ain't Eleanor Roosevelt,' said Grandfather Racket.

'Thank the Lord,' said Shirley. 'There's a real pill if I ever saw one. What I am trying to explain if you would stop interrupting is: we're a family. We're all talking together. It's not what's-his-name there, you know. What was his name, Howard? The one with the peace after the war, that big meeting in Malta.'

'Shirley, please,' said Howard.

'Churchill, that was it,' said Shirley. 'We're not Churchill and Stalin. It's just a family working on something together, Pops.'

'It is not,' said Grandfather Racket. 'We're not together on this. And it was Yalta, you stupid bitch. You don't hear the radio? You're not smart enough to raise this child.'

'Stop it!' Howard finally screamed. 'That's enough, both of you!'

Shirley took a deep breath.

'I know you're tired out, Pops,' she said. 'You haven't slept a wink. So I will have to be the one to rise above this. For the sake of the child.'

'I'm not tired,' said Grandfather Racket. 'Let's get on with my evidence.'

'I'll say sorry if you say sorry,' replied Shirley.

Grandfather Racket stuck his face out at Shirley.

'Howard, he won't say sorry. I'm not talking any more until he says it.'

'Good. Maybe we'll get someplace,' said Grandfather Racket.

'For Christ sake,' snapped Howard. 'This is supposed to be about Lucy. Show us your goddamn evidence and get it over with.'

Grandfather Racket picked up one of the pages on the table.

'My Last Will and Testament. Leaving everything to my beloved daughter, Barbara Jean Racket, under certain conditions which are none of your business, and anyway, she's dead before me. That's one.'

He carefully replaced the piece of paper.

'What?' said Howard, jumping up. 'You're crazy! You left the farm to Babs?'

'That's right,' replied Grandfather Racket. 'And the fine print says if she's dead before me everything goes to her daughter, Lucy Racket, my beloved granddaughter. You think I don't know how to get a lawyer?'

Shirley burst into tears. 'You cruel, cruel man! What does a child want with land?'

'She loves the place,' Grandfather Racket answered calmly. 'We probably got a historicalogical treasure or some such out there where them Indians lived. You'd put up a cemetery. Raymond and me will teach her to do cows, get in corn, slaughter the pigs, cut the hay, you name it. You going to do that work? No. You never did and you never will.'

'I'll contest it,' said Howard coldly. 'You're not fit. It's not your decision.'

'We'll see about that, won't we?' said the old man. 'And if I was you I would cut out that yelling in case Lucy might think you don't know what you're doin'. She ain't used to yellin'.'

Howard sank into a chair.

'Anyway,' he panted, 'that will doesn't prove anything. And I don't give one damn about this dump. You think I care? The whole place stinks of you. Just because Lucy inherits the farm doesn't mean you're the legal guardian, you ignoramus.'

'She's my heir,' said Grandfather Racket. 'That's a legal thing. That's the legal situation.'

Howard paused. He looked at the ceiling and took a deep breath.

'As I was saying,' continued Grandfather Racket. He held up another piece of paper and waved it first in Howard's face.

'Supporting evidence,' he said.

Howard took the thin sheet and glanced over it. He shook his head.

'It's proof,' said Grandfather Racket.

'It's junk,' said Howard, holding his head.

Shirley took the paper from Howard. She read it. She stared at Grandfather Racket.

'Your loan agreement with Sears Roebuck?' she said. 'The payment plan for your new Kelvinator?'

'That's right,' said Grandfather Racket. 'Just read the fine print. Right there. Signatures. Babsie's, mine, and Lucy's. We're a family, us three. Right there on that piece of paper it shows the family line. One missing leaves two. Her and me.'

'Oh, Pops,' sighed Shirley. 'Don't do this.'

'You're the ones doing it,' said Grandfather Racket.

'It's over,' said Howard. 'Finished. There's no more of the way things were, Dad. You aren't capable of raising Lucy. We are. I can't let you go on.'

'And who has *been* raising her?' said Grandfather Racket. 'Answer me that! Who has looked after her all these years with the mother? When the mother went out to work, the mother went out shopping, the mother took classes. Who was sittin' home with the baby?'

He picked up the third piece of paper and read out loud.

'"This note will confirm my intention that should anything happen to me, my daughter Lucy is given over to the custody of my father. This is my wish and intention. Signed: Barbara Jean Racket."'

'Is it notarised?' asked Shirley, her eyes darting to Howard.

'Don't need to be,' said the old man.

'Yes, it does,' said Howard. 'Let me see that.'

'I'll just hold on to this if you don't mind,' said Grandfather Racket. 'You heard all you need to know.'

'You're damn right,' said Howard, 'and it's not worth shit. It's not notarised, there are no witnesses. It won't hold up.'

He looked at Shirley.

'That's right,' she said. 'It's no use getting your hopes

up, Pops. That piece of paper carries no weight in the circumstances. She meant well in writing it. She loved you and you loved her. But Babs didn't really know how things would be. Lucy has to come with us, we all know it.'

'She promised she'd write it up official,' said Grandfather Racket. 'You think I'm stupid? I never trusted you two. And this is what she wrote. This is the official version.'

Grandfather Racket stuffed this paper back into the bundle. He retrieved his will and the Sears agreement and did the same with these. One small, folded page remained. Slowly he gathered this up in his fingers. Howard and Shirley exchanged a furtive glance.

'I saw that,' said the old man.

'And it says here,' he continued, 'on this birth certificate, it says "Lucy Racket".'

'Good Lord, Pops,' said Shirley. 'We know she was born. It's that other question we don't know the answer to, isn't that right? If you had a paper on that, now that might be worth something.'

'You're always interrupting,' said Grandfather Racket. 'This birth certificate also says: "Mother: Barbara Jean Racket".'

'Howard, stop him. This is getting ridiculous.'

'Dad, don't make me say things we'll all regret.'

'I got no regrets, Howard, speak for yourself. I only say what I mean. You ought to try it sometime. Now the next line here is called "Father".'

'Right,' said Shirley. 'And we are all aware that line says "Unknown". We saw it at the time, Pops, every one of us, when we asked Babs how did the county handle the case of a bastard.'

'*You* asked,' snarled Grandfather Racket. 'Nobody else. You were the only one. The only one to say out filthy words. Puttin' them words on my daughter and granddaughter! And what you said, you lying bitch, *was*: what happens to the birth certificate in the case of a whore giving birth to a bastard child. Isn't that what you said! Whore and bastard!'

'Well, now—'

'The case of a whore having a bastard child was what you said. Just so the record is nice and straight like I like. And then my Babsie got up out of her chair and poured her Schlitz on your face.'

Grandfather Racket chuckled.

Shirley's eyes filled with tears.

'That was very mean of her,' she said.

'Look who's talking. Some question to ask my daughter. Maybe we should ask the father. What do you think about that? Maybe he'll have an opinion on the county writing up a whore and a bastard.'

Howard and Shirley stared at Grandfather Racket.

'There is no father,' said Howard.

'So why do you sound so nervous?' asked Grandfather Racket.

'I'm not nervous, Dad,' laughed Howard. 'It's just getting pretty absurd the way you're going on.'

'Don't play tricks with us, Pops,' said Shirley, shifting in her chair. 'The birth certificate says "Unknown". Babs showed it to us that day after she got hold of herself. It's in the county records for anyone to see.'

'She never got hold of herself with you,' said Grandfather Racket. 'You think she'd show you two connivers the real thing? I told her no way will you show them the real one, Babsie. Ha.'

He paused. Howard and Shirley stared at him.

'But what I got right here this minute is the one, the actual real-type original.'

'Give me that,' said Shirley, grabbing at the paper in Grandfather Racket's hand.

He jerked it away.

'Relax, Shirley,' said Howard. 'He's tried to be on top all my life. He hates to be wrong and for once he's wrong. For once he's going to lose. It's music to my ears, I can tell you.'

'Here's some music for you, Howard,' said Grandfather Racket. '"Father: Raymond Smith". You think she was a fool? You think she'd show the original to you?'

Howard was on his feet.

'Give me that!'

'Take it,' said Grandfather Racket. 'I got others. Official copies, all certified, all exactly like the record in the county building. And now you've figured it out, haven't you? Oh, we kept it from you pretty good, didn't we, Hazel and Avery and Babsie and me, 'cause we ain't the type to go blabbin' like some folks. And there you two go plottin' and plannin' and schemin' like always, and now poor Shirley ain't goin' to get what she wants. Boo hoo.'

He sat with his arms folded across his chest.

'So where is this great Raymond Smith now?' cried Shirley. 'And where has he been, this wonderful father of hers? Answer that one. Nowhere. That's your answer. You think a court will let a half-drunk farmer who can't get a decent job raise a child? They won't. We won't let them. I *deserve* Lucy. I should have her!'

'We'll just see, won't we?' replied Grandfather Racket. 'Because Raymond and me, we're a team now, we got lawyers. You try to take Lucy, Raymond will put you in jail for stealing his daughter.'

'Raymond can't even get up for Babsie's funeral,' snarled Howard.

'He'll be up,' said Grandfather Racket. 'And then we'll see who's who around here.'

7

23 November, 1944.

Dear Johnny,

Thanksgiving Day, it's after midnight now and everyone's gone home. We decided to do it all together this year, I suppose the reasons are obvious. The Stilmans, the Butlers, Willard and Barbara Jean. So it was a full table. Except for Jenny, Kat, and Bobby, God rest them, killed almost two years now, early in the war when we thought it was just a bad dream that wouldn't last – and you and Fred and Raymond and Joe in parts unknown. Sadie said Grace, it was lovely, I don't know how she and Bert have stood up so well, Jenny and Bobby gone forever. What she said was, keep our beloved children away from danger, O Lord, they are so far from where they're safe and loved, Bless our dear departed Jenny and Bobby, and Carl and Mildred's beautiful Kat, who only wanted to do good in the world, and protect from all harm Fred in Italy, Hazel and Avery's Joe in the Pacific, and their Johnny and Raymond in France or Belgium, Amen. I shouldn't be telling you these things, Johnny, and I probably won't even send a letter like this, it's just to let you know you are on our minds all the time and maybe to put down on paper for myself how life is. But of course I hope I don't need to tell you we are fine and we carry on each day as normal. No mail from you yet, naturally it's too soon, and of course we don't really know where you are. This is my third letter to you, I've sent two to Raymond, and I hope you get them quickly.

The big news here as far as I can tell is the government has decided to stop making whiskey again. You'd think the country wasn't fighting a war and boys and girls dying for the rest of us, to be worried about a thing like that. You remember how in August and September they let up on certain things and said how we'd have refrigerators, canned goods, and so on as soon as Germany lost. Well, now they say we'll have no extras for Christmas. The drinkers are upset because there will be no hot toddys – I don't suppose I should be so hard on them, but the government says they need the alcohol for making rubber (I don't understand how they do that but they probably explain it to you). Especially there is no bourbon, because corn is going to feed chickens for the troops. I heard this on the radio. I'm stocked up on the canned things so we'll be fine, but I can't find the towels I need, none anywhere, not even the Five And Dime. Do you think this means the war is not ending after all? You probably hear more than we do. Maybe the Germans won't give up. No new blouses for Lizzie, either, but I suppose she'll manage, she's just growing all the time like teenagers do, pretty soon she won't like you calling her your little sister. If I can find the material I'll sew them myself but even material can't be had.

Well, our problems are not important compared to what you are doing. A lot of the boys are coming home, it's over for them, and wouldn't it be nice if you were one of them. Now, a lot are crippled and we wouldn't want that, but just to have you home. Thousands more are still going out, though, every day to the Pacific where

Joe is – no word from him for a good while but I'm sure he is fine. I've just been to the school to pick up my new coupon book. We get a little more coffee and sugar this month. The weather has been beautiful but even with surpluses everywhere they say we still can't feed all of you *and* ourselves, so we still have quotas on milk, vegetables, chickens, and eggs, also corn, as I said. This doesn't bother us in the country so much of course because we grow our own and Lizzie's Victory Garden is the envy of everybody. Somebody passing by said *Life* Magazine ought to put a picture of it in the next issue – peas, beans, lettuce, radishes, potatoes, squash, etc., American flags at the top of every row. So believe me we aren't starving. I don't know how the city people manage.

Dad sold all but two cows, Johnny, keeping those just for milk. He told me not to tell you, but with the polio Billy shouldn't be working, even though he does because he feels ashamed with his two brothers fighting, I heard him say it to Dad. I can see it hurts the bad leg and he just isn't up to doing what needs to be done. With you and Joe and Raymond and Fred gone, and most of the others, there's no help around, just enough to get in the late wheat and corn, and so Dad doesn't know if come spring we'll keep all the land. Well, that's another day and I am not going to go telling you our troubles when you have enough of your own. I have finished the third gold star for the white banner in the living room, one for each of you and Joe and Raymond. Bert and Sadie, and Carl and Mildred, they still have theirs up for Jenny and Kat, God rest their souls, with blue stars of course, and they added a red cross to show they were both nurses. We still can't keep in our minds where El Alamein is, even after seeing the map so many times.

Well, it will all be over soon and then back to normal.

Willard blacks out his place every night starting at eight when it's still light out but there's no changing him. He got a scare in '41 over the U-boats off the east coast, and now he says the Germans could try anything when they see they're beat. He wants all of us to go along but Dad won't do it. Oh, it is something how hard he and Barbara Jean can work that farm – she is determined not to let down her end of things with Raymond gone. They're up at the crack of dawn and at it all day. I don't know how they can take it. They're two of a kind. Dad thinks Willard will have to sell off land and cattle if Raymond isn't back soon, he told Willard this and you can just imagine what he said back. Barbara Jean thought Dad was making too much of the whole thing, she says the war will be over in a few months. She comes up to us every evening after Willard puts out all the lights, to say hello and have a cup of coffee (sometimes – whoever has it). We talk things over and many nights she stays quite late, reading a book in front of the fire after we've gone to bed. The war has settled her down a little. Dad doesn't agree.

I can't think of anything else. Are you keeping warm? We hear it is a very bad winter over there and I wish I had made you a sweater and not just a scarf. Lizzie told me to tell you: wear the scarf or else, and you'll know what she means. It must be your own private joke. Dad said to tell you we're fine.

Good night, Johnny. We have all our faith and confidence in you. Everyone is so proud.

Don't worry about us. Just do the job and be nice to the other boys like we always taught you. Some of them might get homesick. And then come back to us. What a day that will be. We see celebrations in the papers every day. All our love.

Mom

8

Grandfather Racket left Howard and Shirley sitting in the kitchen, 8:57 a.m. It was time to go upstairs to Lucy.

Partway into the living room his gait slowed, his confidence failed him.

At the same moment, he found himself passing Barbara Jean's coffin again. Suddenly his blood pressure collapsed, his legs buckled, and he was overcome with nausea. The contents of his head seemed to evaporate, leaving a featherlight shell. He reeled onto the sofa as the room began to spin and darken and the muscles in his arms and legs quivered. He had no strength to grip the cushions, to hold on, as he felt his body fly into an eerie, dizzying orbit.

He willed himself to spread his rubbery legs and hung his head between them. He drew oxygen into himself with jerks and tugs, like a bellows.

Gradually, gulping and heaving, he was able to sit up. He fell against the back of the sofa. He rolled his head to the side and stared out the front window.

He saw Barbara Jean and Lucy's beloved flower gardens: petunias in all shades of red, pink, and purple tumbled up, down, and around the borders of two large, irregular plots. The yellow Coreopsis Early Sunrise, the Shasta Daisies, the Black-Eyed Susans, and the lanky blue autumn asters were all in full bloom. Lucy's favourite, the commanding deep-rose Physostegia, three-and-a-half-feet tall and known as False Dragon Head, was the most numerous, and held sway over the rest like royalty. Unseen by Grandfather Racket, spiders' dewy latticework hung between the stalks of the Physostegia, creating dozens of miniature temples. Glistening drops dangled from the flowers' broad, bold petals like gems.

These plots stretched out on either side of a narrow stone path that snaked up a gradual hill from the dirt road encircling the farmhouse to the main road: New York State Old Route 141, Rural Free Delivery Number Two. RFD #2 also took in Groom, Niskayuna, Defreetsville, Cohoes, and Watervliet. Little Hoosick was the nearest large town, nine miles from Halfmoon on Route 18.

Hundreds of acres spread out in all directions from Grandfather Racket's farmhouse. A wide, rocky stream that began at the junction of the Mohawk and Hudson Rivers, four miles outside Defreetsville, wound its way through his fields like a slow procession.

The land had changed little since the 1600s when the Dutch, and then the Mohawk tribe of the Iroquois Indians, settled in Albany-Rennsalaer. Farmers still planted row after row of corn that swayed in the affable summer currents like columns of dancers. Miles of poised and patient wheat, oats and barley, shifting gracefully to inaudible tones, produced the same image of unity, like a flock of birds choreographed to pull this way and that as one. Elsewhere, fields were planted with the Iroquois 'Three Sisters', squash, beans, and peas; and in a small plot behind the farmhouse, Lucy and Barbara Jean had planted carrots, onions and lettuce.

By the time the Mohawks were slaughtered by French traders in the late seventeenth century, and the survivors driven north to Canada, they had also planted thousands of trees in RFD #2. Trees stood for endurance, continuity and safety: when the Iroquois League of The Five Nations was formed, the pine tree, 'Tree of the Great Long Leaves and Great White Roots of Peace', was chosen as the League's symbol.

Because Grandfather Racket's one hundred and eighty acres had been the site of Caughnawaga, the Mohawks' last and finest settlement in the area, his farm was lushly endowed with birch, spruce, balsam poplar, oak, pine, elm, maple and Eastern hemlock. Stands of these trees bordered fields; they shaded the banks of the Mohawk, the Hudson, and their tributaries, including the stream on Grandfather Racket's land. They sheltered roads throughout the county.

Two miles down Old Route 141, to the west, were Grandfather Racket's neighbours, Carl and Mildred Butler. Two miles in the other direction lived Bert and Sadie Stilman; and on Route 18a, off the main road to Little Hoosick, his closest friends, Hazel and Avery Martin. The families shared equipment, supplies and men for most jobs. A large shed near his barn housed Grandfather Racket's store of machines and tools: a 1946 Ford tractor; two mouldboard ploughs, also known as single-bottom walking ploughs hand-operated and drawn by his horse Slowpoke; a more elaborate version of this plough, called a five-bottom tractor plough, an assembly of five mouldboards; and a four-row trailing corn-planter, pulled behind a tractor, which could be used for all types of seeds. Grandfather Racket also owned a mower, drawn by either horse or tractor, for cutting grass as well as other crops. Additional equipment – a harvester, a silage cutter, a hay baler, a corn picker and binder, and a feed grinder – were owned by the Stilmans, Butlers, or Martins. Grandfather Racket's Ford pick-up was sufficient for light work; the Stilmans' one-and-a-half-ton Ford truck could haul livestock.

Grandfather Racket kept twenty head of beef and dairy

cattle, and eight pigs that lived across the road from the barn in a large pen. He also maintained one small out-building as a chicken coop, and another for curing bacon, separating and pasteurising milk; and sorting and packing the hens' eggs.

After Raymond was drafted in 1944, Grandfather Racket and Barbara Jean had run the farm together: he would never forget those years of intense determination and exhaustion they had shared. He gazed forlornly at the coffin in which she lay inert, like wood now. She carried none of her usual charge, gave off none of her usual flair for enlivening or aggravating or commanding the routine.

In recent times, she would sit most afternoons in the wide wing-backed chair with the faded damask upholstery, her right leg tucked under the left, reading a book while Lucy napped. This chair had been moved to make room for the coffin. When Babs was reading, she kept a mug of black coffee and a Hershey Bar on a stool next to the chair. She would reach down without looking away from the book, take a careful bite or sip, and then replace the mug or the chocolate slowly, with only a slight turn of her head.

Grandfather Racket usually broke from work at 3:30. He always came in the front door and walked the length of the living room, past his daughter, into the kitchen. Neither spoke or acknowledged the presence of the other. Grandfather Racket was reviewing which chores had to be done before supper and how long each would take. The fifteen minutes for his milk and pie were accounted for; stopping to talk with Babs was not.

Babs knew when Lucy would awaken. She had already planned the evening meal and knew exactly when to begin preparing it. She had cleaned and straightened the kitchen after the noontime dinner. Dishes and utensils were back in place for six o'clock. Now was her time for reading. During the last year Lucy had been able to sort and carry items to the table. She arranged them daintily at each place before her nap at 2:30. Raymond took his meals and snacks – portions prepared and laid out by Babs – in his cottage.

Barbara Jean wore her long sandy hair pulled back in a tight pony tail, which made her narrow face seem drawn and severe. The pony tail fell over her left shoulder, and she weaved it swiftly through the fingers of her left hand as she read, releasing it only to hold the book as she turned pages: licking the tip of her right index finger and pushing each page away with a quick, authoritative dash of the finger. Then she would take up the hair again. Her blue eyes moved across the lines of print with alert precision. She wore thin cotton slacks or faded corduroys with second-hand men's shirts and blue Keds, all from The Rummage Barrel in Cohoes. Clothes fell loosely over her trim, lithe figure. *Moby Dick* lay on the chair that was now covered by a white sheet and standing behind her coffin.

Grandfather Racket was breathing freely again. He raised his head slowly. He edged himself off the sofa and stepped gingerly through the familiar silence of the living room. He opened the door at the far end of the room which he had used earlier to reach the front of the house on his way to Raymond's. This time when he entered the hall he mounted the staircase to his left. Gripping the handrail he turned for a moment to study the front door. There was no sign of Raymond. He began to climb the dusty wooden stairs to the second floor. He stopped once to sit down as waves of nausea rolled across his stomach. Lucy's room was at the top of the staircase, Babs' to the left. The wide-board pine floors upstairs had warped since the construction of the house in 1866, and the varnish on the roughly hewn planks of the walls had faded. The blue, red and yellow chintz curtains Babs had hung in every room brightened the drab interior of the house. The exterior was made of weathered flagstones.

As Grandfather Racket reached the landing, he stepped hesitantly, trying to avoid creaking the floorboards. He cocked his head and heard his granddaughter breathing heavily in her sleep. He entered the child's room. She lay on her back. Her tiger-striped cat, Jungle, was stretched across her chest, purring. He lifted his head groggily.

Cards left from Lucy's fourth birthday, 18 August, sat propped along the windowsill. Two sagging balloons were taped over her bed beside a poster from Babs: 'Four Today! What A Girl! I Love You. Your Old Mom. P.S. Eat Your Vegetables!'

This year Lucy had gone to nursery school every morning from nine until twelve. Babs drove her back and forth in Grandfather Racket's dilapidated Ford pick-up. The girl bounced up and down in the rickety vehicle as it chugged over the hilly, potholed roads to the school. She and her mother sang: Over hill, over dale, we will hit the dusty trail, as the caissons go rolling along.

Every morning from the time Lucy was eight months old, Babs worked in the Watervliet Historical Society as administrator of its small library and museum. She took art and drama classes at Albany Regional School, where Lucy attended nursery school; she was head of The Citizens' Committee to Remember Our World War II Dead, and the only member of The Mohawk Valley Committee To Stop The Loyalty Oaths. During the last few months of her life she had sent several identical letters to The House UnAmerican Activities Committee: 'I am writing to you so you will come up here to Halfmoon and Groom from your big-city life in Washington and protect me and my family from Communists! Come on up and we can look for them together!! I saw *one* last Friday in the barn; *two* under the hay mow on Wednesday; and *four*, all kindergarten age, eating *red* popsicles outside Albany Regional School!' In one of these letters Lucy had enclosed a drawing of her friends eating the popsicles. She drew a copy for herself which now hung on the wall next to Babsie's birthday poster. Recently the Committee had written back to say that Communism was not a laughing matter and that Barbara Jean and Lucy Racket were now under investigation. This letter, too, was pinned to the wall.

Grandfather Racket removed a pair of overalls and a small white blouse from the wobbly wooden chair beside Lucy's bureau. He sat down. On the red cotton braid rug which warmed Lucy's feet in the mornings, the girl had carefully lined up side by side the fuzzy pink bedroom slippers he had given her on 18 August. There was a bottle of soapsuds for blowing bubbles on the bedside table. The thin plastic stick with a circle on the end, through which the bubbles would be blown, was placed neatly beside the container of soapy water.

To the right stood a glass jar covered with wax paper. This was secured around the top of the jar with a rubber band. Lucy and Babs had poked holes in this with the tip of a pencil. Inside the jar lay six lightning bugs, captured one night shortly before Babsie's death. All the fireflies had suffocated within twenty-four hours. Lucy told Babs and Grandfather Racket she would keep them by her bed until they had had enough sleep and then she would wake them up. Bits of apple, lettuce, and Hershey Bar had been added to the jar.

Grandfather Racket stood up. He stared at his granddaughter. Long blonde hair trailed off her head onto the pillow. Matted strands of hair stuck to the sides of her face. She had cried last night at bedtime: her Aunt Shirley had not read *The Travels Of Babar* correctly. She wanted to know when her mother would be well enough to read. Shirley replied that it would take a few months. Lucy said, I don't like how you read, I will wait.

Grandfather Racket saw *Babar* on the floor by the

nightstand. On the top shelf of the short bookcase at the foot of the bed were dolls, trucks, games, crayons and paper; on the shelf below, more library books and second-hand books from The Rummage Barrel: *Madeleine, Babar At Home, The Little Auto, The Little Sailboat* and *Goodnight Moon*.

Lucy was lean and strong like her mother. Grandfather Racket's nose and cheekbones were beginning to take shape. She had Raymond's sparkling chestnut eyes. He called her 'Chipmunk': full cheeks when she grinned, a dasher, a sprinter, clever and curious.

Grandfather Racket stepped towards the bed. He was suddenly aware of a prickling in his legs. The knees had locked. The rigid limbs resisted, but he forced himself forward and sat down on the bed beside his granddaughter.

'It's morning, Lucy,' he said. 'We got to get up.'

She did not move.

'I'm not even dressed myself,' said Grandfather Racket.

Lucy was wearing a tee shirt and loose cotton underpants beneath the thin blue blanket. He put a hand on her shoulder.

'Come on now, honey,' he said. 'I'll help you. You had a hard night.'

Lucy's mouth began to move slowly, as if she were sucking. Jungle stood on her chest and stretched. Then he slid down on to the bed beside the girl and closed his eyes.

'Aunt Shirley gave you a pill to calm you down. Last night it was. You'll be all right now.'

Lucy began to stir. Her eyes opened and she squinted drowsily at her grandfather.

'It's me,' he said. 'We'll get ourselves dressed and fix some breakfast.'

'I don't want oatmeal,' she said.

'You can have what you want, honey.'

Lucy blinked and opened her eyes fully. She turned to her cat and stroked him. He rolled onto his back.

'Aunt Shirley makes me eat oatmeal,' said Lucy.

'When did she do that?' asked Grandfather Racket.

'Each single day,' replied the girl. 'Each of the times. When will Mommy be able to make pancakes?'

'She won't be able to, Lucy,' sighed the old man. 'Just sit up now and I'll try to tell you.'

'I'm so happy I be able to visit Mommy today.'

'Mommy's gone, honey. You can't visit her. She didn't get well.'

Lucy turned over on her stomach and reached down to the floor for *Babar*.

'Where did she go? If that hostipal didn't make her better we will take her to another one.'

She sat up. She opened the book. From between two pages she pulled out a piece of red construction paper which had been folded twice, perfectly, to make a thick square. On the front was a picture, in yellow crayon, of a daffodil.

'I have to give her my card,' she said. 'I made a getting well card of all my own writing.'

'Why, that's beautiful,' said Grandfather Racket. 'And don't it look just like the ones we had out by the path in May.'

Lucy grinned.

'You better not forget to open it up, Ganfar,' she said.

The old man hesitated. He stared at the daffodil.

Lucy leaned towards Grandfather Racket and squinted her eyes. Then she put *Babar* down on the bed and patted her grandfather's hand.

'There, there, don't cry,' she said. 'Mommy is only be gone three months, Ganfar. I can cook, I know how to make peanut budder samwidges.'

'Oh, Lucy,' sighed Grandfather Racket.

He opened the card.

'I did it myself,' said Lucy. 'I thought of the whole idea for cheering her up.'

Inside the card, in black crayon, the girl had drawn the side view of a bed. A black stick person lay on the bed, arms at its sides. The large head on top of the body had frizzy, electrified-looking yellow hair and two saucer eyes blanked out in black. Two ears protruded from the dangling hair. The mouth, a thick black line, curved down at the ends.

Lucy pointed to the other side of the card.

The second picture showed the same bed. But standing next to it was a lovely, smiling woman with bright blue eyes and soft blonde hair. The hair was pulled into a pony tail and draped over her left shoulder. In the corner was a pick-up truck surrounded by trees and corn.

'See?' said Lucy. 'All better now. I going to take that to Mommy in the hostipal so she'll know to be well.'

Beneath the second picture, Lucy had drawn four hearts and written: 'Me, you, Ganfar, and Jungle.'

'I can spell you and Jungle,' she said.

'You spell us real good,' said Grandfather Racket. 'And here I thought you went right to sleep last night.'

'I put back on my light after Aunt Shirley left. Then pretty soon my head almost fell over. She gave me a pill all chopped up in a glass of water.'

Grandfather Racket gave a short laugh.

'I might of known you'd outlast some old pill.'

'I will put my card right here inside *Babar* to keep it nice for when we go to the hostipal tomorrow.'

'Honey,' said Grandfather Racket, 'I'm trying to tell you we can't see Mommy any more. Mommy's not coming back.'

'But I have to see her, Ganfar. She needs my card, she needs to see me spell you and Jungle's name.'

'I know, I know,' said the old man. 'But she was just so sick she couldn't get well. She just, no one could do anything, she just went and died, that's all.'

Lucy stared at her grandfather.

He stood up suddenly and rubbed his forehead.

Lucy collected Jungle into her arms and swung her legs out of the bed. She draped the cat over her shoulder. He opened his eyes, then closed them again. Lucy handed him to her grandfather.

The old man slumped back down onto the bed. Jungle purred on his lap.

'I guess I could use some help, couldn't I?' he replied, looking at his longjohns.

'I know how,' said Lucy. 'Don't you worry about a thing. You look terble in those underwears. Mommy will clean them as soon as she comes home.'

The child went to her bureau and pulled open the second drawer.

'There's only socks,' she said, picking out a ball of clean white ones Babs had washed and sorted last week. 'I need lovely fresh underpants.' She turned to her grandfather.

He sighed again.

'I'm sorry, honey. I guess nobody thought to do the laundry. Just wear those same ones again today.'

'I always put a fresh new pair each of the days. I don't wear a same pair the next day.'

Suddenly the girl's soft face looked tight.

'Go get me a new pair, Ganfar.'

Her voice was rising.

'Lucy,' he replied, 'there isn't none. If they ain't in there, then they're still in the cellar, in the basket. I'm sorry. I never thought about the laundry.'

'But if they are in Mommy's basket then she has to wash them for me. We have to tell her right away, she doesn't know I runned out of underpants and she said to me to put a nice fresh pair when I get up.'

Grandfather Racket slipped Jungle onto the floor and stood up.

'Lucy,' he said, 'come here to me.'

'There is no more pair of underpants in my second drawer!' she cried.

Grandfather Racket held her against his chest.

'Somebody will do the laundry for you,' he said. 'Somebody will figure it all out.'

He began dressing the girl in her overalls and blouse. When he had finished, Lucy draped Jungle over her shoulder and took her grandfather's hand. Then they walked slowly down the stairs together.

9

Shortly after Grandfather Racket left Raymond's bungalow, the young man opened his eyes.

He tried to lift his head from the dingy pillow on his army surplus bed, but he felt his skull would split apart. The room was spinning. He gave up and fell back.

He did not remember setting the alarm at two a.m. when he came in. Now the clock lay on the floor by the nightstand where he had pushed it at seven, when the tinny bell sounded. He had no memory of his decision to rise early, nor of his declaration the night before at The Roadside Rest: This has gone on too long. I won't put up with it. She made me keep quiet for the sake of the child, well, where has it left me now? I'll tell her, I'll stand up to her. Billy Martin had replied that Babs kept him quiet for the sake of her father: Won't you admit it, Raymond? For the sake of the farm, for an easy life. That's what she wanted, that's all she cared about, it's too late now.

But Raymond persisted: She wanted *me*, Billy. She wanted us to have the farm and the child *together*, she was just waiting for the right time.

Billy and the others helped Raymond off the table. They walked him up and down the road. Then Billy drove him home and put him to bed.

Raymond turned on his side. The room was swimming.

His hands, his feet, and the bones in his face ached deeply from last night's exposure to the frigid air: since the war he could not tolerate cold.

Everything in his shack made him think of Babs: her curtains, her colour scheme, her idea to hang photographs of the two of them as gawky adolescents. And it was Babs' decision to frame and put up his paintings from the class at Albany Art College in 1932, the year he dropped out of school. Babs was eighteen, Raymond was a tall, swaggering fifteen-year-old with a fake driver's licence, forged birth certificate, and a job at the Mobil station. Any thought of the country at war in ten years would have been laughable: they were going to be artists.

The Albany pictures were on one wall: a clumsy water-colour of corn against blue sky, two misshapen cows in a field, and a painting of Babs as a wraith in a storm. Thick, churning bands of brown and black loomed behind her. She stood cavalier against a telephone pole, a hand propped on her hip. A cigarette dangled from her mouth. Bright yellow hair was piled in rambunctious heaps on both shoulders. Raymond was thirty-two now. Babs was about to be thirty-five when she died.

He began to weep. His lips were like blubber. He shook. Drinking had not succeeded in quelling the nightmares, the ringing in his ears, the pain and flashing behind his eyes, nor the excruciating remnants of frostbite. These torments had started almost as soon as Raymond arrived home from the war, and disappeared within a year as he drank more and more. Lately the agonies were back, too determined for alcohol to contain. Rubbing his hands and feet only made them ache more.

Raymond saw the clock on the floor: 10:00 a.m. The urine on his overalls had dried, but he recoiled at the smell and could not face undressing. He tried to bring the room into focus. He wiped his nose on the sleeve of his tee shirt.

Gradually, fragments of recent days came back to him: Babs had complained of a headache at her meeting in Watervliet. Someone went to get aspirin. Then she threw up and slipped off her chair on to the floor, unconscious. Two days before, Barbara Jean had said she'd been feeling dizzy, probably from too much coffee. She was going to cut back.

An ambulance took her to the hospital in Defreetsville where she lived in a coma for six days. She died in the early hours of the seventh.

Raymond wanted to marry Babs after he came back from the war in 1946, when Lucy was almost a year old. But Babs said it wasn't the right time, she was confused and afraid. She remained in the house with her father and the child while Raymond lived alone in the bungalow. Now he remembered a conversation with Grandfather Racket and he started to cry again.

It was 1947. Raymond had just finished the milking. He was walking with two buckets across the barnyard. Grandfather Racket and the two-year-old Lucy approached from the house. They were going to have a picnic in the large field below the barn, in a cluster of red oaks and maples. As they came near the barnyard fence, Raymond put down the buckets and smiled at Lucy. He stood with his broad, muscular hands spread open on his hips.

Well, are you off on your picnic?

You come, too, Waymond.

I'd love to, but who will do all this work?

I do it later, said Lucy.

Watch out how you set down them pails, said Grandfather Racket. You slopped good milk in the dirt just then.

Raymond leaned over the top of the white wooden fence.

Aren't you a sight, he said to Lucy. Come here to me. Why, look at you. Your jacket isn't buttoned right and your galoshes are on the wrong feet!

Ganfar mixed dis all up on me. He can't see.

Oh, it could happen to anyone, said Raymond. Don't you have trouble with buttons yourself? And don't I always have to show you which is left and which is right?

There's nothing wrong with my eyes, said Grandfather Racket. I was in a hurry. Leave that coat alone, Raymond. Did you hear me? Get back to work.

Aw, now. I'll just straighten out the jacket. Isn't that better, honey? Come up here and get a hug.

Lucy put one foot on the lowest board of the fence and wrapped her arms around the one above. The young farmer hoisted her up. She stood on top of the fence.

Look at me way up here! she said.

Aren't you something, said Raymond.

Come on, come on, said Grandfather Racket. You don't have to make a big production out of it. Get down off there, Lucy, you'll fall. We're going for our picnic now.

The child held out her face and pursed her tiny lips for Raymond. He lifted the girl down to the next plank. He held her and kissed each ear.

She kissed Raymond's cheek.

Bye-bye, she said.

Run down and push open the gate for me, Lucy, said Grandfather Racket. Just push up the latch like a good girl and I'll be right down. You know how.

The girl ran off. Grandfather Racket turned to Raymond.

You're here for one thing and one thing only. To do a decent day's work until you get yourself a job and move out. And don't you forget it.

I'm not a piece of dirt.

Then what are you?

We both know there's more to it now than a job. Babs and I have a child to think of. I've barely had time to settle in. Give me a chance. There's a lot more involved now than before.

Involved? Is that what you call it?

Yes. We have a child. Don't make me say it. That's why I'm here, and because of Babs. We love each other and we have to face reality.

We? We? You ain't the *we* I'm thinkin' of. I'm talkin' about the we that was lookin' after your responsibilities back here while you took your sweet time galavantin' around Europe. As I recollect you was the one all nice and eager for them Nazis all of a sudden. You probably knew she was going to have that child. Goin' off and leavin' us with all this work. Had to sell off land and animals thanks to you.

I was drafted and you know it. Nobody had a choice. Don't talk to me like that. And I didn't know about Lucy until Babs wrote to me.

Then why didn't you write back to her? Huh? And what about me? I don't deserve a letter?

I couldn't.

The war ended '45. You weren't home til '46. What was goin' on is what I wonder, and I reckon you had a mental breakdown over there. That's what I think. Couldn't take it.

Don't you worry about me, I took it just fine. You seem to forget I was the one working this farm with you from 1941 until 1944. We did every bit of work together and kept the place going.

That was then. Now look at you. Drinkin' every night, sometimes into the day. And you act like you know all about farming.

I do.

I'm not stupid! You think I'm stupid? I know what you want. You're after my farm. Well, you ain't going to get it. You're wasting your time. You're hired help, that's all. Babsie made me take you back but she agreed it ends when I say so. And she don't like this drinkin' business neither.

That's a good one. She drinks *with* me. You ought to see how much *she* drinks. We both know what we're doing. You don't think I deserve a night out?

Night out. Ha. That ain't what I call it. And you got no claim on that child neither. Lucy don't know you from Adam. So forget about it. You ain't fit.

I am not hired help, I am the girl's *father*. I won't forget about it. You'll see things differently when Babs and I get married and then you won't be able to talk to me like this. Everything was just fine when you needed me, wasn't it? When I did as I was told. You didn't complain then.

Get married? Ha! That just proves you don't know my Babsie.

Maybe I know her better than you think.

We'll see who knows who and what's what. She was no better than a whore in Akron. Did you hear about that? All them girls goin' around the country workin' for the war, all they wanted was one thing, the best men gone fightin' to save their pretty necks and them carryin' on with the dregs. I knew all about it, I told her what was goin' on out in them places like Akron, but she never listened. Didn't listen to you, didn't listen to me. She ain't going to suddenly quiet down and pay attention. Maybe you ought to try facing that one for a change.

Come on, called Lucy. I waiting too long. Dis latch won't go.

I'd even say she had other boys right here in town while she was carryin' that child. I bet she did.

Raymond struggled up from the edge of the bed. He was weak but he could stand.

He went to the sink and splashed cold water over his head and face. He gripped his ears as a metallic whine bored through them and cut into his brain, causing an involuntary shudder which passed like a shot from his head down through his legs. Avoiding the mirror to his left, he dried himself with a small towel that, several days before her death, Babs had draped over the back of the chair.

10

Rain drove across the sky like a lumbering freight train, pushing through a dense haze that in its stillness foreshadowed the arrival of a powerful force.

22 August, 1942: steadily overtaking the suffocating afternoon heat, the torrent broke up the thickness and washed away the cloying humidity layered on the skins of plants and animals. Farmers and their children in Halfmoon, New York, abandoned tractors and rakes to rip off shirts and stand half-naked in the gleaming rain in fields of hay. They threw their arms up to God, they danced and sang and gave thanks for the cooling, purifying shower.

On her bed, Barbara Jean Racket kicked away the sheet and rolled on top of Raymond. She licked the sweat from his neck, sat astride him on her knees, and ran her hands and fingers like silk ribbons through the damp hair on his chest and across his taut, muscular abdomen. Between his legs he was soft and moist. She eased herself down, opened her mouth, and massaged him with her lips.

In a moment she propped herself up again. She stroked Raymond's face and he opened his eyes. She smiled; he turned his head away. The rain ran over the house like a river. Raymond watched it stream down the windows, seeking comfort in its steady flow and rhythm, and finding none.

It's almost time, said Barbara Jean. We should get up now so we won't have to rush.

Her suitcase stood by the door.

Look at me, Raymond. Please. I wanted to leave you happy.

He turned and faced her.

No, he replied. You wanted to leave. That's all. And that's what you're doing.

I don't *want* to, she protested. There's a war, Raymond. You have a job, you're doing something. The whole country is mobilised. There's nothing for me here. And anyway, I've told you it's only temporary, I'll be back. Of course I'll be back. Why do you want to ruin our last few hours?

She moved away from Raymond and sat on the edge of the bed. The skin on her back glistened. She folded her arms across her breasts and lowered her head.

I'm sick of talking about it, she said. Why do you make us go over and over this? The bus for Albany leaves in two hours.

I go over and over it because *I* am here, replied Raymond. Am *I* nothing?

Barbara Jean grabbed a loose shirt from the end of the bed and without getting up struggled into it. She turned angrily on Raymond.

Everyone is going somewhere else, Raymond. Don't you see what's happening? There is no such thing as *here* any more. How many families do we know – count them – how many are the same as before? None.

Raymond sat up and covered himself with the sheet.

Does it help to add us to the list? he asked. Today another busload – soldiers going one way to God knows where, women going another, to factories. Factories. Think, Babs! Think what this means. I've got an exemption, I was lucky to get it, and the war won't last forever. I'll probably never be drafted with Pops getting older. So there's no reason for you to leave.

He stared at her.

Or is there? he added. You owe me an answer to that, Babs. Not to leave without saying what you mean.

Raymond, I've told you: there's a good job in Akron, there's good money. I'm thinking of *us*. We'll never have enough if we both stay here. We'll never have a life.

What do you call what we've been having?

He pounded the bed with his fist.

What do you call *this*? Money is more important than this? Money from a rubber factory in Ohio? What are you saying?

Raymond leaned forward and held Barbara Jean's shoulder.

Babs, he said. Listen to me. There's plenty of work right here on the farm, important work. If we get married and have a family, they can't draft me, we'll be safe. Don't you see what I'm saying? Things will be fine, we won't end up like the others.

I want to stay, she replied. But I can't. Raymond, look around, you're not looking! Jenny and Kat are already gone and God knows if they'll come back, all our friends have disappeared. Something is happening, Raymond. These are ghost towns – go anywhere – Groom, Defreetsville, Niskayuna—

I go every day, Babs. And every day business carries on as usual. That's what you don't realise: things keep going.

No! They don't, Raymond. Something is very wrong and it may never be right again. I feel sick – if I sit still – I can't explain it – but if I just sit here and watch . . .

Raymond threw off the sheet and swung his legs over the side of the bed.

Then go, he said. You don't know what you're saying. Life doesn't stop just because there's a war somewhere, there have always been wars. You're twenty-eight, I'm twenty-five. We can't wait forever until there's no more war.

Babs turned towards Raymond.

Please look at me, she said. I have to go soon.

He faced her and they held hands across the bed.

It's *not* forever, she said. Just for *now*. I'll be back when it's all over. We'll be all right, we'll be fine. We'll get married. You know I want to.

Raymond studied Barbara Jean's face. He was unable, in either her mournful eyes or in the lines creasing her young brow, to read the future.

They turned their backs to each other again and began to dress in silence.

11

Raymond lifted his head slowly, dabbing his face with the towel.

Suddenly there was a knock. Hazel Martin entered.

Raymond turned away.

'I don't want to see you,' he said. 'Leave me alone.'

He held the table to keep from shaking.

Hazel was wearing a flat, black hat and veil. The hat was pinned to her white hair which was loosely waved and set. She had made the hat, and her dress, a black and white cotton print. From her left arm, across her abdomen, hung a small crocheted bag. With her right hand she carefully pushed the veil away from her face and up over her head. She adjusted her gold-rimmed glasses.

'You mean you don't want *me* to see *you,*' she replied. 'But there's never been conditions between us, Raymond. Over twenty years ago Avery and me opened our hearts to a little boy and took him just the way we found him. It's no different today.'

Raymond wept.

'You're not to blame,' said Hazel.

'How do *you* know?' demanded Raymond.

'Because that's not how it works. That's not how it is. You'll make yourself sick.'

'It doesn't matter, Hazel.'

'Do you want that child, Raymond? It's the only question now, it's what I came to say. I am very frightened.'

'No, I don't want her. Stop it.'

'Where will she go, Raymond?'

'I don't care. Leave me alone.'

'But she needs for you to care. I said the same thing to Willard just before Babs died. I told him the two of you would have to make decisions for the sake of this child. She is your child, Raymond.'

'I can't take care of anybody, Hazel. You know it. Why are you doing this to me?'

'Because I don't know it. Why can't you?'

'I don't do things *right,* Hazel. Things don't work out for me. Stop lying to yourself.'

'Raymond Smith, you are not talking like the boy and the man I have known all these years. And I don't like what I am hearing one bit. You know as well as I do that from the time you moved in with us, when Johnny was six years old, he worshipped the ground you walked on. There were reasons for that. You shared a room with him and you didn't act like you were stuck with a baby. You took him everywhere you went. You showed him how to do things. You kept the bad elements away from him. You sat up nights when he was sick. But you didn't make the war. I know what you are capable of, Raymond. I've seen how you are with Lucy and I know what you mean to her. I know why every farmer in this county wants you to work for him. I am talking to you about what is right here, right now, not about Johnny. That's over. You did what you could. Everyone did their best.'

'How do you know what I did? Who are you to talk to me about Johnny when you don't know what went on?'

'All right then,' said Hazel, 'I can see you're not able to hear me, something has changed. So let's talk about what is in front of us. Today. Howard and Shirley will try to take

Lucy. I have known them a long time. I know what they are capable of.'

'Let them,' said Raymond.

'Let them?' answered Hazel. 'Is this the Raymond Smith I know and love? Just let those two people take your child? Is that what you are saying to me? I am trying to get through to you, Raymond.'

'You take her if you know so much.'

'It's not my job any more, Raymond. Avery and me are tired, we're so tired out. We can't go through it again.'

'I'm sorry,' said Raymond. 'I'm sorry.'

'What good is that? What does "I'm sorry" mean?'

'Nothing! It means nothing! What do you think?'

'I told Willard and I am telling you, Raymond: we will do anything to help the two of you hold on to her, anything to help her. But it is *your* job. Do you hear me?'

'You've said enough, Hazel. Get out.'

'I'm not leaving until I say what I want. She was a shining light in 1945, Raymond. Do you know what it was like for us? Can you imagine? No, of course not, but you pay attention to me now, for *her* sake, for the sake of this child that's at the mercy of things she has no say over. Or that's the end of her. Let me tell you, Raymond, in those days *all we had was war*. Even when it ended in April of '45 the bad news just kept coming. Seeing the boys who came back so hurt and broken! And then in August, Lucy arrived. All of a sudden there was one little eager happy face in the world, one innocent pair of eyes wondering at everything around her. She was the only one who didn't know about the war, Raymond. Why, we woke up in the mornings, all of us, even Avery and Bert and Carl, we all woke up and first thing we remembered was Lucy, and we'd all rush down to Willard's like newlyweds saying, Oh, Barbara Jean, I'll change her diapers, never you mind, you rest, I'll feed her. And there was Avery burping her on his shoulder saying now-now, and grown-up *men* fighting over who would hold a baby, the women had to compete! Sometimes we just put her on the floor, all six of us, and Billy and Lizzie, and watched her every move with Bert saying, See, she likes me best, did you see that look she gave me, Sadie? All Lucy cared about was pointing out the things we'd lost track of. She'd study a speck of dust like it was the encyclopedia! She belongs here with all of *us*, Raymond. Don't you see? It's what she *knows*, this is her home. She's all we have left of Barbara Jean, Raymond. I loved them.'

Raymond retched into the sink and coughed violently.

'You don't know what I am talking about, do you?' said Hazel.

'For Christ sake, Hazel, I'm sick.'

'What does Lucy care about that! Listen to me. What I am trying to tell you is if you don't do it, if Howard and Shirley take her, she – oh – oh, Raymond – please – I – what can a person say about such a thing? I'm sorry. I've lost my train of thought.'

'You can't even keep straight what you're saying,' said Raymond. 'Don't blame *me*.'

'Raymond, how can you make me face another child going?' wept Hazel. 'How could you do that to me?'

'I'm not doing anything to anybody, Hazel. I can't even stand up.'

'You've got to, Raymond. Oh, the Lord help me. To face another child going.'

'I can't do any more.'

'Are you sure, Raymond? Are you absolutely sure? Think! Don't you see? We needed her very badly at one time, and now she needs us. Somebody has to help her.'

'Hazel, leave me alone,' mumbled Raymond.

'I will. Yes. I will. You'll hear no more long speeches from me. I am worn out. Barbara Jean was one of our children.'

Raymond held his head.

'You could get better,' said Hazel, drying her eyes, 'if you put your mind to it. Your whole life you have put your mind to things and they have worked out.'

'That's easy for you to say. But you know as well as I do this won't work out. I don't have a chance.'

'Easy? Easy? No. I might be *wrong*, it might be too much to expect after all you've been through. But don't tell me it's *easy*. You're a grown man now and it's not my place to tell you what you have to do. I don't want to. It's *Lucy* that's trying to ask you, Raymond. Lucy. It *can* work out.'

'That's enough, Hazel.'

'I – I'm sorry, Raymond. No matter what happens I will stand by you. That will never change.'

She turned and walked out the door.

Raymond struggled to the sink, gripped both sides, and vomited clear liquid into the bowl. His stomach was empty but continued to heave. His heart raced and sweat ran off his face until finally he was able to raise himself.

He left the bungalow and started unsteadily down the road to the house.

12

In addition to Babs' reading chair, there were two others in the living room: deep over-stuffed chairs with thick arms and plump cushions. Both faced corners now, covered with white sheets.

A matching sofa stood against the wall where Shirley had pushed it to make room for rows of collapsible metal chairs. On the sofa were a stack of Bibles and Shirley's black pill-box hat with black lace veil.

Grandfather Racket's wife, who died in 1929, had chosen the fabric for the sofa and chairs. One day in 1940 it occurred to him that from time to time she must have cleaned this furniture: he was shocked to notice that the cheap print of pears, birds, and apples was soiled. In a panic, he scrubbed all three pieces with Ajax. The colours ran and faded; in some places the fabric split. Over the years Babs carefully repaired these gashes with brown thread, but some had torn open as the material wore thinner.

When Grandfather Racket and Lucy entered the living room, Shirley was lining up the mourners' seats in three rows of six chairs apiece. Howard and Shirley's Negro servants, a brother and sister in their sixties who had worked for Shirley's parents, stood beside Babs' coffin. Vernon was dressed in a thick wool suit and white shirt. The shirt had a stiff, high collar. The tips of the collar were turned slightly down over a black tie, more like a ribbon, which hung loosely from the neck of the shirt. The weight of the suit and tightness of the collar made him sweat: beads of moisture had appeared across his forehead. At the moment Lucy and her grandfather walked into the room, he had begun to fear that the sweat would run down his face and stain the shirt.

He was a stocky man. His large hands dwarfed the black hat he held respectfully against his abdomen. Only his hair, which had begun last year to be sprinkled with white, suggested Vernon's age. His skin was clear and smooth.

Lillian stood beside her brother in a black cotton dress. She wore a black straw hat and black gloves. In her right hand she held a small straw bag which matched the hat. Her hair was pulled tightly back and shaped into a bun. Vernon and Lillian spent hours each night straightening their hair. During the day his was slicked down with gels and oils.

Lillian, too, was beginning to go grey. The new colour of her hair softened the rough skin of her face. Her eyesight was poor and she wore thick glasses; she had arthritis in her hips and hands. Vernon and Lillian had been raised by an aunt in Alabama until another aunt brought them North, where they entered a segregated school in Albany.

Under the wide brim of her hat, Lillian's eyes were moist, her lips and brow set in a painful grimace as she watched Lucy enter the room with Jungle and her grandfather. Vernon turned his head slowly towards his sister.

Lillian saw this movement out of the corner of her eye. The fingers of her left hand inched into the open top of her handbag. They gathered up a white linen handkerchief and slipped it under her brother's hands which rested on top of his hat. Vernon placed the hat on his head. As his right hand came down from the brim, he stroked the delicate cloth across his forehead. In the same movement he tucked the handkerchief into the top pocket of his suit coat, so that the corners opened out like a morning glory.

Howard sat slumped on the sofa, his head resting on the back, chin jutting out. He was flipping through the pages of a Bible which he held in the air over his face.

'So what's the good Reverend going to read?' he sighed.

'Anything will do,' replied Shirley absently. 'Do you think eighteen is too many? She wasn't what you call popular. Still, you never know. A mother with a young child always brings them out.'

'Maybe I'll tell him to start at the beginning,' continued Howard. 'Heaven and earth. That's where everything starts, isn't it? And finishes at the end. What a laugh.'

'On second thought, it's better to have too few,' said Shirley. 'Then it will look like a lot of people came and we were short of seats. I can always add. Howard, take away two from each row, that's the boy, and prop them up along the side somewhere. We'll do three rows of four each.'

Shirley fidgeted with the wobbly chairs until each was exactly the same distance from the others in perfect rows. Then she distributed the Bibles, one on every second chair.

Howard clamped the extra chairs shut and propped them against the wall.

Lucy and her grandfather said nothing and did not move.

'We've got enough Bibles for everyone,' said Howard. 'It doesn't look right, skipping a chair like that.'

'It gets people to share, How-How. You want a feeling of togetherness. There. That's nice, if I do say so myself.'

Then Howard saw Lucy and Grandfather Racket.

'Well, look who's awake,' he said to Lucy. 'Hello, sweetheart. Did you have a nice sleep?'

Lucy did not reply.

Howard and Shirley looked away.

Then Shirley motioned to Howard. Howard nodded to Vernon, who quietly lowered the lid of Babsie's casket.

Jungle freed himself from Lucy's grip. He jumped to the floor and stretched. He arched against Grandfather Racket's leg.

Suddenly the cat sprang on to the coffin. He prowled along the top, sniffing the shiny wood. Then he planted himself in the centre and settled into a hard crouch. He glared at the family which had fallen silent watching him.

'Well,' giggled Shirley. 'Isn't he sweet.'

'It's time for his beckrist,' said Lucy.

'We'll feed him for you, sweetheart,' said Grandfather Racket.

'I know how,' said Lucy.

'I'll feed him,' said Howard. 'For Christ sake, we're just hanging around doing nothing. We're not accomplishing anything.'

'And then,' said Shirley, 'Vernon and Lillian will take Lucy to Little Hoosick while we have our, uh, meeting. Won't they?'

She winked at the girl.

'You don't want to hang around for some boring old meeting.'

'I can't go to Little Hoosick, Aunt Shirley,' said Lucy. 'I'm going to the hostipal to visit Mommy.'

'Just get it through your head you're not going to any hospital,' said Howard. 'There aren't going to be any goddamn hospital visits. She's dead. Somebody ought to just say it and get it over with.'

'Shut your trap, Howard,' said Grandfather Racket. 'That's just about enough from you in front of a child. I've told her what she needs to know. She can't hear it.'

The front door banged and everyone looked over to the far end of the room.

'Well, well,' said Shirley, looking anxiously at Howard.

Raymond smoothed his hands across his eyes as if he were washing himself again.

Lucy ran to him and threw her arms around his legs.

'What did I tell you?' snapped Grandfather Racket, glaring at Shirley. 'So much for your big ideas. We're taking over now.'

Vernon and Lillian looked quickly at each other and away.

'Oh, no you're not,' said Shirley. 'Let go of that child, Raymond Smith. Howard, do something. He smells like rubbish the dogs brought in.'

'Me?' said Howard. '*Me* do something? For Christ sake, Shirley, what am I supposed to do? Do it yourself.' He picked up a Bible and threw it to the floor.

'Who do you think you are?' said Shirley. She slapped Howard across the face.

He sat down and pointed at his chair.

'Here's my answer, Shirley. A piece of goddamn furniture. Any more questions?'

Shirley picked up the Bible and dusted it off. She stared at Howard. 'You are pathetic,' she said.

'Can't even stand up to a woman,' sneered Grandfather Racket, 'never mind Raymond.'

Howard massaged his cheek and did not reply.

Lucy stared gravely at Raymond.

Howard looked up. 'Listen to me, Raymond, for God's sake. Lucy is going to *our* place. You might as well tell her, Pops, and get it over with.'

'I agreed she'd go up to Little Hoosick for the *day*, Raymond,' said Grandfather Racket, 'then back here for good. That's been agreed.'

'It has not,' declared Shirley.

'You keep quiet,' said Grandfather Racket. 'We'll do our real talkin' later when Lucy can't overhear. Don't you understand anything?'

'Vernon and I will take you, honey,' Lillian said quickly. 'You be no trouble for us to mind. We can bake some cookies. How would you like that?'

'You better make sure it's what happens, Howard,' said Grandfather Racket. 'All I agreed to was the day. And if she ain't back here by seven o'clock tonight, you'll be seeing us in Little Hoosick. Isn't that right, Raymond?'

Raymond tottered on the brink of consciousness. He ceased to be aware that Lucy was holding his legs and did not hear Grandfather Racket speak. He kept rubbing his eyes, unable to free them from an occluding mesh that blurred the details before him. This shroud – filaments of loss woven into more loss and thence into an intricate fabric of self-loathing and self-mutilation – would not lift. Raymond could not let in the sight of Lucy clinging, begging him to pass through the matrix into light and save her. Once before, on a canvas of snow bereft of warmth or colour except for streams of fresh blood, he had looked straight at the searing flame of such a plea. Then, as now, it was hurled against a storm of overwhelming odds and elements, and for his failure to dominate and transform these, Raymond had burned his eyes beyond further seeing. Seeing is hope, and hope had been taken from Raymond Smith.

Suddenly he stumbled backward. He was seeing double, and could not make his legs work.

Lillian rushed forward and took Lucy's hand. 'You stand up straight, Raymond Smith,' she whispered angrily. 'This is a *child*.' She turned and nodded to Vernon.

'I think Lillian may need my help, Mis Racket,' he said.

'Do what you want, Vernon,' renlied Shirley. 'We're used to him by now. It's poor Lucy who needs us.'

'He's all right, he's all right,' insisted Grandfather Racket.

Vernon walked slowly over to Raymond. Lillian brought Lucy to Grandfather Racket. She clutched his legs and buried her head.

'Raymond,' demanded Grandfather Racket. 'Pull yourself together. Lucy is askin' you.'

Every bone in Raymond's trembling, floating body seemed to snap under the weight of his suffering and left him no structure to mount against the forces amassed somewhere in the vacancy before his eyes.

Vernon gripped Raymond under his arms and pulled the tall young man into a hug.

'Come outside with me,' urged Vernon quietly. 'We can't let that Howard and Shirley see this or you got no chance at all. Hold still now. I'm goin' to turn you and walk you. Put one foot then the other.'

'I can't do it, Verne,' wept Raymond.

'You got to try. Slowly, Raymond, one step at a time, and jus' maybe you be able to beat them.'

Vernon walked Raymond outdoors and released him gently.

'Now go on,' he said. 'Let's see you walk. I'm tellin' you, you got to.'

The servant turned and went back inside.

Raymond propped himself against the door.

In a moment he pushed his body away from the house and staggered onto the dirt road.

'Raymond,' [illegible] 'Don't [illegible]' [illegible]

Every nerve in Raymond's trembling [illegible] body screamed [illegible] to step under the weight of [illegible] and [illegible] him [illegible] against the [illegible]

[illegible] Raymond [illegible] arms and pulled [illegible]

[illegible]

[illegible] 'I'll go and [illegible] you and wait [illegible]'

[illegible]

[illegible]

[illegible]

[illegible]

[illegible]

[illegible]

13

'Thank you, Lillian,' said Shirley. 'Thank you, Vernon. So much for him. Just over an hour until the meeting. Everything is ready. How about that breakfast, Lucy? Some for you and some for your nice little kitty. A big hot bowl of oatmeal and then off to Little Hoosick.'

Lucy burst into tears. 'Where did Raymond go?'

Grandfather Racket put his arm around the child. 'He'll be back, don't you worry. Just gone to do the chores. And you ain't eatin' no oatmeal,' he said. 'Aunt Shirley and Uncle Howard are not in charge. I'll make the decisions.'

'I don't believe this,' said Howard. He folded his arms across his chest, a scowl on his face.

'Jungle is hungry,' wailed Lucy.

'All right, all right,' said Howard. 'I'll feed him.'

He jumped up from his chair. 'Come here,' he said to the cat on the coffin.

Jungle stared at Howard and did not move.

'What's the matter?' said Howard. 'You deaf? I said come here. It's time to eat.'

Howard approached to pick him up and suddenly Jungle bared his teeth, spat, and lashed a fist of claws at Howard's hand. He retracted his paw as deftly as he had struck out, like a magician, and settled back into a rigid hump. His eyes never left Howard's face.

'You little bastard!' cried Howard, leaping away. 'Look at me!'

Blood began to ooze from two holes on the back of Howard's hand. The skin was already turning black and blue from the force of Jungle's paw.

'Shut your mouth, Howard,' said Grandfather Racket. 'You got what you asked for.'

'He's hungry,' sobbed Lucy.

'He can go to hell,' said Howard. 'Look at my hand! He's a vicious animal. We ought to put him to sleep.'

He whipped his arm through the air.

'Get out of here, you stupid cat. Shoo!'

Howard sucked the back of his hand.

Jungled hissed at him and did not shift.

'Well, now. I guess we're all a little upset,' said Shirley. She looked reproachfully at Howard. 'And therefore we ought to keep our tempers down. The most important thing is Lucy.'

'She's not a thing,' said Grandfather Racket.

'We know that, don't we, Lucy,' said Shirley. 'You're a very good girl. And I would appreciate your cooperation after breakfast in going along to Little Hoosick with Vernon and Lillian, to bake some lovely cookies.'

'It's just until tonight,' said Grandfather Racket. 'Then they'll bring you back or I'll come and get you.'

'I don't want to,' said the girl.

Lillian turned to her brother. He looked at her.

Vernon said, 'Why don't Lillian and me help you feed that cat, Lucy? We could manage him together.'

'Thank you, Vernon,' said Shirley. 'That's very thoughtful. And, by the way. As you will be spending a lot of time with the child from now on, there are to be no more first names. Yours, I mean. She is to call you Mr Vernon and Miss Lillian. Her mother let things go and I will be trying to put her back on track.'

'Don't you sound like the Queen of Sheeba,' said Grandfather Racket. 'You call anybody what you like, Lucy.'

The girl looked at her grandfather.

'Go along,' he said. 'They'll get you and Jungle something to eat.'

Lillian held out her hand to Lucy, and they left the room. Vernon scooped up Jungle with one hand and nestled him between his chest and his arm. With the other he pushed through the door and went in to the kitchen.

Grandfather Racket stood still for a moment. Suddenly his eyes widened and he bolted to his bedroom.

It was way past time to bring in the cows and milk them. Then he had to go across the road with buckets of feed and scraps to the muddy plot where he kept the pigs. Normally he and Raymond had these chores completed by ten o'clock. The old man had forgotten his animals.

In his bedroom he yanked his overalls over the longjohns and fumbled with his bootlaces. He tried to think when the late corn would be ready, how long it would take to gather, what he would do if Raymond could not help. He thought about the wheat, the weather, the salt blocks he had to replace, when he should sell four head of cattle.

And he could not stop turning over and over in his mind how to make certain Lucy would remain with him.

As he careered down the hallway from his room, he vomited down his trouserleg and onto the floor. He wiped his mouth with the back of his hand, stepped through the foul liquid, and kept going.

14

Hazel Martin was twenty-seven when she saw the Albany-Rennsalaer Home For Wayward and Abandoned Children, and Raymond Smith, for the first time.

She had been living in Halfmoon, eighteen miles from the rambling converted mansion known as Bennett's Gorge, since her marriage at the age of twenty-two to Avery Martin, who had inherited his family's farm on Route 18a. The couple had one child, Joseph, aged three, and Hazel was newly pregnant with the second.

Most of the families in the area were devout members of the Halfmoon-Watervliet Presbyterian Church. Hazel and her neighbours, Sadie Stilman and Mildred Butler, were also active on the Ladies' Committee for the Worthy Poor and Destitute, organised by the church's minister, the Reverend Ethan Barker. The group visited mental asylums, hospitals, bread lines, soup kitchens and Salvation Army shelters, where Reverend Barker preached redemption through hard work and self control, and the ladies sang hymns. At Christmas and Easter they took baskets of food, toys and decorations to all these places, and to families living in squalor beside railway lines or underneath bridges.

Up until several weeks before Hazel visited the Home, it had been located almost ninety miles away near Albany. The authorities, however, felt that the children, ranging in age from several months to fifteen years, would benefit from being in the countryside, so when the estate at Bennett's Gorge became available, the decision was taken to move before Christmas.

The children left behind staff and nurses they had known for months or years, and regular charity visitors like Hazel and her friends who were a sustaining presence in their lives. In many cases, the women developed strong attachments to particular children. They spent extra time with these children, brought special gifts, and from time to time, invited them to their homes for a meal. On rare occasions one of the visitor families might even take a child home to live, while he or she remained legally a ward of the State.

Six women from the Ladies' Committee agreed to go on a Christmas visit to the new orphanage, with the understanding that this was to be the first of many regular outings to the institution.

The group planned an afternoon of carols, hymns and prayer. They also prepared sacks of carefully cleaned and wrapped used toys, and Avery Martin agreed to be Santa Claus.

The entourage started out early in the day to arrive for a noontime dinner. Bundled in blankets and nestled in a bed of straw, they made the journey in a horse-drawn sleigh driven by Reverend Barker.

The ambling dirt roads between Halfmoon and Bennett's Gorge were layered with packed snow which had fallen all week. The surface was smooth and soft, and the runners of the sleigh moved across it with a confident *swoosh*, as if buoyed by a cushion of air. Snow-laden pine trees gleamed in the stunning light from a pure blue sky; the parishioners had to shield their eyes from the glare of the white fields. The horse held his head high, nostrils flared in the cold, as his hooves hit the downy path with a delicate, padded thud. The gentle rocking of his body clanked the row of bells on his bridle. Avery Martin, a stocky, reticent man of thirty-four, pressed his cotton beard close to his face. The tassle on his red and white cap danced in the breeze. Underneath a blanket, he and his young wife held thickly-gloved hands.

Gradually, the sounds of the sleigh and the horse wove into a deep, melodious hum. This, and the sway of the carriage, shielded the little band against the cold, and lulled them into a peaceful communion with the landscape.

When they arrived at Bennett's Gorge, they were greeted by the Directress, the Administrator, staff and nurses, who led the party – minus Santa and his sacks – into a huge reception room dominated by a blazing fire and sparkling Christmas tree.

On either side of the tree, in groups set apart according to age, sat fifty rustling children over the age of three years. The younger ones were held by several attendants, or contained in groups of ten or twelve in large metal pens with high sides and bars. Infants remained lined up in cots in the nursery. Each child wore a coloured tag bearing name, age and dormitory number. A small cluster of teenagers sat in sullen apathy far from the others.

As the visitors entered the cavernous room, the Directress stopped and held up her arms. The children immediately fell silent. The staff fanned out noiselessly among the children, positioning themselves beside their assigned charges and motioning them to wriggle in together.

The Directress nodded to one of her staff who then cupped her ear and called out: 'What do we say to our visitors, boys and girls?' A tinkling chorus replied: 'Thank you for coming, Reverend Barker.'

Some of the children lagged behind the pace of the response and the delayed words echoed from various points in the room. The Directress, her arms still raised, looked snappily at her staff, and several stunned children were promptly yanked up off the floor and whisked from the festivities.

The Directress lowered her arms. She gestured with a hand and Reverend Barker came forward. He greeted the children, showed them how to clasp their hands in prayer, and taught them to say after him, 'The Lord is my shepherd, I shall not want.' He then recited the Twenty-Third Psalm in full, introduced the Ladies' Committee, and led them in two hymns.

Finally he announced that after dinner Santa would arrive with gifts for each child. The staff and Directress smiled and made no attempt to stifle the squeals which rippled through the clusters of children. When it was time to lead them in to the dining hall for dinner, the Directress asked those who had been designated Santa's Helpers to come forward to meet the Ladies' Committee, with whom they would share a table during the meal.

From the sea of orphans, six four and five-year-olds emerged, wearing red and white caps like Avery's. They were led to the front of the room.

While the other children began to move out quietly, the Directress eased the six helpers under her arms like a mother hen. She whispered to the ladies, 'These are some of our worst cases.'

One at a time, she nudged each child towards a visitor. Hazel was standing next to the Directress as she took the hand of the last child to be paired, a sturdy boy with a wan face. His eyebrows were pushed into a deep frown. He bit and peeled scabs from his lower lip as he stared intently at a tiny pool of melted snow on the floor by Hazel's boots. His Santa hat was too large, and without looking up the boy kept pushing it off his forehead with two fists of gnawed fingers. He wore high, scuffed leather shoes several sizes too large and tied with torn and knotted laces. His baggy brown trousers were rolled up at the cuffs. The sleeves of a girl's blouse and cardigan fell just below his elbows and could not be buttoned.

The Directress said to the boy, 'Raymond, you will go with this nice lady, Mrs Martin.'

She said to Hazel, 'We can't get him to talk. He only came to us in October and then we moved here. He is a very serious boy. Aren't you, Raymond?'

The orphan tucked his hands into each other and held them against his waist. He continued his grave study of the small gathering of droplets beside Hazel's boot while his right hand gently rubbed the left.

Hazel was not prepared for the silence of the child's torment. To her shame, she removed her wool cap and looked away from him. She was suddenly confused and distraught. She tried smiling at the lines of bedraggled children shuffling to the dining hall, but none smiled back and she was overcome with despair at their rigid masks of indifference. The narrow, pale faces revealed a reality beyond Hazel's comprehension.

This look reminded her of her elders: men and women who she had always believed started life with the innocence and curiosity bestowed upon all children, and who grew pinched and hardened only after many years of labour and sacrifice. They wore their masks as a matter of principle, with the Calvinists' pride in self-denial.

What Hazel saw at that moment in Bennett's Gorge made her feel she had lived a life of lies and ignorance. She was overcome with guilt and self-loathing.

She heard the Directress say, 'Mrs Martin, are you ready to take Raymond into dinner? The others have gone.'

'I – yes,' she stammered, 'of course.'

She looked down at Raymond who did not raise his eyes. All of a sudden Hazel was on the floor, kneeling beside the child.

'How old are you?' she pleaded.

Raymond looked up and regarded Hazel thoughtfully. He appeared to give consideration to her question. But after a moment his gaze fell back to the floor.

Hazel struggled to stand up.

'I – I'm afraid I've got the most awful headache,' she said. 'Perhaps I shouldn't stay.'

'I understand,' replied the Directress. 'Come and eat now and you will be all right.' She addressed Raymond.

'You're five years old, aren't you, Raymond? Say to Mrs Martin: "I am five years old, Mrs Martin."'

His head still lowered, Raymond turned to Hazel and slowly lifted the index finger of his left hand until it touched the badge on his cardigan.

Feeling that she might faint, Hazel averted her face. Then her arm rose, extended in Raymond's direction. For a moment it hung in mid-air. Finally, at ten minutes past twelve, several feather-light fingers came to rest on the back of her hand.

His index finger still affixed to the red cardboard circle on his sweater, Raymond walked into the dining hall with Hazel Martin.

15

Willard Racket had just turned seventeen when his father's farm burned down: a barn, a silo, two storage sheds and the family's run-down, two-storey house. Blackened crops of wheat and corn had to be destroyed. Ten head of cattle – the entire herd – plus one horse and three boys burned to death. This farm was less than twenty miles from where Grandfather Racket now lived.

The summer of 1888 was hot and dry. Rainfall was the lowest in seventy-five years. The air was charged. Buildings sizzled, scorched grass snapped underfoot. Temperatures rose daily beyond one hundred degrees. Wells failed. Babies, animals and old people died.

A farmer's child was never to light a match in heat or drought. No open flame was permitted anywhere. Fire was the summer nightmare.

Children went to a one-room school only when they were not needed on the farm. Grandfather Racket's father allowed him to attend two or three days per week until he turned fifteen, as long as work was completed to his satisfaction.

During summers there was little for young people to do. Even if they could reach a distant town by horse and flat-bed cart, few shops and no saloons would admit them. Saturday night barn dances, and a secret stash of local moonshine, were the teenager's only relief from labour and poverty.

Another pastime the boys enjoyed was the crafting of corncob pipes for the forbidden smoking of dried cornsilk. July and August were perfect: there was plenty of corn, and sun to harden the cobs and parch the silk.

At seventeen, Grandfather Racket ran the largest and most successful business in illicit teenage smoking in the County of Albany-Rennsalaer.

First he shucked the corn and put aside the moist silk. Then he scraped the kernels off each cob with his penknife, fed the tepid mush to the pigs, and cleaned the cobs in his ration of water.

On a sloping patch of brown grass behind the barn, where his father never went, the boy spread crisp old newspapers. He untangled the sticky wads of cornsilk and separated hundreds of strands into long, even clusters. He arranged them carefully on the papers to dry.

He crafted small bowls from chunks of the slippery cobs: square bowls, round ones, oblong, shapes made to order. All were the proper thickness and would not burn through during smoking.

The last step was to make an opening in each bowl for the hollow reed through which the burning silk would be smoked.

The tiny pots forged, they lay on the paper beside the silk, turned and rotated daily. Just below was a straight line of precisely-cut six-inch pieces of reed. One complete pipe cost two cents; with dried silk, three.

Boys came after dark with flashlights to survey the wares and make their purchases. On a good night, Willard Racket would be visited by six or more boys of all ages. Each was required to bring his own matches for the midnight smoke which bound buyer and seller to the evening's transactions. The young entrepreneur provided a small bucket of wet dirt for used, smouldering cornsilk and piles of spent matchsticks.

Sometimes, as on Saturday night, 28 July, 1888, one boy or another brought along jugs of moonshine stolen from a father's illegal still. Following Iroquois custom, the boys sat in a loose circle lighting and smoking their new pipes. They all tried to achieve the touch and sound of a perfect draw: a series of patient kisses on the hollow shaft held gently between the lips.

After two long draws, the pipes were passed clockwise in silence from boy to boy, one full round until each participant was finally handed back his own pipe.

One portion of cornsilk rarely lasted the whole round. The hot, charred wad would have to be emptied into the bucket at regular intervals, replaced, and re-lit. Each attempt at lighting required three or four matches. This ritual was accompanied by much sucking, gagging, and coughing. At the moment of victory, when smoke began to rise steadily from a boy's pipe, he was rewarded with a swig of acrid whiskey.

That night the drink provided was strong. Silence and composure could not be maintained. Participants began standing up, shouting, boxing, and then rolling on the ground in fits of laughter. Despite their inebriation, all knew how the host's puritanical father would view their clandestine activities. One after another, the boys bellowed at each other to keep quiet.

Between swills from the crude bottles, Willard Racket implored his friends not to waken the old man. He ordered them not to drink the remaining liquor.

Gradually the group found its way through the darkness into the barn. They dove and sank into mounds of hay. They struggled uproariously to find their feet against the rising tide of drunkenness. To the complaints of the animals housed in the barn, the boys replied on all fours with vigourous lows and whinnies.

Struck with fear, which welled up to challenge the seduction of the moonshine as he and his friends entered the barn, the young Grandfather Racket made a final, wobbly plea to his friends for caution and restraint.

On his own he reeled back over the path taken into the barn. He stomped on the band's smouldering supplies. He scooped them up at random and plunged them haphazardly into the bucket of sand. He sniffed and searched the circle. He kicked up clumps of dirt to expose and stamp out any lurking hazards. Finally he stumbled back to the barn to join his friends.

Small undiscovered fires at the original site began to burn widely. These spread to nearby fields.

Others, started by pipes and matches carried into the barn, ignited the bales of hay there, which in turn lit the adjoining silo and its stores of corn. The near side of the house burst into flames from the intense heat of the raging barn and silo.

Willard Racket's mother and father were both slightly deaf, his mother also in ill health. But Mr Racket was a stern watchman. He monitored his land, his animals, and his family with unfailing vigilance.

From within sleep on the night of 28 July, 1888, Mr Racket thought he heard his cow Bessie May giving birth to twins. But this was impossible. The previous year, 1887, Bessie had had twins. She could not be delivering now because she could never have calves again. She had suffered hours of labour, the wrenchings and twistings of frantic neighbours trying to shift the lead calf, who was breech and would not shift. It was finally ripped out of the screaming cow, dead. A second dead calf followed, nearly killing Bessie May.

Her plaint came to Mr Racket again. He tossed and turned.

Then new sounds began to register: cattle and horse slamming their heads and chains against the stalls in the barn. Mr Racket shot up in bed. He smelled the fire and heard the snap of his timber.

He shook his wife and shouted her name. She started and awoke. She cried out as Mr Racket swept her instantly into his arms. He staggered down the stairs. The hallways were filling with dense smoke. The steps and floorboards seared his bare feet.

On the first floor, the sitting room to the right swarmed with flames. They fled from the house which had been built for them by her father, and given on their wedding night, out into the balmy air which popped with the false heat of the fire.

Mr Racket ran with his wife away from the house, the barn, and the silo, several hundred yards. He laid the crying woman on the ground.

Then he bolted up. He ran to the house. Driven back by the heat, he ran to the barn. He ran again to the house, again to the barn. He returned to his wife and collapsed beside her. He closed his eyes and held his ears against the screams of Bessie, nine other cattle, and Mabel, his horse.

Suddenly his son appeared: from behind the barn, next to the silo, Mr Racket could not tell exactly. The young man's hair and clothes were scorched. He was sobbing and rolling on the ground with two other boys who were on fire. Three were missing.

Two days later, a doctor told Mr Racket the boy would survive his burns. The father beat his son with a paddle of charred timber and then sold him to a prosperous lawyer who owned a large farm nearby. A week later Mr and Mrs Racket moved to her sister's in North Dakota.

Young Willard Racket was a strong, determined worker. He did as he was told. He attended meticulously to every detail of the farm. He ate little.

Eventually he married the lawyer's niece, who boarded at the house and cooked and cleaned for the family. The couple continued to live on the farm, which was bequeathed to Willard Racket in 1912.

Now, in 1949, as he made his way shakily to the cows and pigs who needed him, he met Raymond Smith holding his head and walking in circles on the dirt road near the barn.

16

Monday, 11 December, 1944.

Dear Mom, Dad, Lizzie, and Billy,

I think I'm somewhere in *France*! Not bad, huh? Did you get my other letters?? We never know if mail makes it over there – we hand it to some guy in a jeep and he drives it to HQ and then if we're lucky he brings letters back to us from the good old US of A. And don't forget the censors, so I hope I'm not saying anything wrong (giving away secrets!) But we never know when or if mail ever gets through. Probably we ought to shoot it over to you with one of our rolling 57mm howitzers. Let me tell you, Mom, these babies will really scare the Krauts. We won't be sending letters to *them*! (well, a different kind, if you know what I mean.) The first time I saw these guns I couldn't believe my eyes. Hopefully I'll get the chance to try one out for real – training isn't the same thing. Anyway I got *two* letters from you yesterday, thanks for all the good news, everything sounds great and it really cheers me up. The guys who didn't get mail were really jealous. The pictures made me sort of think about everybody, especially with Christmas coming, but then I showed the pictures all around and Raymond and me told the guys all about RFD #2 and the swell times of late. The guys from New York – there's even two *Jews* in our unit and although they're definitely different, they are really great – they can't IMAGINE what there is to do on a farm. So, boy! Did we have a lot of fun telling them! (nothing you don't know already, Ma, ha-ha) There's also Italians, three from Brooklyn. You should hear the jokes they tell. I'm not sure what's the laugh in most of them but I go along because all the guys stick together. They probably don't understand *me* half the time either, but they don't mind me kidding them and all, so there's no problems. This is no time to be fighting among ourselves, we've all decided that.

Just in case you did NOT get my other letters – you didn't mention getting any and I can't tell by the dates on yours. I mean I can't remember the date of *my* letters, so just in case, here's a summary of what's been happening. I'll be writing every few days to keep you up-to-date. I don't miss you or anything like that, I just thought you might like to know the details, and I want to give you a quick rundown now because they told us we'll be setting up in our new position (somewhere – I'm not allowed to say just in case you tell the Krauts!) tomorrow or the day after, and who knows if we'll get any letters out after that. Not because of the enemy, Ma, don't worry – they figure we won't be in a real battle for a long time, if ever. Which we are really upset about, because when we came over here they (by they I mean top brass: Middleton over us, Hodges over him, then of course Eisenhower over everybody) *promised* it wasn't too late in the war to see action, and here we are just riding in trucks, no enemy anywhere. Well, I suppose how could there be, after we kicked them out of France back to where they belong. So, all the big guys want us to do is wait someplace near Germany so when the time is right we just go in and finish them off. I wonder if Joe is in the thick of it. The word going around on my end is the Pacific is tough but the Japs are no match for our boys. Have you heard from Joe? I can't remember the name of the place he was supposed to be headed. I wrote to some address over there but I never heard back. Oh, well. I'm going to bring home at least one Kraut helmet and I hope he'll get another one off a Jap. Send me any news from Joe. At least Raymond and me got in the same battalion.

You should *see* what the Germans have done over here. Villages are like piles of stones. They just knocked down whatever they wanted to. I don't know how the people manage. These little places in the countryside all cheered us when we drove through, a lot of them were even crying, so you get an idea of what's been going on. Every day is *COLD* and *WET* and most of the native people we saw hardly had a coat, they dress practically in rags. You ought to see the French girls!! Oo-la-la!! (Don't read this part, Lizzie) There is snow everywhere and tons of rain, too. How they get anything to grow after these winters, Dad, I don't know because the rain freezes on the spot, deep down. They say it's the worst winter over here in a *hundred* years. But still I hear they farm the land real good. I don't know what the people do for heaters. I can tell you we are chilled to the bone every minute. I'm wearing the scarf you and Lizzie knitted for me, Mom, and it helps a lot. I don't take it off, even at night. I'm glad we don't have to walk, thanks to you guys rationing gas and tyres.

I almost forgot what I was saying. And by the way one of the guys just told me we're in *Belgium* now, not France – I can't keep it all straight, one country from another. This guy who told me it's Belgium carries a map and he actually reads *French*. He's from Georgia.

So as I was saying, after Raymond and me left New York we got to a place in England in six days more or less and spent Thanksgiving eating the *WORST* turkey I ever had. I missed your cooking that day, Mom and Lizzie. But we played a lot of poker, which we also did on the ship coming over (boredom is our biggest problem) and Raymond won hundreds of cigarettes! He doesn't even smoke! He'll trade them for other things when the time comes, that's what we all do who don't smoke, the smokers will trade anything for one of them. But that Raymond can sure play poker! I never knew that about him. He stays quiet, looks around at everybody from behind his cards and no one knows what he's up to, a real poker face. Not trying to trick you or anything, just watching what's going on and sizing up the situation.

Then we sailed for France. We landed near where Normandy happened!! It was a great moment. The padre (he doesn't mind they guys calling him that, we don't mean any harm, and he's not like a priest at all, so say the Irish guys) he didn't say a word, just knelt on the sand and bowed his head. So then we all did. There wasn't a sound. I have to admit, I said a few words to the Man Above myself. Not that we're heading for trouble, Mom, Don't Worry. It was just because of what the guys in D-Day went through for the rest of us. And now the 108th will finish things off once and for all. I can't believe I've got this chance because that's where we're headed, the end of the war!! All the coffee we want! No more coupons! Our C-rations have the best hunk of chocolate I've ever tasted – here's a little piece for Lizzie and Billy. I hope it doesn't crawl out of the envelope by the time you get it! (ugh)

Raymond told me to say hi to everybody. He doesn't think I know but he is pretty upset over something. Not one word from Willard, which isn't right. He walks off by himself and pretends to be cleaning his gun when the mail gets handed around. He did say he got two letters from you, Ma, didn't give the details, *and* I think he got a letter from Babs last week. He kept to himself for a few days after so it can't be *good* news. She's probably breaking up with him, the worst that can happen to a guy over here. Maybe he's just homesick – a guy from St Louis, he was even crying in the foxhole the other night, but his buddy from home said he always was a Mama's boy.

Can you read this? Some of it I wrote in our truck bumping along some pretty lousy roads, and the snow and the rain were coming down hard, with me jammed up in a corner. But I want to get this done in case they collect mail tomorrow where we're settling in. Lizzie, take care of yourself and I'll be home soon. Billy, go easy on the work – Dad and I agreed to hire a few extra hands while Joe and I are away and I don't want to hear about you overdoing it. I know polio doesn't actually hurt but still you shouldn't be putting a strain on that leg. If anybody is writing to Joe: thumbs up. Who knows what's going on. I'm fine, Ma and Pa, there's nothing to worry about, the war is *NEARLY OVER!*

I love you. Don't forget to write.

Johnny
Pvt. John Martin, age 22, that's me!
Battery A, 548th Field Artillery Battalion
108th Infantry Division
AND PROUD OF IT!

17

'We got to do the animals,' said the old man. 'They don't know whether we're comin' or goin'.'

He kept walking.

'I'm sorry,' said Raymond, following.

Across the road, pigs jammed together at the fence shoved and snorted as they caught sight of the two men.

'Why don't you just call it what it is?' said Grandfather Racket.

He said to the pigs, 'Hold your horses. You think I can do two things at once?'

He strode past Raymond's bungalow to the gate which led in to the field below. Four cows with bulging udders had gathered nearby, pressed against each other. They stared forlornly at Raymond and Grandfather Racket.

'You're all right now,' cooed the old man. 'I know we're late. I told you before, our Babsie went and died.'

He turned to Raymond.

'Dry those tears,' he said, dabbing at his own eyes. 'We got serious business to figure out.'

He unbolted and swung open a heavy wooden gate.

The fields basked in soft August light. Hills behind the barn seemed to expand and contract in the shifting hues like patterns in a kaleidoscope.

The cows waddled through the gate-way. Grandfather

Racket patted the last one. They followed Raymond down the slow incline to the barnyard, where he opened another gate and led the animals through to the back of the barn. Grandfather Racket followed and closed the gate.

There were six small stalls in this section of the barn. The hard-packed dirt floor was thickly covered with straw. Two bare bulbs and two small encrusted windows lit the space. The cows shuffled obediently into their assigned cubicles and Raymond moved slowly from one to another, draping a loose circle of heavy brown rope around each animal's neck. He yanked the connecting lines to make sure they were held securely by the bolts in the wall.

In silence Grandfather Racket and Raymond took two buckets apiece from long nails on the wall near the door. Grandfather Racket pulled up a stool on the right side of the cow in the first stall and spread his legs. Raymond did the same behind the low partition separating his stall. First they warmed and readied the cow's teats by holding and gently pulling each one in turn. Grandfather Racket kept one hand propped on his thigh.

'We got to take them two big steers to Defreetsville,' he said.

'When I go to town,' said Raymond, 'I'll check the prices. I have to get gas for the tractor. We might do better to wait.'

'I don't want to wait,' replied Grandfather Racket.

Raymond did not respond.

'This one's a little sore, isn't it?' Grandfather Racket said to his cow. He stood up and took a tube of cream from a shelf above the animal's head and sat down again. He applied the ointment to his cow's teat and replaced the tube.

Then he grasped two teats and began the steady, rhythmic stroke: the subtle grip, the long squeeze, the delicate loosening of hands. Separate strokes merged into one continuous flow, a symbiosis of the hand and teat. Milk pounded in to the bucket, clanging the metal with the force of its thick stream. As the bucket began to fill, the only sound in the barn was a soothing thuck-thuck, thuck-thuck, as new jets of milk plunged into the frothy liquid.

'You get what I'm saying, Raymond? I ain't going to fool around with you.'

Raymond's hands were trembling. The cow shifted, and turned her head to evaluate him.

'Hold still,' he said. 'Relax. You're all right.'

'She can feel you. And I can hear it in your voice. Pull yourself together.'

'That's the girl,' Raymond sighed. He butted her swollen sack with his fist, the way a calf would with its head. For a moment there was silence and then milk began to flow. Raymond lifted his head towards Grandfather Racket's cubicle.

'I'm fine now.'

'We'll see.'

'They're going to take Lucy. That's what they're up to. They'll just do it.'

'Goddamn it, Raymond,' snapped Grandfather Racket. 'Where's your old spirit? What happened to the young man who told that ornery daughter of mine not to go galavantin' off to Akron?'

'She went anyway, didn't she?'

'But you told her! You told her good! That's what I like to see. And you can do it this time, too. I already put Howard and Shirley in their place, I told them you and me is in on it together. And then what do you do, you go and collapse like that after I went and stuck up for you.'

'Don't bother. Nobody asked you.'

'Well, aren't you just somethin'? Don't bother, he says. I'm tellin' you, Raymond, the fact of you bein' the father, the police won't allow strangers to take her. You *got* to bother! I showed them two the birth certificate and they got worried then, oh they sure did.'

'I doubt it,' said Raymond. 'They'll do what they want.'

He could barely move his hands or hold up his head.

'Listen to me,' said Grandfather Racket. He cocked his head towards the partition.

'You listening, Raymond?'

'I told you I'm fine!' he shouted.

'I'm trying to put backbone in you before it's too late.'

Grandfather Racket's voice began to rise. His cow rustled her head.

'Soon's we're done here,' he said, 'and Lucy's gone, you and me are going back down to the house so as you can own up to your full responsibilities.'

'Leave me alone,' said Raymond. 'It's over.'

'Shut up! You know dang well what I am saying. You are going to tell them straight out, no ifs ands or buts, that Lucy Racket is your child and you are taking her, being that the mother is dead. Let them try and stop you.'

'Take her where?' said Raymond. 'To that shack I live in?'

He rested his elbows on his thighs and propped his head in his open hands. The cow turned again and pleaded with him.

'No!' yelled Grandfather Racket. He bounded up from his stool and stumbled into Raymond's cubicle. He slapped the young man across the back of his head.

'With me. She'll live with me in the house. You're not listening!'

'You hurt me,' cried Raymond.

The old man ran back to his stall, picked up the stool and returned. He sat close to Raymond.

'Pay attention, Raymond. I never liked you. I don't like you now. I just manage to tolerate the sight of you. You're a lazy poacher that took advantage of my daughter after all

I tried to do for you, and I'm happy to say you didn't get what you were after.'

'I didn't want anything,' said Raymond. 'And you know it. Except Babs. I never imposed, I never took extra. You *did* like me. You *do* like me. You just won't admit it.'

Grandfather Racket propped his hands on his rickety thighs as if they were an old chair.

'You never stood up for yourself, Raymond,' he said.

'I need a drink, Pops. I'm really bad.'

'You don't need no drink! Listen to what I'm sayin'. Just take it easy and you'll be all right. I'll help you. Didn't I always? Didn't we always do things for each other?'

He stared at Raymond.

'Where do you keep it?' he asked.

'Behind the bales under the window,' answered Raymond.

Grandfather Racket found the bottle of whiskey. Raymond gulped it.

'You better get a handle on yourself,' said Grandfather Racket. 'That's all I'm givin' you today. We got to think. You all right now?'

Raymond did not reply. He stopped drinking and held the bottle.

Grandfather Racket clasped his hands in front of his chest as if to pray. He lowered his voice to a gravelly whisper.

'Howard and Shirley want to move our Lucy up to Little Hoosick. That's the story. You know it, I know it. And I reckon you're right, they'll take her today if they can get away with it. I agreed for the day 'til after the funeral, but they're about as low as you can get so nothing would surprise me. I showed them papers, drawn up legal and all, before you came down – and what did they do? Practically spat on me. Well, we'll see who spits on who around here.'

'Why don't you just talk to them again,' mumbled Raymond. He held his head.

'*We*, Raymond. *We*. It ain't just me. It's you. And as long as you can open your mouth, that'll do. I can sit you in a chair. You just tell them you're the father and you're taking over your legal and proper rights, end of story. I'm talkin' about the two of us together. You understand?'

'Get me a glass of water. And the aspirin. Over there on the shelf.'

'Answer me, Raymond Smith,' ordered Grandfather Racket, fixing the young man with an icy stare.

'Get off my back,' snapped Raymond.

Grandfather Racket stood up and jabbed a finger at Raymond. 'I'm not finished with you,' he said. 'This thing ain't over by a long shot.'

He patted his cow. Her bewildered eyes drooped, and the old man stroked her.

'Aw, now, you'll be all right. Sometimes you got to wait.'

'I'm going to be sick,' stammered Raymond.

'You're not going to be sick! Where is the damn aspirin, Raymond? I don't see no glass neither. What you don't put me through.'

Raymond waved his hand and did not look up.

'They're up there somewhere.'

Grandfather Racket found the glass and filled it at the tap on the side of the barn. When he came back Raymond wolfed down four of the tablets and slurped the water.

'She's not going to live in that dump with you,' declared the old man. 'That's obvious. You can help her with her homework but that's it. And teach her the farm.'

'That's better. Thanks, Pops.'

'Don't thank me. And don't go calling me Pops. Nothing has changed. Stick to the subject. You're going to tell those crooks you're the *father* and that Lucy stays right here at her proper home, starting tonight. You got that? No back-talk. There's a child needin' you down there.'

Raymond turned away and took a deep breath.

Then, danger suddenly welling up inside him, he leapt from the stool and charged towards the door of the barn to escape. He grabbed the handle, and at the same moment, the door burst open. The cows started and yanked against their ropes in fright at the crack of Raymond's head against the old wood. Grandfather Racket jumped up, kicked over the bucket of milk, and fell against his terrifed beast.

'What's got into you?' he cried, stumbling out of the stall.

The young man lay on his back, stunned by the sharp blow. Vernon and Hazel rushed into the barn, fearing what they had struck.

'Raymond,' said the bewildered woman, kneeling in the dirt and straw.

'What happened?' he mumbled.

'You ran yourself into the dang blasted door like some kind of nut,' said Grandfather Racket. 'That's what happened. I swear, Raymond, if you ain't—'

'Let's help you up, Raymond,' said Vernon. 'Take my hand, that's it.'

Hazel rose without dusting her dress and held Raymond around the waist as Vernon lifted him to his feet.

'Give yourself a minute,' said Verne. 'Go easy.'

'Nothin' wrong with him a little sense wouldn't cure,' complained Grandfather Racket. 'I just finished tellin' you, didn't I, Raymond, just finished tellin' you what you got to do, and now look.'

'Willard,' said Hazel, 'get him a stool, for pity sake. Your carrying on won't help anyone.'

'Huh! You're a fine one, Hazel Martin,' retorted the old man, plunking the stool down beside Raymond. Vernon took Raymond's head in his hands and examined it as Raymond leaned against him and gave way to the gentle exploration of the servant's fingers.

'He's not a baby any more, Hazel,' Grandfather Racket persisted. 'As of today he's got responsibilities, you know it as well as me, and it don't help him neither, you pamperin' him like this, treatin' him like a child.'

Hazel glared at her old friend and neighbour.

'God help me, Willard Racket,' she said, 'but sometimes I wish you'd just be quiet.'

'Well,' he pouted, 'if that's how you feel I'll go and shut up then.'

He folded his arms across his chest. He stared at Hazel, his eyes clouded with tears.

'Oh, Willard,' sighed the woman. 'I am truly, truly sorry.' She stepped forward and wiped his cheeks with both hands.

'Hazel, he's got to do it,' pleaded the old man. 'If he don't do it—'

'He will,' said Hazel. 'Verne and me came to talk to him again, and I know he will be able to do what he's got to do. But he'll have to pay attention right now because Lillian is in the car with Lucy. They're going to take her to Little Hoosick in a few minutes and people are starting to arrive for the funeral.'

'So we don't have much time,' said Vernon, holding Raymond away from his chest. 'Raymond, listen to me,' he said. 'I'm your friend.'

'I know, Verne,' answered Raymond weakly.

Vernon looked up. 'Get me some water,' he said.

Grandfather Racket refilled the glass and set it beside him.

Suddenly Vernon smacked Raymond hard on one cheek and then the other, picked up the glass and poured the freezing water over the young man's head.

'More,' he commanded, without moving his eyes from Raymond. He held Raymond's shoulders and jostled him, shouting 'Raymond! Raymond!' as the amazed young farmer coughed and sputtered, his eyes wide and gleaming.

Grandfather Racket returned urgently with another glass of water. Vernon threw it into Raymond's face, calling out his name again, and shouting, finally, 'Lucy needs you!' Then he administered sharp taps over and over to Raymond's reddened, icy skin. Raymond began to quake and sob and Vernon held him securely.

'I'm sorry I got to touch you like that, Raymond,' said the servant quietly, 'I don't like to touch nobody so hard, but we got no time left, the Lord has left us so little time. The child needs you now, she don't need you later. A child can't wait.'

As Hazel and Grandfather Racket stood by in stunned silence, Vernon released Raymond. The young man looked up, his eyes clear and open. He did not turn away.

Vernon took Hazel's hand.

'All right now,' he said, 'I'm going to Little Hoosick. I'll bring Hazel up to the house first. Then what I want you to do, Willard, is you give Raymond a little while to put himself together. And when he's ready you go on up to the house, too, and do your business.'

He led Hazel out, pulling the old barn door gently behind him.

18

The bus from Albany seemed to float over the dusty road and down the slow incline toward Cohoes, 3 November, 1944.

A group of men, women and children stood in front of the General Store and Post Office. They did not stir or speak. They fixed their mute faces like road signs in the direction of the rumbling in the distance.

The bus rounded the last bend outside Cohoes, then rose like a mirage at the end of Main Street. The still assembly at the Post Office stared as one, held in time like images in a photograph, without registering the vehicle's arrival or the sighing of its brakes as it came to rest. The driver swung open the door and then, as if some primitive reflex had been tapped, the people surged gently forward like a wave.

Raymond and Grandfather Racket stood back from the group. The first passengers to descend were two soldiers in trim, bright uniforms and caps. The first limped, and held a crutch with one hand, the door of the bus with the other. The boy who followed had no legs, and was carried by two more soldiers who somehow squeezed with their friend down the narrow steps of the bus and reached back to receive his wheelchair from the driver. The parents, grandparents, wives and children of these men separated themselves from the group and stepped forward, speechless. They touched hesitantly, suddenly unknown to each other. Tears carved rivulets down their grim faces as the quivering leaves on nearby trees witnessed the passage of time and place.

Then the boy with no legs began to howl plaintively to these decaying leaves and to the bleak autumn harvest for salvation, and an eerie wail of doom rose up from the grandparents.

Barbara Jean Racket stood inside the bus at the top of the steps, her eyes fixed on the crowd in a glassy stare. For a moment it seemed she would not descend, until another young woman took her arm from behind, whispered encouragement, and eased her down.

Raymond and Grandfather Racket came forward slowly, and as Barbara Jean stepped onto the ground, the old man began to sob. He had to be supported by Raymond, who held out his other hand to Babs and led them to the truck for the short drive to Halfmoon.

Barbara Jean sat between the two men. Raymond eased the old Ford onto the road.

When are you leaving? she said to the windscreen.

The day after tomorrow, replied Raymond. Johnny, too.

They did the training together, mumbled Grandfather Racket.

You said that in the letter, replied Babs. And Hazel wrote that Joe is in the Pacific.

Raymond and Johnny are only just home from the training camp, said Grandfather Racket, wiping his nose with the back of his hand. And now they send them right over to God knows where without a decent rest, and us behind in the work, everybody selling off land and cattle.

He stared at his daughter.

It don't look like you suffered too much in Akron.

She did not reply.

I sure hope you're ready for some real work, said Grandfather Racket, 'cause there ain't no men left.

I know how to work, said the young woman.

Good. We got lots of it, I can tell you. The dang government has left it all to the old people and the women, the whole government is off-duty down there in Washington after they went and said it was all over, after we supposedly beat the dang blasted Germans and got the Japs on the run, and they told me Raymond was exempt, they got nothin' but liars down there.

Suddenly Raymond pulled the truck to the side of the road and jammed on the brakes.

What's goin' on? snapped the old man.

Raymond turned to Barbara Jean and reached out for her hand. The skin was still so soft, how could it have stayed so sweet, so far away? He thought all sweetness had left the world. There had been no softness, nothing that would yield to touch, in two years of war and labour.

Babs, he said.

His brooding eyes gathered up the reality accumulating between them as she silently nodded her own understanding of the ominous journey awaiting them.

We have to get home now, Raymond, she said.

He accelerated back onto the road and sped towards Halfmoon.

19

The people waiting at the house included the owner of the blacksmith and machine repair shop in Defreetsville, two women who worked with Babs at the Watervliet Historical Society, Hazel Martin, the Stilmans, and the Butlers. The hardware store owner, the proprietor of the general store, the man who ran the Mobil station, and several farmers in overalls and their wives, had just arrived.

There was a man in a stiff black suit standing in a huddle with Howard and the minister, Reverend Bates. They were beside Babs' coffin, which was still closed. Raymond and Grandfather Racket did not recognise this man.

The other guests clustered just inside the living room door. The men had removed their hats and fingered these anxiously as they glanced around the room. The women leaned together, whispering. Shirley was rushing between the chairs, pushing them together and adding extra ones.

Everyone turned and fell silent as Grandfather Racket and Raymond entered the room.

The old man's eyes filled with tears. He stiffened his back and pursed his lips.

'Well, now,' he said in a tight voice. 'Babsie sure would've appreciated this.'

He moved slowly into the room, shaking hands with the men and receiving silent embraces from the women.

Raymond followed, his head lowered. The Stilmans, the Butlers, and Hazel Martin stood together, stone-faced. Grandfather Racket nodded to Hazel as he walked towards them.

'Avery?' he asked. 'Billy and Lizzie?'

'They couldn't manage it,' replied Hazel.

'Too many funerals these last years,' said the old man. He shook his head. 'I can't reckon how it happened.'

Sadie Stilman said, 'I am sure sorry, Willard. It isn't right at all.'

'We been friends a good long time, haven't we, Sadie?' he said.

'Yes, we have,' she answered. 'And it don't stop now. That means you, too, Raymond.'

She held his hand. Raymond stared at Sadie, studying her acceptance of him.

'Just try to take what I am giving to you, Raymond,' she said. 'We are not far away. Do you hear me?'

Raymond nodded and replied, to his surprise, 'Yes.'

The guests fell back and some went outdoors by the cars as Raymond and Grandfather Racket moved towards Babs' coffin. By now Shirley was standing with Howard, Reverend Bates, and the stranger.

'As you can see, we're *both* back,' Grandfather Racket said to Howard.

Raymond straightened himself and walked to one of the mourner's chairs where he sat down.

'You're not looking too well, Raymond,' said Howard.

The young man glared at Howard without flinching.

'Never mind about that,' said Grandfather Racket. 'He's fine. Now, Reverend, the family is having a private meeting before the service. Then you can bring the people in and get started. Has Lucy gone up to Little Hoosick? I don't want her around for this.'

'We've taken care of that,' replied Shirley. 'She left with

Vernon and Lillian a short while ago.'

'What about the cat?' asked Grandfather Racket. 'Lucy don't like to leave Jungle.'

'They took him,' said Shirley. 'Vernon promised to look after it. But I told the child I'll have his claws taken out if he acts up on my good furniture.'

'Just like you did to Howard,' said the old man.

'Oh, don't start that again,' said Howard. 'Haven't we heard enough from you?'

'This is Tyler Hughes,' interrupted Shirley, introducing the man beside her.

He shifted uneasily.

'A neighbour of ours from Little Hoosick. Isn't that right, Tyler?'

'Why, yes,' he coughed. 'Sorry. Bit of a cold. My condolences.'

'Nice of you to pay your respects,' said Grandfather Racket. 'Now if you don't mind.'

'We've asked Tyler to meet with us,' said Howard. 'To stop you from making any more goddamned remarks like that last one.'

'The family can handle itself and its goddamned remarks, Howard. I ain't never noticed you and that wife of yours short for words. Whatever him and the Reverend want to do, long as it's according to some custom or other, I don't mind. Babsie and me never knew one church from the other, no disrespect intended, Mr Hughes.'

'Anything is okay,' said Raymond. 'Babs never had a religion.'

'Oh, that's a big help,' said Howard.

Raymond's long legs stretched out from the cheap metal chair. He crossed his ankles at the top of his laced workboots and massaged his forehead. The collapsible crossbars propping up the chair bowed as his bulk depressed the flimsy seat.

'You always got by on your looks, didn't you?' said Howard. 'And now when somebody needs more from you, you haven't got it.'

Raymond raised his head. He blinked at Howard.

'Watch yourself, Howard,' snapped Grandfather Racket. 'That there is the father of my granddaughter, plus which I reckon he is your biggest problem right now.'

'Howard, I want you to get to the point right this minute,' said Shirley. 'I won't stand for you not taking charge. I mean it.'

Raymond blinked again. Then he said to Howard, 'You don't even have looks going for you.'

'Hey! Who do you think you are?' Howard retorted.

'Pardon me,' interrupted Reverend Bates. 'Perhaps I should attend to the mourners.'

He went quickly to the other end of the room and escorted the remaining guests outdoors.

'You think I have to take any crap from you?' continued Howard. 'Just because my sister let you get in bed with her?'

Raymond smiled vaguely and stared out the window.

'She didn't let me,' he said. 'She dragged me.'

'Oh!' said Shirley. 'This is about as much as I can take!'

Grandfather Racket chuckled.

'Do you hear this, Shirley?' said Howard. 'Do I have to listen to some drunk insult me and my sister?'

'You certainly do not,' replied Shirley. 'And I'll tell you something else, Raymond Smith. My husband doesn't need appearances: he has substance.'

'Too much, by the look of it,' said Raymond. He lowered his head and began rubbing his temples.

'Jesus Christ,' said Howard, who began to pace in circles.

He raised his fists.

'You want a punch, Raymond? You're asking for it.'

'I'd like to see that,' said Grandfather Racket.

'Pardon me,' said Mr Hughes, 'I wonder—'

'Why don't you just shut up,' said Grandfather Racket. 'It's none of your business.'

'And another thing,' said Howard, jabbing a finger at Raymond, 'if you think you're so hot, I'd like to know how come *you* came back from the war and not Johnny Martin. Who do you figure was yellow over there?'

'That's a good question,' replied Raymond.

'Pretty obvious which one ran,' added Howard.

'The Army wouldn't even take *you*, Howard,' said Grandfather Racket. 'Shirley's got you softer than a cow's titty.'

'It was my eyes. They turned me down over my eyes and you know it.'

'Your eyes is perfect. I don't see no glasses. You was kicked out on account of flab. And who the dang hell are *you*?' added the old man, suddenly turning on Howard and Shirley's friend. 'I don't like the look of you and I never heard the name Tyler Hughes.'

'Tyler is representing us,' snapped Howard. 'He has a few things to tell you and Raymond that ought to straighten you out.'

'Now I get it,' said Grandfather Racket slyly. 'A fancy lawyer.'

Mr Hughes took an envelope from the inside pocket of his suit jacket, which he handed to Grandfather Racket.

'Well, now,' he said nervously.

'Well now what?' said Grandfather Racket, waving the envelope. 'I'm not deaf. Speak up! How much did he pay you? Huh? You know how he makes all that money, don't you? Dead people. They both love 'em like that. So this is what's going on. Sit up there, Raymond. Pay attention. You're the father, you're the one in the legal position. Mr Hughes is going to say out all the fancy talk that's in this envelope, aren't you, you crook?'

'Now see here,' said Mr Hughes. 'I will not—'

'Don't you use your nasty tone on my friends!' cried Shirley. 'What a disgrace. Howard, I won't have it.' She stamped her foot.

Howard jammed his finger into the air in front of his father's face.

'And I won't either,' he said to his father. '*You* pay attention. And hear every word. Because this is the last time I talk to you about it out of court.'

'Well, well,' said Grandfather Racket. 'Scare tactics. Don't worry. Raymond and me won't miss a thing, so's we can report to our team of lawyers. Isn't that right, Raymond?'

Raymond lifted his head and managed to dominate a surge of nausea that pushed up his throat. His head was spinning but he had found that if he focused rigidly on each person as he spoke, he was able to continue. He stood up and held the back of the chair.

'Mr Hughes,' he said. 'I am the girl's father. There is nothing to fight about. I am going to take Lucy and raise her. We can settle everything right now.'

'Mr Smith,' said Tyler Hughes, 'it is fine for you to come forward, uh, however, the problem we have here is that you never married Miss Racket. It does appear that no one will dispute you fathered the child. However, you did not enter into a legal relationship with the mother. And my clients inform me there is no proof whatever that she intended for you to raise her daughter. Nor, I am afraid, any proof to date that you would be in a position to do so.'

'What are you talking about?' replied Raymond. 'I have a home right here and it's where she has been living. Babs wrote to me in Belgium about our plans to get married, we both wanted that. I have the letters as proof.'

Howard and Shirley looked at each other.

'And what precisely was in these letters?' Mr Hughes asked carefully.

'Her plans for us. The future. That we'd get married and

make a proper home for the baby. How much she loved me and missed me. It was always her intention that I raise Lucy.'

'You must be kidding,' said Howard.

'No, I am not kidding, Howard,' replied Raymond.

'Excuse me. You say you have these letters?' enquired Mr Hughes.

'I'd have to look,' said Raymond. 'But I'll find them. Don't you worry.'

'In any case,' said Mr Hughes, 'the fact remains that you and Miss Racket did not marry.' He paused. 'I wonder why?'

'Don't answer a sneaky question like that,' retorted Grandfather Racket. 'Just what are you getting at, Mr Tyler Hughes? This man has worked for me for years. I can vouch for him. And that child loves him.'

'Oh, Pops,' said Shirley. 'Just look at the state he's in. That's all anyone needs to do to get their answer.'

'I was later coming home than expected,' said Raymond. 'I was wounded. So our plans were delayed. That's all there was to it.'

'Really?' replied Mr Hughes.

'She was going to marry him,' interrupted Grandfather Racket. 'But my daughter was a stubborn girl, Mr Hughes. She couldn't be pushed. She told me herself she was going to eventually, she just had to get to know him again. I told her not to wait too long, for Lucy's sake.'

'She needed time,' said Raymond. 'Meanwhile we took care of Lucy fifty-fifty.'

'For Christ sake!' exploded Howard. 'This whole conversation makes me sick. Babs would never have married him, Dad, and you know it. You were in on it. I can just hear you: "He won't be good enough for you, Babs, you can do better, Babs, what about the farm, Babs?" And now I know you were going to leave her the place so it all makes sense. You didn't want *him* to end up with it. You just wanted to use him in your old age, get him to do all the shitwork. Isn't that right? And she knew all about it, didn't she? You planned it together. Admit it! You were two of a kind.'

He kicked one of the folding chairs and it fell over on to the floor.

'Howard!' cried Shirley.

'After your lovely wife fixed them up so nice and neat in them rows,' said Grandfather Racket. 'You're just talking lies, Howard. Lies is all you're capable of.'

Howard turned on Raymond and laughed.

'Oh, she was something, Raymond, she was really something,' he said. 'You're a fool. They *both* dumped you. Don't count on any favours now from the same man who did that. He's chewing you up and he'll spit you out when he's ready.'

'Ignore him,' sniggered Grandfather Racket. 'He's on a fishing trip. He knows he's got no legal position with Lucy and he's scared.'

Raymond looked back and forth between Howard and Grandfather Racket.

'I'm the only one here with rights,' he said coldly. 'I don't need any of you. I'll find those letters and they will prove what I am saying. In the meantime, Lucy stays here with me.'

'You won't find those letters,' said Shirley. 'You never kept track of anything in your life. You can hardly stand up, never mind raise that beautiful child.'

'We'll see,' said Raymond. 'Maybe you shouldn't be so sure of yourself.'

'Perhaps,' interrupted Mr Hughes, 'if I just continue outlining my assessment of the situation to Mr Smith and the elder Mr Racket. I think that might clarify things for everyone.'

'Thank you so much, Tyler,' said Shirley. 'You are our rock.'

'He can outline anything he wants,' said Raymond. 'But—'

Suddenly feeble, he could not finish the sentence. He quickly sat down again, managing to muster an air of competence, as if he had planned all along to sit.

'But he knows my position,' he continued, 'and I am not going to change it.' He held the sides of the chair to steady his hands.

Howard and Shirley pulled two chairs from the rows and sat close together.

'To finish what I was saying, Mr Smith,' continued the lawyer, 'it would be the position in state law that a man who fathers a child but is not married to the child's mother must satisfy three conditions in order to be granted custody of that child in the event of the mother's death: one, he must establish that he and the mother lived as man and wife for a substantial period of the child's life; two, he must prove that it was the mother's intention that he have custody of the child in the event of her death, usually by presenting a notarised, witnessed will; and if conditions one and two are satisfied, then, three, he must be deemed by examination of the court to be mentally fit and financially able to rear the child.'

Mr Hughes paused and looked at Raymond.

'What's the matter?' snapped the old man. 'What are you lookin' at him for? Lost your breath? Too many big words?'

'Mr Racket, I am trying to be sure you and Mr Smith understand the implications of what I am saying.'

'I understand exactly what you're saying,' answered Raymond. 'But you're wasting everyone's time.'

'That's right,' said Grandfather Racket, 'and don't worry about me neither. Hearing good is right up my alley.'

Howard rolled his eyes and groaned.

'Well, then,' said Mr Hughes, 'I am afraid, based on depositions my clients say they are prepared to give me, that there is no possible way Mr Smith could satisfy a court on these three points.'

'What about the point of a child being used to a place?' asked Grandfather Racket. 'Of where that child actually lives? Huh? Where's your point on that?'

Raymond sighed and began to rub his head again.

'With all respect, Mr Racket, state law attempts to establish what is in the best interest of a child, regardless of where he or she may be domiciled. The view would be that what a child is used to is not necessarily what is best.'

'In this case they're the same thing! You know it, every one of you right here knows what I'm talking about!' Grandfather Racket exclaimed.

'Don't be ridiculous, Mr Hughes,' added Raymond. 'I was living on the farm with Babs, I saw Lucy every day. There's no question of what's best and you know it.'

'If I am not mistaken, however,' said Mr Hughes, 'you and Miss Racket resided in separate dwellings. At no time did the child actually live with you or consider you to be her father. Would that information be correct?'

'We didn't want to confuse her,' replied Raymond. 'If you want an example of thinking of the child's best interests, that's one right there.'

'Perhaps. But I am afraid from the point of view of your rights in the present situation, it was not a favourable decision. And a court would probably feel that the mother wanted to keep this information from the child for some reason.'

'There you go again!' said Grandfather Racket. 'Tryin' to sneak up. The only reason was stubbornness. I told you already. And the war. Everybody coming and going, the upsetness, trying to get settled.'

'But my clients believe, and are prepared to state, that it was because Miss Racket considered Mr Smith unfit to care for her daughter. Her only written communication on the matter granted custody in case of her death to you, Mr Racket. Not to you, Mr Smith.'

'See what I mean, Raymond?' laughed Howard. 'They were doing a few things behind your back.'

Raymond stared at Grandfather Racket.

'Don't look at me,' said the old man. 'I didn't encourage her. I had nothing to do with it. You know how she was when she put her mind to something. She just wanted Lucy to keep the family name, that's all. It don't mean nothing. Anyway, what's the difference? I'll get custody and we'll all be here together just like we planned. You can still be the father.'

'She said things to me,' replied Raymond. 'And she meant them. I am the one who should have custody of my own child.'

'Tyler,' said Shirley, 'we've got to get things moving. There are people waiting out there. You've told Raymond his situation. Now tell Pops.'

Raymond folded his arms across his chest and stared out of the window again. His mind was moving rapidly, covering this point and that, suddenly alert to signs and signals and possibilities, unexpectedly in command of his speech and actions, despite the intrusive persistence of alcohol. The prickling and tingling of early withdrawal from the drug – the agitated clamouring, the false energy of cells deprived of their sustenance and then complaining – helped mobilise Raymond's thoughts rather than fragment and confuse them.

Mr Hughes turned to Grandfather Racket.

'As I was about to say, the statement from your daughter which my clients tell me you have in your possession – the statement regarding her wish that you should have custody of the child in case of her death – would carry no weight in a court of law. If I am not mistaken, Mr Racket, it was neither witnessed nor notarised. And probably not dated. My clients are prepared, one, to contend that you forced this statement from your daughter during the week she was suffering from the headaches which preceded her death; and two, that because of advanced age you are mentally and physically incompetent to provide the care which this child needs. I will further submit that the girl requires the presence of a woman. Therefore, under the circumstances, my clients have today filed for temporary custody of this child pending their application for adoption, and I see no reason why the court would deny this motion. A county social worker will visit both residences and submit home assessments to the court. After that, I will be in touch with you and Mr Smith to let you know when a hearing on the adoption matter is scheduled. I expect the whole process to move quite quickly, given the child's age and circumstances.'

He turned to Howard and Shirley. 'I will be going now. Good day.'

Mr Hughes adjusted his suit jacket and walked briskly towards the door. Howard and Shirley jumped up from their chairs and ran after him.

Grandfather Racket shook his fist and shouted, 'There ain't no social worker comin' in this house. Over my dead body!'

'Let them go to hell,' said Raymond. He stood up and took the old man's arm, and led him outside.

'By God, they won't get away with it, Raymond,' said Grandfather Racket.

'No, they won't,' answered Raymond.

The guests stood close together in a large group. They followed Tyler Hughes' car with stone faces as it disappeared over the road by the barn.

Reverend Bates came out of the crowd towards Raymond and Grandfather Racket.

'Why don't we begin,' he said. He put his arm around Grandfather Racket and motioned to the other mourners. They followed him inside, and filed into the rows of chairs. Grandfather Racket lost his balance and stumbled as Reverend Bates eased him onto a seat in the front row. Raymond sat beside him. Shirley rushed in, panting, and stood in the back with Howard, who was pacing again.

Reverend Bates walked slowly to Babs' coffin. He opened the lid and turned around. He clasped his hands and looked at the silent gathering.

The hot August sun languished behind a veil of clouds. In the fields, Grandfather Racket's cows chewed sleepily, mashing wads of grass or cud in the steady, rotating grip of their jaws as jowls swayed underneath like fans. The hogs were asleep in a puddle near the trough.

And by then Lucy had arrived in Little Hoosick with Vernon, Lillian, and Jungle.

20

The small boy waited on a chair in the reception room. It was Monday morning, ten minutes to twelve.

His feet did not reach the floor. He crossed them at the ankles and let them float. 'Do not suck your hand, Raymond,' said the Directress, 'or Mrs Martin will not want to see you.' He slipped the withered fingers of his left hand from his mouth, licked tiny strings of blood from around the nails, and made his fists into an embryo which he tucked up under his sweater. He was six-and-a-half years old.

The Directress pointed at the large round clock on the wall.

'You remember that Mrs Martin arrives when both hands reach the top,' she said.

Raymond rolled his lips together and watched the woman leave.

His heart began to twist as the emptiness of the dark room engulfed him. He looked hungrily at the clock, determined to make sense of what the Directress had told him. But the dial appeared to the small child as a whirling chaos of spots, lines and numbers. He turned away in terror as the clock defeated him and he was left in a timeless abyss.

He could not find a point on which to hook the knowledge that Mrs Martin always came when promised, every other Monday at twelve o'clock, in time for dinner. He finished his lessons at 11:30, was carefully washed and groomed by one of the staff, and then, on those days, led into the reception room by the Directress at 11:50.

Often she found him sitting in this chair on Wednesdays, Saturdays, Tuesdays, or any other day. The calendar in Raymond's classroom made as little sense to him as the clock. The Directress would then reprimand him for expecting extra visits from Mrs Martin, and deny him sweets or puddings for not listening to what he had been taught.

It was now 11:55. The little boy's chest tightened. He squirmed in the chair. His hands longed to re-enter his mouth, but he must obey the Directress or Mrs Martin would not appear: it had happened that way several times, on a Thursday, a Friday, and a Tuesday, when he had not been able to resist the temptation and Mrs Martin had not come. He felt that his chest would crush beneath an anonymous weight bearing down on him.

Then he heard the heavy oak door of the Home open. He heard it bang shut. Mrs Martin would enter the room just as he reached the number ten. Raymond began his slow count. At the same time, he sat up very straight, and in the cocoon of his sweater cemented his hands together.

The Directress and Mrs Martin appeared in the doorway of the room just as Raymond was thinking: 'Ten'. He stared at Mrs Martin and did not move.

Hazel was wearing a flowery dress and a light cardigan: it was April. Her thick blonde hair was pulled back in a bun and strands of loose hair fell across her face. She pushed these away and smiled shyly at Raymond. Today, in addition to her handbag, Hazel was carrying a home-made cloth sack with twine handles.

The Directress said, 'We'll see you at lunch then. 12:05. He has been a very good boy.'

She was about to turn away when, to Raymond's astonishment, Hazel addressed her. This had happened only once before in Raymond's presence, when Hazel had asked whether she might give Raymond a sweet to hold until after the meal. The Directress had said no: it was not fair to show that some had more than others.

Now Hazel said, 'It is such a lovely day I thought Raymond and I might take a picnic outdoors. I made some sandwiches for us.' She smiled at Raymond again.

Raymond noticed the other woman's eyes widen and twitch. For a moment she did not speak.

'Then we could come back,' continued Hazel, 'and read a story. He might like the fresh air.'

The Directress replied, 'I wouldn't want him to get into the habit of this sort of thing.'

'It's just for today,' Hazel replied firmly.

Raymond's heart was pounding. His eyes twinkled. He took a breath that filled and expanded his chest, and the rush of air dislodged the knot of tension in his lungs.

The Directress said, 'Isn't Mrs Martin very good to you, Raymond? I want to hear you say thank you.'

Raymond stared at the Directress and did not reply.

'I know he appreciates it,' said Hazel. 'He is always very polite.'

'He must learn to say it,' replied the other woman.

She nodded to Mrs Martin and left the room.

Hazel stepped closer to Raymond and held out her hand. He wriggled off the chair by himself without releasing his secreted fists. He and Hazel walked down the hall and out the front door in silence.

When they reached a sunny clearing not far from the Home, Hazel took a small blanket from her sack and spread it on the ground. Raymond reached into the bag and took out two packets of sandwiches cut in triangles. He arranged these in a circle on the blanket. He also removed two apples and a bottle of milk. Hazel opened her handbag and gave Raymond a bar of chocolate. He handed it back to her.

Hazel laughed. 'The chocolate is for you, Raymond.'

She tried to return the sweet to him, but he would not take it. She placed it on the blanket between them.

They ate the picnic without speaking. Occasionally Hazel would point out and name a bird or a flower. When they had finished and Hazel was packing up the blanket, she asked Raymond, 'Would you like the chocolate now? Or will I save it for another day?' Raymond did not reply and Hazel tucked the bar into her handbag.

When they returned to Bennett's Gorge, Hazel read two books to Raymond, sitting beside him on the couch in the reception room. When she had finished, she said, 'Now I have to go. You know that I always leave after we read.' Raymond gripped the two books in his lap until his knuckles turned white.

The Directress appeared in the doorway and said something to Mrs Martin which Raymond could not make out. He did not feel his feet touch the floor as he accompanied Hazel and the Directress down the corrider.

As usual, the Reverend Barker was waiting in a car. Hazel waved to Raymond before she got in and drove off.

21

Raymond was eleven years old when Bennett's Gorge refused to keep him any longer. The Martins' first child, Joseph, was nine; their second, Johnny, six; and a third, Billy, had recently turned one.

Hazel, and sometimes Avery, had visited Raymond regularly since their first meeting. By the time he was seven he had begun to talk. At eight he could read and write.

In the year leading up to his expulsion he had begun to steal. Children in the Home did not have private lockers, nor were they allowed possessions. Toys, books, and clothing – even those given as gifts to individual children – were stored in locked closets and distributed at the discretion of staff.

Raymond broke into these closets and took sweaters, scarves, trucks, toy soldiers and stuffed animals. Sometimes he just sorted through and rearranged items on the shelves. He also pried open kitchen cabinets and ice boxes, and stole cookies, bottles of milk, raw hamburger, leftover food and matches. He managed to get into the groundskeeper's shed and remove or rearrange trowels, rakes, hoes and seeds.

No one ever saw Raymond steal any of the missing goods. Most were never found. Staff grew impatient as one after another of their plans to catch or thwart the thief failed. The loudest and most disobedient children were wrongly accused and punished.

Finally Raymond was identified when a nurse discovered him in the corner of the dormitory at four o'clock one morning: he sat cross-legged and barefoot staring into a dainty crackling fire made of twigs, socks and paper balls neatly formed from pages of books. The fire was encircled by an army of toys and tools. It gave off a pungent odour, and a light grey smoke which strolled through the dormitory and awakened the other children.

Raymond did not hear their cries, he did not notice the nurse rush into the room. His unflinching gaze was entwined with the hot dancing light of the flames and he was devouring a piece of cake intended for dinner. Crumbs cascaded from his lips down the front of his thin cotton nightshirt. The nurse raised the alarm, doused the nascent blaze, and grasping Raymond by the back of his neck, herded him and the other children into the corrider.

Raymond was denounced in assemblies, paraded as an example before the smaller orphans, deprived of food and special outings. He was made to sit alone in a corner at the back of the classroom.

On the first Monday Hazel was scheduled to visit following his discovery, Raymond managed to sneak downstairs from the captivity of the dormitory. From his hiding place, he could not see his friend, but he did hear the Directress forbid her to make further visits. The woman angrily accused Hazel of contributing to Raymond's criminal tendencies through over-indulgence. The Directress outlined the Home's plans for his punishment and rehabilitation, and stated that if the plans failed, Raymond would be sent to a locked detention centre in Albany. He heard Mrs Martin protest and demand to see him. He heard the Directress usher Hazel out, and he heard Hazel's voice rise just before the gigantic slab of door crashed shut. Raymond crept back to his dormitory.

The next day, Hazel returned with Avery and the Reverend Barker. Raymond glimpsed their arrival from the window of his classroom. His heart leapt as he saw Avery take Hazel's hand and march up the path. He lost sight of the trio as they rounded the corner of the building, but he heard the knocker on the main door bang repeatedly. The banging paused and then resumed, until finally Raymond heard the door open.

His chest was suffused with a heat that poured into his arms and down his legs. He thought his heart would explode as it drove up to his throat and tried to push out. Quickly pretending to stifle a cough, he clasped his mouth with both hands, one sealing another, to shut off the cry which was struggling upwards towards oxygen like a flame.

For days after this visit, the Martins did not return. Raymond's every waking breath was expended keeping alive his vision of Hazel and Avery striding up the path to Bennett's Gorge.

Two weeks later, on the regularly scheduled Monday, Hazel and Avery arrived at the appointed time, spied upon by the ubiquitous Raymond. The Directress turned the couple away at the door. But this time Raymond was caught off-guard when no voices were raised and no protests lodged. During the next fortnight he lived in isolation and despair. He resumed stealing and fire-setting and welcomed the floggings and privation. For the first time in six years he did not anticipate the normal visit with Hazel.

On Monday, 19 November, 1928, when the Directress, carrying a satchel, took him from the classroom at 11:45, he thought it was Wednesday and he believed he was being sent with the weekly post to Albany. At the thought of the detention centre he felt nothing. He simply followed the Directress into the reception room to meet the postman.

Raymond and his body no longer had anything to do with each other, or with any living place or presence on earth.

At first he could not adjust. When he saw Avery and Hazel and the Reverend Barker standing with a fourth man who looked official in a dark suit and hat, he wondered why they should be going to Albany. Possible reasons for this cruel turn of events twisted in his mind like a knife. Within seconds his head was stabbed with pain and he felt his skull would fly apart.

The Directress passed the satchel to Avery. He took it and glared at the woman until she turned away from him. This gesture of Avery's thrashed at Raymond's brain, another assault to jam and jumble the well-worn order of its pathways. In a sudden flash Raymond thought he had figured things out: the postman must be sick.

But then he heard his name.

Until that moment, the only sound his ears had admitted was the anticipated chug of the postman's car motoring to Albany. He was dizzy. He tried to see where his name had come from. The postman: the postman must be ready for him, he was not sick after all. And yet, somehow, he was not in the room.

Then he saw Mrs Martin: Mrs Martin.

Her eyes did not leave him. They have brought her here to say good-bye, thought Raymond.

She repeated his name.

He could not bear the parting. He went cold. All transfer of emotion froze. Discs of ice seemed to descend upon his eyes, and so he was able to hold Hazel's gaze without taking her in.

Suddenly the Directress turned and left the room, saying nothing.

Hazel said: Raymond, you are coming home with us. Avery and I want you to live with us.

There is a mistake, he thought: Didn't they tell you? I am going to Albany, I am going to prison.

Then he looked at Avery. The intimation of a smile brushed across the man's lips.

Raymond kept looking. He was not mistaken: Avery was smiling.

The delicate stroke which had graced Avery's lips then passed over Raymond's eyes, evoking the suggestion of a spring thaw: a tentative melting away, a cautious dilation like the opening of a flower in unaccustomed light.

Raymond turned back to Hazel, whose resolute countenance awaited him.

He knew what he had heard.

His arms stiff at his sides, the orphan wrenched his face to the ceiling as his lungs burned and his neck and cardigan flowed with tears.

22

'So you're the kid that set the fires at Bennett's Gorge,' said Howard, eyeing Raymond as he chewed a large bite of Hazel's Thanksgiving turkey. 'How old are you?'

Raymond sat at the Martins' table with his hands locked together underneath and out of sight. He stared at Howard. This was his third day in his new home.

'Shut up, Howard,' snapped Grandfather Racket. 'You never can think of a nice goddamn word to say, can you?'

'What's the matter with you?' said Howard. 'I can't ask some kid how old he is? Everybody's heard of him.'

'Eat that dinner Hazel put in front of you and keep quiet,' replied Grandfather Racket.

Barbara Jean, seated on one side of Raymond, turned to him.

'You look about ten or eleven. That's what I figure anyway.'

At the head of the table Avery Martin rested his elbows on either side of his plate and propped his chin on his fists.

'Now let's just take our time,' he said. 'Raymond has been with us only a few days and we want to make him feel at home.'

Howard shrugged. 'All the same to me,' he said. 'I don't care.'

'Well, now,' said Avery, 'we do. So you'll just mind your manners.'

'All I'm saying,' continued Howard, 'is for a kid that got kicked out of Bennett's Gorge he doesn't look like much.'

Grandfather Racket reached across the table and struck Howard across the side of his head. 'Did you hear what Avery's been sayin'? I hope that fancy college you're going to can straighten out your manners. We'll just see.'

'I'm nine,' said Joseph. 'Johnny there, he's only six. He's still a baby. Look at him, he can hardly use a knife and fork or behave himself at the table.'

Joe sat up straight and cut his turkey into even pieces which he lined up on his plate.

'Joseph,' said Avery, 'that will be enough.'

Johnny was seated next to Raymond, perched on a stack of books. He was concentrating with every ounce of his strength on the knife and fork with which had had lanced a slice of turkey. He was scowling at the meat. Suddenly he let the utensils crash onto the plate and began to pick up bits of carrot, sweet potato, and stuffing with his fingers.

'See?' said Joe, looking at Raymond and Howard for approval. 'He's stupid.'

'*You* stupid,' replied Johnny, slurping.

'Both of you,' said Avery, 'will leave the table if you say another word. Johnny, pick up your knife and fork and cut your food properly. You will not eat with your fingers.'

Raymond brought his hands up from under the table. He reached over to Johnny's plate, took up the knife and fork, and began cutting the meat.

'You got to hold them further down,' he said quietly.

'They too heavy,' said Johnny.

'It's how you hold them,' said Raymond, returning his hands to their hiding place. Johnny grasped his fork and began to stab the bites of meat into his mouth.

Barbara Jean smiled coyly at Raymond. 'You're at least eleven, aren't you?' she said. 'You're no ten.'

Raymond turned away.

Hazel returned to the room.

'At last,' she sighed. 'Billy is asleep.' She sat at her place.

Avery said, 'Everyone fold their hands now while Mother says her grace. We already said ours, Hazel.'

'Bless this home Oh Lord, this table and the bounty you have generously placed before us: the food, and the gift of children. Please welcome Raymond into Your heart as we have. Amen.'

She lifted her head and smiled. 'Now,' she said, 'don't wait on my account.' Avery carved more turkey for Hazel and heaped sweet potatoes and stuffing onto her plate.

Grandfather Racket stuck his chin out at Raymond.

'Tell me something, young man,' he said. 'What do you know about ploughin'?'

Howard laughed. 'He doesn't know anything, Dad.'

'I bet he does,' said Barbara Jean.

'Give the boy a minute,' said Grandfather Racket. 'I'll be the judge of what he knows. You got to understand, Raymond, my son over there thinks he's pretty dang smart, but if you left him alone at my place for a few days he'd starve. So what with him gone to college and bein' no use anyhow, I'm lookin' for a helper.' He cocked his head towards Avery. 'Avery mentioned him and Joe was showin' you some things these last few days. So just go on and tell me what you learned.'

Raymond sighed deeply. His eyebrows scrunched into the centre of his forehead.

'I don't think he's been listening,' said Joe.

Avery held up a hand to his son.

Hazel said, 'Raymond listens very carefully and he will speak when he is ready and not before.'

For a moment Raymond studied his untouched plate of food. Without looking up he said, 'The purpose of ploughing is to prepare a good seed bed for planting.'

Avery smiled.

Grandfather Racket sat back in his chair, chortled, and slapped his thigh. 'Now there's a fine start, knowin' why you do the thing in the first place.'

Raymond took a deep breath.

'I hope I never need him in an emergency,' said Howard.

'Go to hell, Howard,' said Barbara Jean. 'You're not so fast yourself, you tub of lard.'

'Barbara Jean,' snapped Grandfather Racket. 'You are a guest. I'm sorry, Avery, I don't know what's got into them but I'll tell them a thing or two when we get home. There'll be no more of *that*. Fourteen years old and listen to you, Barbara Jean Racket.'

'Barbara Jean,' said Avery, 'you may not use that language in this house.'

'I'm sorry, Avery,' replied Barbara Jean coyly. She snuck a glance at Raymond. 'I was just trying to give Raymond a chance to answer. We'll be working the farm together. I hope.'

'I appreciate that,' said Avery, 'but we do not use curses or insults in front of our children.' He turned to Grandfather Racket. 'As usual I am talking to all three of you.'

'I'm doing my best, Avery,' said Grandfather Racket. 'They just don't show me the proper respect.'

'You don't deserve it,' said Howard.

Hazel said, 'Howard, I would like you to leave the room.'

'You heard her,' said Grandfather Racket. 'Get out before I take you out myself.'

'My pleasure,' said the boy. He got up and kicked his chair away from the table. As he went out of the door he turned and sneered at the gathering.

Barbara Jean whispered to Raymond, 'Forget about *him*. He's a jerk.'

Johnny said, 'Where is Howard going?'

'He wasn't speaking nicely,' said Hazel, 'so I asked him to leave the room.'

'Oh,' said Johnny. He quickly folded his hands and put them in his lap.

'The plough is not a simple tool,' Raymond said to his plate.

'Good boy,' said Avery.

'Different designs,' Raymond continued.

'It depends on the soil, don't it, Dad?' asked Joseph eagerly.

'That's right,' replied Avery. 'And what else?' He shook his finger at Grandfather Racket. 'Not a word out of you, Willard Racket. This is for the next generation.'

'The climate,' said Raymond. 'And the terrain.'

'That's not fair!' cried Joe. 'I knew it as well as him.'

'Of course you did, Joseph,' said Hazel. 'And you knew it first. Raymond is just learning.'

'Yeah,' said Joe. 'I knew it before him.'

'What's he mean, terrain?' asked Grandfather Racket suspiciously.

Avery laughed. 'You go over it every day, Willard.'

'Don't act smart, Avery Martin, just answer me in plain English.'

'It's how the land is. Rocky, hilly, flat. What the plough has to cut through. Then you adjust the vertical hitch between the ploughshare and the horse, depending. Nothing new to you.'

'Well, good Lord, Avery, just bring the boy over to me and let him watch me at it. You'll have him all confused.'

'That's a single-bottom mouldboard walking plough you'd be talking about there, Mr Racket,' said Raymond.

'Yep,' said Grandfather Racket. 'You said it exactly.

That bottom part Avery is callin' the share, that's the business end of it, cuts up the dirt and turns it over. See? I know how to say it out myself. It's a beautiful thing as long as you got control of your horse, two jobs at the once. But don't you worry about that, I'll show you.'

'Dad lets me do the ploughing already, don't you Dad?' said Joe.

'I sure do, because you're careful,' replied Avery. 'You do a fine job. You're nice and strong.'

Raymond's heart sank.

'I'm strong,' said Johnny politely.

'And I know Raymond will be, too,' added Avery, smiling at the boy. 'He just needs to do it awhile.'

'Don't worry,' said Joseph proudly. 'We'll teach you.'

'I think he knows a lot already,' said Barbara Jean. 'But I bet there's a few things *I* could teach him.' She grinned at Raymond.

'You stop that, Barbara Jean,' said Grandfather Racket. 'Don't you go carryin' on. What did I tell you?'

'Barbara Jean is boy-crazy,' said Joe. 'That's because her mother is sick in a hospital and can't watch her.'

'That's enough, Joseph,' said Hazel.

Beneath the table, Barbara Jean placed her hand on Raymond's thigh. He stared ahead in a panic.

'The other type is a disk plough,' he mumbled. He shifted his leg and Barbara Jean removed her hand.

'Stilmans, our other neighbours, got one of them,' said Willard. 'We share it around. A real beauty. It takes two horses to pull that, very tricky. What else you know about it, Raymond?'

Raymond was perspiring now: Barbara Jean was touching his leg again. He wiped his forehead nervously.

'Are you all right, Raymond?' asked Hazel.

'Uh – yes,' he replied. He jerked his leg away and the hand

fell off. 'They work good on hard ground. The mouldboard maybe can't cut through.'

'That's the boy,' said Grandfather Racket. 'Avery knows what he's been teachin' you, don't he? Bert's getting a stalk-cutter, too. That's what you do before you plough – you chop up them old stalks of corn so they can get ploughed under and make the soil full of all the stuff that's in 'em. The cutting's a big job by hand.'

'Mr Martin told me that's why you have such good crops,' ventured Raymond. 'You take the time to cut old crops before you plough.'

'That's right,' said Willard. 'Got to be thorough. Now that disk plough, after—'

'After you use it to plough,' said Raymond, 'you can adjust the height of the disks and use it as a harrow.'

'I want to get down,' said Johnny. 'I'm tired.'

'Well, then, let Raymond lift you,' said Hazel.

Johnny held his arms up. Raymond leaned over and pulled him off the stack of books, which fell to the floor.

'Would you please pick those up for me, Barbara Jean?' asked Hazel.

Barbara Jean left her chair and stacked the books neatly under Johnny's chair. Raymond held Johnny on his lap.

'Raymond's going to take me ploughing with him,' said Johnny, yawning. He rested his head on Raymond's shoulder. Raymond blushed and saw Joe smirk.

'When you're feeling better,' said Hazel. 'When you're all over being sick.' Johnny closed his eyes and was soon asleep.

'How is he, Hazel?' asked Grandfather Racket. 'What's the doc say?'

'He's not over it yet, Willard. He says rheumatic fever can affect a child a long time, especially like with Johnny when the heart muscle got damaged. We just have to be patient and the Lord willing, he'll be a fine young man. But he'll likely be weak and tired a good long time, he had such a high fever. We thought we'd lost him, didn't we, Avery?'

Avery looked at Johnny for a long time.

Raymond grew restless and self-conscious. He did not know what to do with his arms. Johnny was beginning to slide off his lap. He wanted to hold him, but Joe was still watching and would call him a baby. Suddenly Johnny turned in his sleep. Raymond glared at Joe, put his arms fully around Johnny, and pulled him up to his chest.

Hazel smiled. 'Thank you, Raymond. Take him to bed for me now, he's worn himself out.'

Raymond held Johnny close as he lifted himself off the chair and carried the small boy up to the room they shared.

23

Most of the American elms near the Racket Funeral Home were lost in 1946 to Dutch elm and phlegm necrosis diseases. These trees, and a generous scattering of bur oaks among them, used to border Main Street in Little Hoosick on the bright grass which ran along both sides of the street next to sidewalks, nearly forming an arch over the broad road, and on the plush lawns in front of the sprawling white houses with their wooden wrap-around porches.

From her room on the second floor, facing Main Street, Lucy would be able to look out on a wide expanse of manicured lawn cut in the middle by a concrete path which led from the porch of the funeral home to the sidewalk. The path was defined on either side by two rows of low shrubbery. These were planted when Howard and Shirley's elms, one in the centre of each large section of lawn, died.

Here, and up and down Main Street, tree surgeons sawed and chopped the diseased trees for firewood. Then they gouged out the stumps because new egg-shaped buds, already infected, would continue to push up in an effort to restore the amputated trees. Craters from the massive stumps were filled with soil and planted with grass or shrubs.

From her window Lucy would also see Howard and

Shirley's driveway and parking lot, and the back of a large white sign with black lettering on the front: The Racket Funeral Home, Howard and Shirley Racket, Proprietors. In the parking lot, white lines were neatly painted to make spaces for mourners' cars.

Around the side of the house, where Lucy would not be able to see, were two parking places marked with 'Reserved' signs. One was for Howard's black Chrysler, the other for the hearse, a specially designed black Cadillac. From this spot Howard and Vernon moved bodies, transported mainly from hospitals or private homes, through the cellar door at the back of the house down to Shirley's embalming room. After a service in the funeral parlour, the casket would be carried by Howard and one of the male mourners through a hidden corridor to the side door. From there it would be placed in the waiting hearse at the head of a procession of cars and driven by Vernon to the cemetery. Howard or the minister sat in the passenger seat.

The downstairs of the cavernous house consisted of several heavily carpeted rooms in the front and smaller ones in the back, including Vernon and Lillian's living quarters and a small kitchen. All the rooms were connected through a series of halls, or sliding double doors of hand-carved mahogany and inlaid Tiffany glass. The most spacious back room served as the funeral parlour.

As mourners entered the house, they found themselves in a wide, comfortable reception area with sitting rooms to either side. Each of these was linked in turn to a more intimate room, referred to by Howard and Shirley as Consultation Rooms One and Two.

The interior of the downstairs was elaborately decorated with oak and mahogany: dark, brooding timber, sideboards, and tables which seemed to pull at the bright exterior of the house as a forest draws in and stifles the sun. High, broad windows, covered by thick burgundy drapes, nearly touched the floor and shed little light. The downstairs swam in a murky aura emanating from heavy brocade lampshades.

A mourner had recently told her minister that entering the house reminded her of riding the Ghost Train through the Tunnel of Terror with the child she was now burying. Customers at the County Fair were lured to the tunnel by a conspiracy of freshly-painted billboards depicting monsters frolicking in a sunny meadow, by the twinkling Ferris wheel and organ music across the way, by the croupiers hawking innocent games of chance where the most to lose was a nickel, by dolls dancing on the ends of sticks, and by the gossamer cotton candy spun magically on a stick from an ethereal whirl of air and sugar. With all this, said the woman, who could be scared of a silly amusement ride?

But as the little train with its squealing customers lurched forward into the pitch-black tunnel, a light suddenly went on and a headless corpse appeared, blood spurting out its neck. From inside the figure a hollow voice moaned, 'Help me', and customers felt drops of liquid on their hair. The train jerked left and a cackling witch with only a mouth on her face was thrust in front of the train, eating a screaming baby and sucking its blood which clung to the witch's lips. The train careened to the right and another light clicked on, revealing a jail cell where hooded executioners sawed arms and legs off pleading children.

By then, said the woman, our cries were real. The children screamed for us to end the ride, but we knew we were trapped.

We had been fooled by the cheery appearance out front and now had to endure the nightmare inside.

24

Vernon eased Howard's Chrysler alongside the curb in front of the Racket Funeral Home. Lillian took Lucy's hand and helped her out of the back seat. Then she opened the front passenger door and lifted out a box containing Jungle. She leaned in to Vernon.

'You take your time comin' back, Verne, they'll only upset her.'

Vernon nodded. Lillian closed the door and her brother drove slowly away from the house, on his way back to Halfmoon for Howard and Shirley.

'These is very high stairs,' said Lucy as she began the ascent to the family's quarters on the second floor. 'I going to rest on each one.'

She was lugging a Five And Dime shopping bag decorated with snowflakes and reindeer. On it was printed 'Merry Christmas To All, 1948'. The girl plunked the bag down next to her as she paused on each step. She could not reach the heavy oak banister and grasped instead the beautifully turned and carved posts as she negotiated the staircase. Lillian carried Jungle.

'We just goin' to put these things down, Lucy,' said Lillian, 'a place to put them, and then we go and bake.'

At the top of the stairs they entered what was to be Lucy's room. The small child paused.

'Who is these clothing?' she asked.

She was looking at the wide bed. There was a black velveteen dress with long sleeves and a high lace collar laid out on the bedspread. Beside the dress in a neat row were a pair of girls' white cotton socks, white cotton gloves, and a pair of black patent leather shoes with straps. There was also a black lace veil.

'They for you, honey,' answered Lillian. 'From your Aunt Shirley.'

With one hand covering the other, Lucy clutched the handles of the shopping bag. It dangled down to her feet, and occasionally she poked her knees against it to make it swing.

'Why don't we open up that bag and put away your nice things?' suggested Lillian.

The bag had been saved from last December's shopping trip with her mother. They had bought a scarf for Grandfather Racket, a wool cap for Raymond, and fruitcakes for the Stilmans, the Butlers, and the Martins. To buy secret presents for each other, Babs told Lucy to go down aisles one and two, while she would look in aisle three for Lucy's gifts. Lucy chose a bottle of spray perfume with a pink top for Babs and rushed to aisle three to show her. Then she proudly tucked the perfume under her sweater and gave it to the check-out girl while her mother was not looking. When Babs arrived at the counter, Lucy danced in a circle and jabbed at her mother's bulging coat. Babs tickled her and slipped the gifts to the smiling attendant at the cash register. Then she chased Lucy down aisle one.

On Christmas morning Lucy found a gleaming red tractor with three attachments – shovel, mower, and hay cart – from her Grandfather; a boxed set of six Little Golden Books from her mother; and white Frosty-the-Snowman mittens from Santa. Raymond gave her a big red card containing a dollar bill.

All these items, and her mother's half-used bottle of perfume, were in the bag now, along with the jar of disintegrating fireflies, *Babar At Home, Madeleine,* a red cardigan, and crayons and a colouring book purchased by Vernon and Lillian on the way to Little Hoosick. Jungle was sitting on the floor in his cardboard box, which Vernon had found at the farm. It was tied across the top with heavy twine.

'But I have clothes on me already,' said Lucy. 'And I brought clothes for Mommy, too. So we are fine already.'

'What do you mean, honey?' asked Lillian. 'Clothes for your mother? Show Lillian what you got in that bag.'

'I can hold it myself,' replied Lucy, pulling the bag away from Lillian. 'I washed her Keds because they had mud.'

'Is that what you were doing before we left, darling?' said Lillian. 'And what all did you wash? Can you tell me? Did you wet everything?'

Lucy stared at Lillian and did not reply.

'Well, then,' said the woman, 'those Keds need some fresh air to dry off. Why don't you give them to Lillian and I'll put them right here on the window seat to dry.'

Sunlight poured through the huge window facing Main Street. Reclining underneath, on the wide, cushioned seat, were several stuffed animals: two bears, a rabbit, a dog and an owl.

'We'll just move these little fellas over, will we,' said Lillian, 'and you give those sneakers to me, honey, like a good girl.'

Lucy set the bag on the floor. She separated the handles and reached in with both hands, producing two soggy blue sneakers which she handed cautiously to Lillian.

Then she picked up the bag and held it again with both hands. She watched Lillian place the shoes in the sunlight.

Lucy looked at the stuffed animals; she looked at the dress again. Her eyes wandered around the room.

The walls were freshly painted a bright white. The smell of the new paint irritated Lucy's nostrils and she scrunched and rubbed her nose. There was a thick pink carpet on the floor, and drapes covered with pink and white bears holding coloured balloons. The bedspread matched the curtains. Over the bed hung a mobile of gently rotating birds. There was a set of drawers, also painted white, a full-length mirror, a child's desk and chair, and a toy chest decorated with circus animals.

Lucy walked suspiciously over to the toy chest. She transferred her shopping bag to one hand and lifted the lid of the box. It was full of new toys. She did not look in the drawers of the bureau, which were filled with girls' underwear, socks, blouses, shirts, and shorts. The closet held several new pairs of shoes, and dresses.

Lucy lowered the lid of the toy chest and again grasped her bag with both hands. She saw that Lillian was watching her. Suddenly the woman turned away. She unpinned her hat and held it tightly in her hands.

'Did Aunt Shirley have a new baby?' asked Lucy.

'No,' replied Lillian quietly, 'your Aunt Shirley didn't have no baby.'

'It won't be able to sleep on this big bed,' said Lucy. 'It will roll over and fall out on its head and it might run down those big staircase we just came up on.'

Lillian turned around and faced the child. 'Honey, you know your Aunt Shirley and Uncle Howard don't have no children.'

'Then who is this big room we are in, Lilleran? It's not polite. I want to go home.'

Lillian shook her head slowly.

'I'm sorry, honey. I am truly sorry.'

'It's time for me and Jungle to go back home,' repeated Lucy.

Lillian sighed.

'You've had a bad shock today, honey, so you don't know what we're sayin' to you. But Vernon and me will try to make it easier if we can.'

Again Lucy stared at the woman without speaking.

'You are going to stay here with me today, sweetheart,' said Lillian. 'I know you don't want to, I really know. All I can keep sayin' is how sorry I am.'

'But Jungle wants to run around now. He doesn't like a box for staying in.'

Lucy tipped her face down to the box and peered in.

'Come on, Jungle, time to go! Come on now!'

The cat did not stir. Lucy moved her bag to one hand and picked up Jungle's box by the rope with the other. She struggled to the door of the room.

'Lucy, honey, you can't go,' said Lillian. 'I don't want to say it but I got to. You're going to stay here just for a few days and we'll have a nice time together.'

'But I have to tell Ganfar, Lilleran. He'll be worried. We'll go and tell him if it's okay, then we'll come right back.'

'He already knows,' said Lillian.

'He doesn't know!' cried Lucy. 'He misses me. Come on, Lilleran. We have to go.'

The girl stumbled through the door, dropping the Christmas bag. Her mother's shirts, socks, and trousers fell out, then the lightning bugs from the ripped top of the jar, and the red tractor.

'*Now* look!' she bawled.

Jungle's box fell from her hand and she collapsed onto the carpeted floor of the hall outside her door.

Then, from downstairs, came the sound of the front door opening as Howard and Shirley returned from Babsie's funeral.

25

'Yoo-hoo!' called Shirley. 'We're home. Where is everybody?'

'Christ,' said Howard, slapping the mail on the table. 'You act like we've just been to a wedding.'

For a moment there was silence. Inside Lucy's room Lillian listened carefully. She knew Shirley would hold Howard for a moment. Lucy, curled up on the landing, stopped wiping her tears and lifted her head.

Shirley said, 'I'm sorry, Howard. I got carried away. I just thought it would be best to put on a cheerful face for the child.'

Howard began to cry.

'It's too soon,' he said. 'Babsie just died. And it's a mess with Dad and Raymond, we don't know what they'll do next.'

Shirley spoke softly.

'Howard, they won't be able to do anything next. The important thing is what *we* do. And that's clear. Tyler has his instructions, and he told us it won't be long before everything is finalised. The worst is over. Lucy needs to get settled in, starting today. That's our message to her. She has to know right away where she stands. She is going to be upset and she needs our help.'

'I won't be any help to her,' said Howard. 'It was when

we put the coffin in the ground. Then I realised. I don't know why Babs and I couldn't get along, Shirley. Maybe I didn't try hard enough.'

Howard's knees gave way, and, sobbing, he slid down against the wall on to the floor.

'Take my hand, sweetheart,' said Shirley, 'and try to be a little quieter. That's it. We don't want to scare the child.'

Lillian tiptoed to the door of the bedroom and closed and opened it loudly.

'Is that you, Mis' Racket?' she called. 'I thought I heard someone.'

'Why, yes, Lillian,' answered Shirley. 'Mr Racket and I have just come in from the cemetery. A lovely ceremony. Did you put the child down for her nap?'

Lillian quickly picked Lucy up from the floor and packed the spilled items in the bag.

'Oh, yes, Mis' Racket,' said Lillian, from the landing. 'She had a lovely rest.'

Lucy squinted her eyes at Lillian.

'But Lilleran, I—'

Lillian held up her hand and shook her head slowly.

'She just fine,' called Lillian. 'Probably ready for a snack now.'

Lucy scowled at Lillian and called down the stairs to her aunt.

'Okay, Aunt Shirley, I all ready to go home now. So is Jungle, he don't like the box Vernon made for him. We're not hungry.'

Lucy clutched the rope around Jungle's box and took up the shopping bag. Jungle meowed and scratched the inside of the box.

'Good boy,' said Lucy. 'We going home right now to wait for Mommy.'

Lillian tried to take the box, but the girl pulled it away.

'I do it myself, Lilleran,' she said angrily.

'I'm bringin' her down to you now, Mis' Racket,' called Lillian.

Lucy held tight to the rope and let the box bump and slide down the first half of the imposing staircase to the next landing. She lifted the shopping bag deftly from one stair to another. By the time she and Lillian reached the landing, Jungle was meowing loudly and pushing at the top of the box.

'Don't do that, Jungle!' screamed Lucy. 'I told you we going immeditly.'

Again Lillian tried to take the box from Lucy.

'What did I tell you!' she cried, yanking the box from Lillian.

As she turned the corner of the second landing to start down the stairs to the reception area, Lucy saw Shirley waiting with her arms outstretched. She was holding a balloon and a basket of candies. Howard was sitting on the floor, his head propped in his hands. The girl paused. Then she started down, hauling her cargo behind. Lillian followed.

'Thank you, Aunt Shirley,' she said, 'but I have to be going now. Maybe the next day I would be abailable.'

'Surely you have time for some nice candy.' Shirley winked at Lillian.

'No thank you,' replied Lucy. 'Jungle needs to catch mice now and Mommy is waiting for me.'

'Where are her new clothes, Lillian?' asked Shirley. 'Didn't I tell you to bathe and dress her after the nap? We have the Baker funeral at four o'clock today.'

'Yes, Mis' Racket,' said Lillian, 'you told me. But the child has a terrible rash on her neck and arms and I was afraid the new dress might make it worse. I was sure you would want to see it for yourself and not have me go makin' a wrong decision.'

Lillian took a step towards Lucy, turned her back to

Shirley, and rubbed her hands rapidly around the girl's neck and up and down her arms.

'Stay still, honey,' she whispered. 'Lillian tryin' to help you.'

'Stop that!' cried Lucy, pushing at Lillian's arms. She dropped Jungle and the bag again.

'See?' said Lillian, turning back to Shirley. 'I thought you wouldn't want to take no chances on this. She just might need a cream. I didn't feel I could do anything without you being here.'

'Yes, Lillian, very good. That was exactly the right approach. As I told you, I will be the one to take action with Lucy in case of illness or mishap. I must always be called. Now. Let me have a look. Oh, Howard! Come here and see this. Her little skin is all red! It's no wonder, the hygiene they had over there. I want Dr Blake called immediately. What do you think, Lillian? Do you think he needs to see this? I'm not sure. Lucy! Do not squirm while I am examining your rash. This could be a serious matter.'

Lucy began to cry.

'What about her bottom, Lillian? Did you check her bottom? Now that would concern me very much.'

'Oh, yes, I check her behind and she is jus' fine.'

'Good. And what is your opinion about Dr Blake? Would he want to see this? How serious do you think it is? Will it spread? I mean, isn't that always the question in these situations? Turn around, young lady, and no more of your back-talk.'

Shirley rotated Lucy, scrutinising her face, neck, and arms.

'Thank you, Aunt Shirley, I feel fine,' sniffled Lucy. 'I want to go home now, it is a very serious matter.'

'For Christ sake,' said Howard, 'why don't you just wait and see if it goes away? I didn't notice a goddamn rash on her this morning.'

'That might be a good idea, Mr Racket,' said Lillian. 'I could keep my eye on her while you do the Bakers. You know, some rashes, you put cream on them too soon, they get worse. I can watch it and then we see what we do after I report to Mis' Racket and she give her final opinion.'

'Yes, I agree with that plan, Lillian,' said Shirley. 'Excellent. We'll wait and see. Now. Young lady. Because of this rash, you will be sorry to hear you will not be putting on your new outfit. Your skin needs air. I was hoping to get her started today, Lillian. Well, I suppose tomorrow is time enough.'

'Oh, yes,' said Lillian, 'that will be time enough.'

'Do you understand what I am saying, Lucy?' smiled Shirley.

Lucy shifted and looked at her aunt.

'What I am talking about is that now, since you will be living with Uncle Howard and me and be our new daughter, you will learn the business just the way I did as a child. Isn't that wonderful? And we are going to start with you helping me greet the guests – we call them mourners – as they arrive for the funeral of their loved ones. Vernon and Uncle Howard bring the deceased into the parlour while we comfort the bereaved. And that beautiful outfit upstairs on your bed, that's what you will wear. We'll do everything together, Lucy, I'll show you everything. You'll finally have a real family.'

Shirley put down the basket of sweets and tied the balloon to the hall table.

'But you won't do nothin' today, honey,' said Lillian. She bent down and put her arm around Lucy. 'You're too tired. So you and me is going to jus' bake cookies, go for a little walk, take it easy.'

'I bought a nice red collar and leash for Jungle,' said Shirley. 'So he can go out, too.'

'I don't *want* to!' screamed Lucy. 'I am going home right

this minute. I don't live here, you know me and Jungle live in Halfmoon. It's not nice to lie, Aunt Shirley, Mommy and I don't like liars.'

Shirley gasped.

'What did you—'

'I can't take any more!' yelled Howard, jumping up. 'I shouldn't have listened to you, Shirley. This is crazy, it's out of the question. Listen to this child, look at her. She doesn't belong here, Shirley, you know it as well as I do. We've got to face it now before it's too late. I'll take you home, Lucy, come here to me, we're both upset.'

Lucy had laboriously taken up the box and the bag again. Jungle was hissing and meowing desperately now, pacing back and forth in the wobbling box.

'You will do no such thing, Howard Racket' said Shirley. 'I forbid it. Did you hear what she called me?'

'Thank you, Uncle Howard,' said Lucy. 'Mommy is worried about me, she needs to see me right away.'

'Of course she is,' said Howard, 'she loves you very much. You need to be at home, don't you?'

'Yes,' sighed Lucy. 'I'm getting tired now.'

'It's the right thing, Shirley,' said Howard. 'Don't tell me you don't know it.'

'It's not the right thing,' said Shirley. 'Do you hear how she talks to people?'

'She's upset,' said Howard. 'What do you expect, for Christ sake! She doesn't want to be here. She's going back.'

'Howard, don't do this,' Shirley said quietly. 'I know how you feel, but it will pass, it's only the first day. Remember how we discussed this? We always knew the first day would be the hardest, she's not used to us, she has bad habits. She can't go back there and you know it. What about Tyler? All the papers are signed and filed. Just think for a minute. You're upset about your sister, I understand that.'

She opened her arms to Lucy.

'Can I give you a hug, honey? You've had a terrible week, haven't you?'

Lucy nodded.

'Come here to me and we'll talk about it,' said Shirley. 'I think it's best if you rest here for now and we'll just try to get used to each other and work this whole thing out together.'

Shirley took the girl's hand and sat next to her on a small loveseat. Exhausted, Lucy allowed herself to nestle in the crook of her aunt's arm.

'Will I go make some coffee, Mis' Racket?' asked Lillian. 'And apple juice for you, honey? Would that be nice?'

'Thank you, Lillian,' said Shirley, 'what a good idea. Wouldn't apple juice taste good, Lucy? If I'm not mistaken, you love apple juice.'

The child did not respond. Lillian disappeared behind the partition separating the stairs from the reception area, and then through a sliding double door leading into the first-floor kitchen. This was connected to the three rooms she and Vernon shared.

'I won't have any coffee,' said Howard glumly. 'It's after two. I'll go below and help Vernon get Baker set up.'

He walked over to Lucy and kissed her forehead. For a moment he watched her face and eyes.

'You even look like my baby sister,' he said. 'The spitting image.'

'I never spit,' replied Lucy. 'It's not nice.'

'No,' sighed Howard, 'it isn't.'

'I drink my apple juice, Uncle Howard, and then you drive me in your car to my house.'

'Okay, honey,' he said, 'we'll figure out something. We'll do our best. And maybe you'll stay with us awhile. Okay?'

Shirley reached out and took Howard's hand.

'It is so good to see your masculine spirit come alive, Howard,' she said. 'You make me proud to be a woman.'

'Bully for me,' replied Howard.

He walked to the far side of the reception area and through a door leading to the basement stairs.

When Shirley turned back, she discovered that Lucy had fallen asleep. Her head slumped awkwardly off the woman's arm. Dirt and tears stained her cheeks.

Lillian appeared, carrying a tray.

'She's asleep,' whispered Shirley.

Lillian nodded slowly. 'That's good,' she said.

26

Friday, 15 December, 1944.

Dear Johnny,

I should have written sooner, I just couldn't, so I hope you got my last letter written on Thanksgiving night. I don't like you to go without a letter. Of course I won't send this one, I won't burden you, I just need to put down what's happened and then maybe I'll be able to write something later to cheer you up with all you have to face, and then wait to give you the bad news until you get home and we can be together and comfort each other. I don't know what to do, it helps if I feel I am talking to you.

Johnny, word came that Joe is dead. Oh, how can I even write out such a thing. A man in uniform, a few days ago. It is the knock on the door you dread. I knew what it meant because of Sadie and Mildred, what they went through when they heard about Jenny and Kat. He took off his cap, Dad and Billie were at the cows, so poor Lizzie was with me, fixing the dinner, it was noontime. She's still so young, Johnny, to hear things like this. Why, even Joe was only twenty-five, you're just twenty-two, it is always the young people. They say he was taken prisoner by the Japanese, I can't remember the name of where it was, and then we won a battle there and went in and took over, and inside the camp they found Joe and many other boys who had died there. Lizzie burst into tears and ran to her room. I guess Dad and Billy saw the army car because they came up from the barn, Billy was walking as fast as he could, trying to keep up with Dad. Then the two of them just stood staring at the officer trying to get their breath, Dad went all pale. The poor soldier couldn't speak, he twisted his cap in his hands and bit his lip, staring back at Dad. He was young, too, Johnny, I feel they could have sent an older man. I said nothing, suddenly words failed me. Then finally Dad said, Which one? and the poor boy replied, Joseph, Sir, I am very sorry. Isn't it strange how a mind works, it never occurred to me it might be you – maybe that you've just gone, only a month or so, and we've had your letters from the ship so I know you're well. And I suppose I don't think of you as being away, Johnny – I guess everyone feels the war is nearly over, not really a war any more, but of course Dad was right, it could have been you, the war isn't over. I guess I just didn't want to imagine it. Probably because Joe always fit in so well with Dad, while you were more with me, which I think started with the rheumatic fever when you were a baby. Dad looked after Joe, I had to watch you every minute, keep cool cloths on you. I don't mean I favoured you, I hope Joe never thought that, or you, Johnny, that Dad doesn't love you the same as Joe. It's just that Dad put a lot of faith and responsibility in Joe, him being the first he took him everywhere and taught him everything about the farm. He did the same with you as you know but I always thought Dad and Joe saw eye-to-eye on things – and yet now I am remembering it was Joe who made me the valentines, Joe more than you even who liked me to tuck him in at night, and of course he had that way when he was a teenager of saying Oh, Mom, you don't have to tell me, I know. So there wasn't any favouritism – I'm not sure what it is I am trying to say. But when the officer said Joseph, Sir, Dad just turned away and walked back to the barn. He was moving ever so slowly down the road, he seemed like a ghost. Billy cried, No, Mom, and buried his face on me. I put my arm around him. Even now I feel I am speaking of someone else, Johnny, when I tell about Joe. I wonder if it's normal not to feel anything. I don't even remember what I said when I first heard the words. The officer was fighting back his tears and finally he said, I am sorry, Ma'am, please tell us if there is anything we can do. I think I said no, I appreciated his coming and I knew this must be a hard job for him. He said yes it was. He walked back to his car and drove off. Then Billy asked for Lizzie, I said I thought she'd gone to her room and he hobbled in – his leg is giving him a lot of trouble, he insists on helping Dad though everyone has told him not to but he feels that with you and Joe off fighting he is useless. Dad has been so patient with him but of course Dad is overworked, too. We had two young boys help for a while but they came drunk and somehow drank all day. I guess I just stood in the doorway quite a while, I don't know. All of a sudden there was Sadie in their old Ford, I didn't even see her coming, and Mildred was with her. They opened the doors and stepped out slowly, looking at me. I couldn't think why they had come, I looked at my watch, it was after twelve and I wondered had I forgotten something. Isn't that ridiculous, Johnny. Of course they had seen the Army vehicle pass and realised it was coming to us, but I must have looked blank. I heard myself say – it seemed like someone else's voice – Joe is dead. Mildred said, We'll take you inside now, Hazel, and she and Sadie held my arms, I remember this part because I replied, It's time for Dad's dinner, and Sadie said, We'll fix his dinner, you just come in and sit down. They led me over to the sofa and sat one on either side of me, and all of a sudden, I don't know where it came from, I just howled, the tears wouldn't stop coming, and Sadie kept saying That's it, Hazel, that's it, and then Mildred rang through to the operator to fetch Bert and Carl, I overheard her say, Mabel, get Carl and Bert, Sadie and I are with Hazel, it's Joe. Tell them Avery's gone down to the barn, *go to Avery in the barn*. I'm worn out telling you all this, Johnny, why, I don't even believe what I am telling you, it is just words. Sadie and Mildred are making the meals, Bert and Carl are doing Dad's work, he hardly gets out of bed, and Billy and Lizzie sit together under the maple by the old chicken coop every day, just looking out on the fields, even in the light snowfall we had yesterday, a sprinkling across the land. They hold hands, I think they are writing poetry, school is out of the question. Billy is seventeen, Lizzie only fourteen. Aren't they too young, Johnny? They're not ready.

I have to go to sleep. God watch over you, Johnny.

Mom

27

The tractor swept up and down the field, pulling the wide hay rake with its dozens of gently curved and rotating pitchfork-like fingers. Occasionally a rock would fly up and bang against the steel wheels of the machine or its intricate system of spokes. The Ford tractor, with a small turn-around radius, was ideal for this job. Raymond manoeuvred it deftly and efficiently at the end of each row, and after dozens of passes up and back, he had created a trail of perfectly linked mounds called windrows that resembled flaxen braids.

It was five o'clock. The funeral was over and Babs buried. Lucy was due home at seven.

Raymond finished raking and parked the tractor. He climbed down from the worn metal seat. This was a typical late summer's evening, spare and cool. He was wearing only the tee shirt and overalls he'd slept in and worn all day, and the air – drained of warmth as the sun slipped beneath the horizon – chilled him.

He sat down on the running board of the tractor and opened the tool box fitted just behind it. He pulled a new bottle of whiskey out from under a packet of nails and cradled it in his hands between his knees, turning it over and over.

He had never understood his grief at the decline of summer, nor why he suffered so deeply from the cold.

By September he had to wear layers of underclothes and sweaters, and still he shuddered as the sun began to recede. Babs would have put a wool jacket and scarf on him today. She always said that for Raymond winter began in August. With each passing day he seemed to mourn another ounce of sunlight lost. Probably she would have found and removed his whiskey from the toolbox, too: neither of them understood what besieged him, but she had decided he would not handle whatever it was with alcohol, and had begun the effort to take charge of his supply.

He set the whiskey down on the ground. He rubbed his aching hands, his legs. Then he crossed his arms and held himself while he surveyed his work.

It had been a radiant summer with just enough rain. In the next few days he would borrow the Stilmans' baler, a new machine that made cylindrical bales. This type had begun to replace the tightly packed square bale, which tended to trap excess heat and moisture in the centre. The warmth and wetness set in motion a process of internal oxidation that often led to the spontaneous combustion of the hay, with disastrous results. The cylindrical bales were more loosely packed and air could enter through either end. Raymond and Babs had finally persuaded a suspicious Grandfather Racket to make cylindrical bales after numerous fires in nearby towns.

When the baling was done, Raymond would begin preparing the silage which would be stored in the silo, and used to feed the cattle who would be bereft of green pastures through the long winter months. Although in the southwestern states sorghum was used in making silage, for Raymond and his neighbours in Albany-Rennsalaer corn was the principal silage crop. The Butlers' corn-picker, pulled behind Grandfather Racket's tractor, would remove ears of corn from the stalks. Raymond and Grandfather

Racket had recently purchased a standing corn-sheller, operated by a gasoline engine, which would in turn remove the kernels from the cob for storage or grinding as additional livestock fodder. Then, using the Stilmans' field silage cutter, pulled behind the tractor, Raymond would cut the corn stalks off at the ground, chop them up, and blow them into the Stilmans' one-and-a-half-ton Ford truck, all in one operation. At the silo, another blower attachment, connected to a barrel of molasses, would transfer the mixture of corn stalks and sweetener into the silo through the top. As the silage mashed down, it would begin to ferment. By November, the succulent, nutritious concotion would be taken from an opening at the bottom of the silo and fed to the cattle. Raymond and other farmers in Albany-Rennsalaer also added various grasses to the silage, a technique which they believed enhanced the fragrance of the intoxicating goo.

Raymond and Babs used to review these details hunched over mugs of coffee at the table in his bungalow. He talked and she kept a small notebook: how many bushels they might expect of each crop, the likely price per bushel, the weather forecasts. There was always the question of when, depending on price, to buy and sell cattle or hogs, and how many should be kept for their own needs. Grandfather Racket thought his daughter had a head for figures and planning; in truth, she relied completely on Raymond. When she reviewed the monthly calculations and scheduling with her father, the old man believed that he and Babs had done the figuring and made the decisions.

Babs and Raymond also discussed how much money Raymond should have each week. Babs would draw this amount out of the account she and Grandfather Racket kept in the Albany Savings Bank, provided Raymond had not drunk in the morning more than three times in a seven-day period. If he had, she reduced his allowance by half and refused to accompany him to The Roadside Rest, or to bed. At the time of her death, she had not been with Raymond for three weeks, and had threatened to cut off his money altogether.

Raymond looked across the shorn field. It was his favourite, bordered on the east just below the fence by the farm's clear, tumbling stream, a tributary of the Mohawk River.

When he was a boy, living with the Martins, he used to take Johnny Martin with him to do his jobs on local farms. In the hot summers they got relief by sitting in this stream. They left their overalls in a heap on the bank and went about building dams, racing twigs and digging clay from the rocky bed. They made pots for Mrs Martin, and cannons, horses and Indians for themselves. Hazel Martin baked these creations in her oven and used the lopsided pots for jam and sugar.

Whenever Raymond mowed this field or mended its fences, he imagined Johnny was with him again. Sometimes, since the war, his eyes and ears played tricks and he thought he could hear and see two boys kicking and hooting through the stream. This experience was like the trance of watching a movie in a darkened theatre: at those moments of remembering Johnny the only light which existed in the world for Raymond was the screen in front of him. All else surrounding his vision blacked out as he sat hypnotised by the montage unrolling before his eyes. This film could run forward from 1932, when Raymond was fifteen and Johnny ten, or play back to 1930 when they became 'blood brothers' by pricking and pressing together their index fingers.

Unexpected scenes from all seasons could appear: the two boys firing snowballs at each other from warring snowforts; chopping down and hauling pine trees from town to town on sleighs to earn extra money for Christmas; choking on whiskey and cigarettes behind the barn; lying on their backs under fiery maples in October, gorging themselves on ripe red apples; collecting beetles from stalks of spring corn. Raymond's library of these documentaries was vast, but he had stopped noticing long ago that none bore a date later than November 1944.

He took the cap off the whiskey. He lifted the bottle, tipped it back, and felt his body shed an unnamed grief as the liquor glided over his lips, into his mouth, and down his throat. When he stood up, his legs were light and delicate. He drank again and felt himself float up from the ground to the seat of the tractor. Now he was ready: he would go to Lucy, and make the life Babs had once wanted.

He gulped more whiskey and turned the key. He raised the rake off the ground with the lever behind his seat; he locked the mechanism into the correct notch. Then he swung the tractor out of the gate and drove down the dirt road.

28

Raymond pushed open the flimsy screen door which led into the kitchen, and stomped his feet on the linoleum.

Grandfather Racket sat at the table, poring over Babs' notebook of calculations, crossing out and adding lines with a pencil.

'It's too cold to have that door open,' slurred Raymond, shutting it. 'We've got to keep the place warm for Lucy. Seems worse than usual for this time of year.'

'You say that every summer 'bout now,' replied the old man, not looking up. 'This August ain't no different, Raymond. You just forget one year to the next. I don't know where you go in between.'

Raymond shrugged his shoulders and took off his boots.

'How many times have I told you, clean them boots outside, not on my nice floor,' said Grandfather Racket. 'We got a child to look after.'

Raymond looked at the cracked, worn linoleum. He chuckled.

'What's so funny?'

'Nothing. Is there any coffee?'

'On the stove, and there's some dinner there, too.'

'What is it?' asked Raymond, peering into a pot.

'Soup.'

Raymond stirred the mixture without interest.

'You been drinkin', Raymond?'

'Why would I be drinking?' replied Raymond. 'Don't I know as well as you Lucy is due back here tonight? That's all I've got on my mind. What time is it?'

'Six-thirty. I already been upstairs to straighten her room, I put a nice jar of flowers in there. You better not of been drinkin'. This is a child we're talkin' about. You got responsibilities.'

Raymond put a bowl of soup and a mug of coffee on the table and slumped into a chair. 'It seems like you and Babs are always trying to tell me my responsibilities.'

Grandfather Racket looked up. He slapped his pencil onto the table and stuck his jaw out.

'And why is that? Huh? Why? Because of you doin' all the time what you're doin' now: lyin'. Just when I got things to talk to you about.'

'I am not lying,' said Raymond angrily. 'Lying about what?'

'Drinkin', for starters. Look at you. And Lord knows what all else. Like tellin' us you don't remember what happened in the war when every man over there came home with a story but you, and you say you don't have no stories and so I just wonder what really went on, what you're not sayin'. And now you tell me you ain't been drinkin'. You test my patience, Raymond.'

'I was cold,' said Raymond. 'I just had a little to take the chill out.'

'So eat hot soup if you got a chill,' said the old man, looking away, distracted again by the notebook. 'Warm you up quicker than booze.'

Raymond slurped the soup. He spat it back into the bowl.

'What the hell did you put in here?'

'Don't ask me, ask Campbell's. But never mind about that, Raymond, look at this paper. I don't understand her figure on the late corn. What does she mean, "$++"? It's for October, she says that all right, but what's this "plus-plus" stand for?'

Raymond smiled.

'If I'm such a drunk, why would you ask me a question like that? Are you sure I'm up to figuring it out?'

'Don't go funnin' with me, Raymond,' replied Grandfather Racket, watching the young man's glassy eyes.

'Okay,' said Raymond. 'And don't *you* go insulting me.'

Raymond's eyelids began to droop and he slumped down in the chair.

'If you're so dang upset about what you call them insults, maybe you could sit up straight and start payin' attention and then I wouldn't have to insult you.'

'Tell me what you're doing with that notebook,' replied Raymond, recovering his posture and concentration, 'and I might just be able to remember what "plus-plus" means.'

'I'll tell you what I'm doing: I don't know how much money we got.'

'The two of you had a bank account,' laughed Raymond. 'Just look at the balance. She put the receipts in at least once a month as far as I know, sometimes twice, depending on when we sold things. She never told me more than that. You can see in the notebook we were doing well. In January we got rid of two nice steers. We couldn't have spent all that, plus the grain came in good, demand was up.' Raymond sighed. 'All she meant by "plus-plus" was the corn crop for October looks extra good. Extra money.'

Grandfather Racket took a bank book out of his pocket and laid it gently on the table.

'That's simple enough,' he said. 'Now the real problem, Raymond, is there was money goin' out every month and I don't know why.'

'What do you mean, money going out? She paid me

before she put the money in and she never took money out. Did she? Why would she?'

'And we kept the food money in the thing says flour and she put that in before the deposits, too.'

He got up and took a large tin cannister labelled 'flour' from a shelf. He set it on the table and pried off the lid with his fingertips.

Raymond leaned across the table and looked inside the container.

'There's at least five dollars in there, Pops,' he said. 'What are you worried about? Are there things you forgot? The new stuff for the kitchen? How much did you put down on the Kelvinator and the cabinets?'

Grandfather Racket eased the bank book over to Raymond.

'That's all accounted for,' he said. 'It might be my eyes, Raymond. Maybe I'm seeing things. I want you to look for me.'

'You don't have to show me this, Pops. It's not my money. You've paid me, fed me, put a roof over my head. We've each done our part of the bargain, fair and square. You don't owe me a thing.'

'It's yours now,' replied Grandfather Racket. 'Yours and mine. I'm going to change over this account to both our names. So you got to help me figure out what's wrong.'

Raymond laughed again.

'You shouldn't put my name on anything. I've never managed money in my life. I can tell you what I think. But that's it. And probably not worth much.'

'You might be a bungler, Raymond, but you're no thief. I'm doin' this for Lucy. We're her family now and we got to get us a lawyer and now I don't even know if we can afford one and still get by. We don't know how long she can stay here if we don't fight back. And there's something in this book I just don't understand. There's a lot of money missing, Raymond, unless I'm reading the dang thing all wrong.'

Raymond tried to puzzle out what Grandfather Racket was saying. His head felt light, his stomach queasy. He had touched no more of the soup and none of the coffee. They were cold now, each covered with a thin, greasy film. The sun had nearly set, leaving the sky caught between light and darkness. The tops of the hills seemed detached, floating against a panorama of sharp lavender-gold hues, cut off from the fields below which had already disappeared from view.

Raymond took the bank book and held it: a threshold Babs had forbidden him to cross. He opened it shyly and saw Babs' and Grandfather Racket's signatures on the first page, along with the account number, and the words 'Payable To Either Or Survivor'.

He studied each of the pages which followed, struggling to concentrate on the tight columns of carefully penned and dated entries.

'You see, Raymond?' asked the old man urgently. 'You see what I mean?'

'I'm not sure,' he replied slowly. 'It all looks the same, sort of, until here.'

He paused. The whiskey made it easier to hold back his shock: in April, 1948, the book showed a balance of $9,687.32. By the beginning of August, 1949, it had dropped to $415.84.

Raymond looked at the book again.

'Just follow on from there, Raymond,' said Grandfather Racket. 'From April, 1948.'

He ran his finger down the column on one page, then turned to the next.

'Do you remember taking money out, Pops? Think for a minute. Maybe you've forgotten.'

The old man shook his head.

Raymond leaned forward.

'Pops,' he said, 'did you touch the account at all? Did you look in this book?'

'All the bills, we just laid out cash as they came in. You know how we did it – repairs, gas, insurance on the truck and the tractor, all them type of thing. I never had cause to look in the book.'

'So the deposits listed here are your Social Security, her salary from the Historical Society?'

'That's right.'

Again Raymond ran his eyes over the string of withdrawals beginning in April, 1948: there was at least one a month, in some months as many as three. The total amount withdrawn each month ranged from four to six hundred dollars.

Raymond took the pencil and notebook from Grandfather Racket.

'Pops, that's more than $9,000 taken out.'

'So you see it, too. It ain't my eyes. Or my imagination.'

'The bank must have made a mistake. It's impossible.'

'They don't make mistakes, Raymond.'

'What branch was this?' He turned back to the first page. 'Defreetsville. But they know you and Babs. They'd notice a thing like this, they'd wonder about such big withdrawals, they'd point it out to one of you, ask if anyone else had use of the book.'

'They never saw *me*,' replied Grandfather Racket. 'I hate the dang bank. Babsie did all that.'

'Maybe it didn't get all taken out at Defreetsville,' said Raymond.

'I thought of that. Maybe a person could get another branch to give it out to them if they said they was a member of Defreetsville or some such. Look at all them branches listed on the inside there. Probably all they got to do is check do you have that amount and if so they could just give it out. So then maybe Defreetsville wouldn't know.'

'Where did you and Babs keep the bank book, Pops? Maybe somebody was stealing it.'

Grandfather Racket paused.

'She had it in a drawer in her room.'

'Was that the usual place?' asked Raymond.

'Nope.'

'What are you saying? What do you mean?'

'I'm sayin' that when I went to look for the book in the cupboard in the sitting room where it belongs, all I found was the notebook.'

Raymond closed the bank book.

'I don't see what you're getting at.'

'When you was out doin' the hay I was thinkin' what we'd need to get a lawyer. Maybe a decent car. Plus a woman to come in. Somebody's got to cook and clean, Raymond, this ain't no life for a girl the way I put up a meal. I don't even know where we keep a broom. Might not even own one, I couldn't find it tonight. Babsie wasn't much of a cleaner neither. So then I said, hell, there's enough to take out for whatever we need, what am I savin' it for anyway. When I finally found the book and opened it up, I thought I was seein' things.'

'Look,' said Raymond, 'it's the bank's fault for letting someone have access to your account. I'll go in there tomorrow and demand an explanation. They have to return the money, they're responsible.'

Grandfather Racket folded his hands and rested them on the table.

'Did I ever tell you where I got all that money, Raymond? I bet you never knew I had $9,000.'

Raymond laughed.

'You sure never told me.'

'My mother.'

'Your mother?'

'Inheritance she got from her father. Must have lied to my old man, the stubborn cuss. They was livin' out West a long time, then one morning a cheque arrives. "I will love you 'til the day I die", the note says. They had a flowery way of talkin' in them days.'

He sighed.

'I'm sorry, Pops,' said Raymond. 'I didn't know.'

'They moved away from here and I never saw her again,' said Grandfather Racket.

'Well, then, somebody owes you an explanation,' said Raymond angrily, 'and your money. This is outrageous. I'll be in the bank first thing in the morning, we won't stand for this.'

Grandfather Racket shook his head.

'No, Raymond. Don't waste your time. You don't want to see it, do you?'

'See what? An unauthorised person has taken your money, Pops. Someone fooled the bank, they let a false signature go by, they owe you that money.'

'No. Somebody fooled *us*, they didn't fool no bank.'

'What do you mean? You said yourself you never looked at the book, never had any dealings with the bank.'

Raymond was starting to feel confused again. The alcohol was wearing off, his head was throbbing, and he could not make sense of what Grandfather Racket was saying.

'I don't feel well,' he said, rubbing his forehead. 'I have a headache.'

Grandfather Racket leaned forward. He opened the bank book to the first page and pointed.

'It was Babs stealing my money, Raymond.'

Raymond looked at the old man.

'My own daughter was robbin' me right under my nose.'

Raymond fumbled with the book, turning pages back and forth.

'Open your eyes, Raymond, and see what's starin' you in the face. There's only two names on that account. The bank don't give out money except to names that's official in the book and on their records.'

'I'm looking at these figures,' stammered Raymond, 'give me another minute, let me just look it again.'

'The only thing you'll find on them pages is how much she stole. You won't find any other names.'

Raymond could not stop his fingers running up and down the columns of figures. One number bled into the next until the pages were awash with meaningless ink. Suddenly he wanted to bolt from his chair.

'You heard me,' said Grandfather Racket. 'My own daughter was robbin' me.'

'It's impossible,' mumbled Raymond. 'She wouldn't do that to you.'

'It ain't impossible, she did it. Apparently she treated me the same as she treated everybody else.'

'There's got to be a simple explanation,' said Raymond. 'Did she leave a note, anything like that?'

'Nothing. I been through the whole place. The minute I seen the book was gone from the cupboard, I searched her room, and the book was all I found.'

'Nothing else? Are you sure, Pops? Nothing at all?'

'Why would there be, Raymond? She was up to something she didn't want us to know about. She didn't give *you* the money, now did she? No. I know she didn't. And she never bought nothin'. So where's it gone to?'

'I don't understand,' said Raymond. He stumbled up from the chair, knocking it over behind him. 'Maybe if I just get a little fresh air, I can't seem to think straight.'

'Oh, no you don't,' snapped Grandfather Racket. 'I thought you said you was cold out there. You're aimin' to go get a drink from some bottle you got stashed away. Not while I'm in charge you ain't. Just stay right where you are.'

'Some fresh air,' repeated Raymond. He held on to the edge of the table.

'Sit down, Raymond,' commanded the old man quietly. 'Pick up your chair and sit down here with me. We got to help each other now. My guess is she was figuring to go off someplace, leave us both, take the child, or maybe not take the child. Who knows? Maybe she got herself a bank account under a new name. Or maybe she had somebody else and give him the money to keep for her til she could get away.'

Raymond stared out the back window. Near-darkness obscured the outlines of the rolling hills. It seemed to sway like an eerie wall pressing at him and barring escape. His skin felt tight and prickly. He covered his ears against a high-pitched scream.

'Take them hands down, Raymond Smith,' snapped Grandfather Racket, 'and listen to me. Because we got another problem: it's past seven and there ain't no sign of our Lucy.'

29

13 December, 1944.

Dear Mom, Dad, Lizzie, and Billy,

Well, here we are. I can't figure out why there's no letter from you (not that I'm complaining!) and what about Joe?? We hear things are hot over his way – have you heard from him?? Please write and tell me everything. Anyway, I'm fine. You should see us trying to get organised. When you figure the number of guys (I'm not allowed to say how many regiments, top secret, but believe me it's *a lot*) then you can imagine. Some Corporal even said, what we need around here is a MOTHER! That got a good laugh! We're actually in an open field, high up, which they call something to do with snow and it's a good name because the whole place is covered with guess what?? And when it isn't snowing the rain comes down in buckets. Then the sky clears a little, you can see trees all around, the tallest pines you could think of. I can't figure how they get like that over here and not at home. Maybe it's just there's so many all together. Well, anyway, my gang, good old Battery A, along with Battery C, just got some very good news about where we're being placed, a position that's a real compliment to us, which obviously I can't tell you about but I bet you can guess, and boy, how we kidded some of those poor guys in B that won't be with us. We told them Eisenhower knew they had a yellow streak a mile wide. They know we don't mean it, so we had a good laugh – nobody around here is scared *or* yellow, I can tell you that, it was just such a boost to us to know the big brass have confidence in us so if anything happens (which it won't, Mom – the Krauts are done for already) it will be up to *US* to take care of things. You could hear the Indian whoopees when they told us, we danced in circles holding our M-ls like big tomahawks. Mind you now, this was in *mud*! Up to our ankles. But we didn't care, even some of the guys that already have infections on their feet (blisters, fungus, you name it – our feet go in for a pounding) we were all having a ball, the best news since we got here.

Speaking of feet, I don't think I told you about our boots. The rubber boots with clips are supposed to go *over* the leather lace-up boots. But if you do that your darn foot is HUGE and you can hardly walk, so none of us can figure out how a guy would be able to chase Krauts in a get-up like that. So some of us, Raymond and me for example, we just wear three or four pairs of socks inside the overboot, no leather boot at all. My feet are cold but I figure they get air and I must be right because no fungus, just blisters, and if we walk a lot or jump around, we keep the circulation going pretty good. The trouble is the ground is not great and the rubber sole isn't that thick. Everyone complains about their hands, too. Of course we all got good gloves but you can't eat or clean your gun or pitch a tent in them, or write letters. Nobody thought of all this (like right now, my fingers are numb and I have to keep rubbing them and blowing on them between sentences.) We warm our hands by the little tin stoves – no shortage of wood but we have our supplies of kerosene because of course (what else) the wood is *wet*. We have little field cookers, too, for when we're on the run (never!).

I am taking a break in the mess tent. Nobody bothered to tell us about trying to sleep in a foxhole – or should I say trying to stay *awake* in a foxhole – it's impossible to do either and we spend an awful lot of time in them. Raymond and I have a reputation for digging the best foxholes in the history of war. But for some reason I didn't sleep too good last night. It's only about five a.m. right now, the mess tent is freezing, and I'm wearing: wool 'beanie' under thick fabric 'flyer's helmet' with flaps, gloves when I can't stand it and then I have to take a break from writing, M1941 field jacket, thick wool trousers, *and* socks socks socks in those darned rubber overboots. We have thick over-trousers, too, made of the same stuff as the tents but you can't move in them (never mind if you get a call from nature, you're a goner). You'd tip over like a clown trying to get anywhere in a hurry. Of course we have our M1 helmets, no use in this cold, but great as water-carrier and wash basin! Aren't we clever! And made of solid steel in case of Kraut bullets – just a precaution. You'd think I was in a fashion show, telling you all this. It's just to give you the idea. Our M-1s take eight-round clips and our M1923 belts hold ten clips, that's eighty rounds. The only problem is, so we hear, is when a clip is done it pops out automatically and if a Kraut is close by he can actually *hear* the sound of that and knows you're out of ammo and have to re-load. So in our spare time we practise loading and re-loading. Raymond has the fastest time in our group, which is so fast you can hardly even time him and what's more he has some technique for muffling the sound when the clip pops out. I'm not bad myself but Raymond keeps insisting I have to do better. Anyway, we are fresh as daisies and ready for anything and pretty soon it will all be over. Once in a while we go on patrol just to keep sharp, remind us how important our job is. We're trying to get used to the idea that we won't actually see battle – once we're in Germany it will just be a matter of showing our might, mopping things up. I just hope this weather clears when we *do* start to move – you can't see a thing. All we can hear besides the wind is an occasional sound, you won't believe it, like traffic, most likely what's left of the German defences, this is what we're told anyway, trying to figure out our next move. It's OK, Mom, they're nowhere near us, and wouldn't dare try anything. Our front line is solid and they're way beyond it. We've got great anti-tank guns and bazookas that pack quite a punch. These are small rocket launchers and Raymond and me are getting good at them already. He is very strict about making me practise, he can keep at it for hours without a word. He also managed to get hold of (I can't say how but he didn't really do anything wrong) two .45s, Colt automatic pistols. These take seven rounds in a magazine and they're supposed to be the thing if you meet the enemy head-on – they're only for short range. There's plenty of ammo for these, so Raymond's got us shooting at pieces of wood in our spare time, his aim is perfect and he says I have to improve mine. I think he is worrying over nothing, but he is collecting and storing up all kinds of spare things, kits, ammo, clothes, (c-ration packs, maps – one special one he marked with a red crayon to show where we are and how we got here. The rest of us are *lost*!) He is actually careful about eating his rations now, he says you never know when they might come in handy. And he practises packing all this stuff on to *himself*. He's quiet but he's always thinking. He has got hold of *both* a shoulder holster and a belt for carrying the .45's – they're printed with 'Milwaukee Saddlery Company, 1944' so they're practically brand new. Mom, you should see us all decked out in our M-1s, .45s, and layers of cartridge belts! We are quite a sight. I've asked a guy from Long Island, he has a camera, to take our picture one of these days with *all* the gear on so you get the idea. He has some method of developing the film – you meet the most incredible guys here, everybody has their own gimmicks and ways of getting by. Raymond looks so serious when he's all decked out, like he's really getting ready for trouble, he looks like a walking general store. He even has pine needles stuck in the netting over his helmet and has sewn special pouches and pockets on the *inside* of his jacket and trousers for carrying anything, you name it.

And by the way I think he is still pretty low. I asked him was Babs breaking up, not to pry, but he said no, he's just worried about how the farm is going and so on, that he did get a letter from her but that's all it was – about how hard it is keeping things up without him. A lot of the guys get pretty bad after the mail. I am trying to cheer Raymond up.

Only eleven days until Christmas. Drink some of your famous eggnog for me, Ma. Probably no chance we'll beat the Krauts by then. Oh well. I hope everybody is okay. Lizzie, I've been meeting some real nice guys over here, they're dying to meet you – handsome Greeks and Italians from New York! (only kidding) One guy called Dominick, he's beginning to think farm girls are swell after what I've been telling him! Seriously, these are the greatest bunch of fellows you could know and I've invited them all to Halfmoon when it's over. I love you and please don't worry – I'm fine.

Johnny

30

In September and October, 1944, German U-boats landed special scientific teams around the Arctic Circle. These units escaped detection by Allied patrols and established a weather centre that relayed coded data to Berlin.

The data showed that in December the Ardennes would be blanketed by rain, fog and heavy snow. Such conditions would cripple superior Allied air power, leaving British and American ground troops on the front line unprotected against a surprise attack. German meteorological experts calculated that the worst of the predicted weather pattern would begin in the early hours of Saturday, 16 December, and last for two weeks.

16 December was therefore chosen as the day on which Germany, nearing defeat, would launch an all-out offensive on the Western Front, in a desperate effort to reach Antwerp and sever the Allied armies.

In October, under cover of fog and darkness, and using intricately deceptive tactics, the German High Command began amassing the tons of supplies and thousands of troops needed for the Ardennes offensive. In the First Assault Wave, the Germans planned to encircle the Schnee Eifel and trap the two forward regiments of the American 108th Infantry Division.

By 13 December, German forces and *matériel* had succeeded

in moving to within twelve miles of the Allied front line. On 14 December, they were within six miles. And on 15 December, they were poised to attack two miles from the Schnee Eifel.

By 5:30 on the morning of 16 December, the hour at which the First Assault Wave was scheduled to overrun the 108th Division, the predicted snowfall had begun, and the German plan had achieved total surprise.

* * *

Wednesday, 20 December, 1944. 10:00 p.m.

Dear Johnny,

I am beside myself with worry and even though there is no use in writing I have to do something – there are reports coming over since yesterday of a surprise attack by the Germans in the area where I think you are, it began on 16 December. It was on the radio yesterday and now all over the papers. Dad wasn't here when the news came on, I think we keep the radio on all the time, he was down at the cows with Billy and Carl. So when he came up I said nothing and when he asked me, anything on the news? I said no, just the usual. He has had about as much as a person can take, and anyway there are no details being given as yet so most likely there is no reason to worry. Of course Dad did hear it that night and read it in the morning paper. So we are trying to find out *exactly* where your regiment is, Johnny, and that will help. There was no way to keep it from Billy and Lizzie. Nobody thinks about anything else any more, we sleep with the radio on. I can't believe it is almost Christmas, one thing just swims into another, Joe is to be buried over there, wherever it is, they told us we will have to pay to bring him back or else wait til probably the end of the war. Who makes these policies, leaving us with a decision like that? But we had to, Johnny, I'm sorry if this hurts you – but there is no money for such a thing and many, many families are reduced to this. No proper funeral, no proper burial in their own towns. Willard and Barbara Jean have been up to us every day since the early reports from Belgium, she is very agitated, demanding the government find out what's going on. As you probably already know, she is pregnant with Raymond's child and in that way of hers she is determined to marry him, she says the war can't stop people's lives, and Willard told her – they were here in the house – he won't permit it. He is just as determined as Barbara Jean, it makes no sense at all but he feels Raymond abandoned the two of them and says there is 'no dang way' he'll let Raymond have one square inch of his land (you know how he talks.) Please don't tell Raymond, Johnny. You know how Willard and Barbara Jean are, they could change their minds a dozen times before you and Raymond set foot back here, arguing all the while. I can't remember whether I told you – Bert and Sadie heard that Fred will be back from Italy soon, he is fine, just a broken pelvis from a parachute jump, his other wound from '43 has healed though they think there will always be a weakness in the chest and he won't be doing any of the heavy work from now on. Thank the Lord he lost only one lung, it was shrapnel, and at first they thought he would be blind, too, but no, his sight has been saved. The news is coming on the radio so I'll go now. Of course I won't send this letter, I don't know how so much worry and sadness got into every line. We love you, Johnny, our prayers are with you every minute. I'll write again tomorrow.

Mom

31

The old Ford pick-up veered along the winding dark roads from Halfmoon to Little Hoosick. Grandfather Racket decided to take the back way as far as Cohoes, then County Road 47 from Cohoes to Defreetsville and on in to Little Hoosick. The feeble light from the vehicle's headlamps dispersed uselessly in the fog that had descended upon the Mohawk Valley.

An occasional skunk or woodchuck darted across the road, and Grandfather Racket, hunched over the steering wheel, kept jerking the truck from left to right to avoid the animals on one side or potholes and a ditch on the other. As he approached Niskayuna, he suddenly screeched the truck to a halt, reached across Raymond, and popped open the glove compartment.

'What are you doing?' said Raymond. 'It's pitch black out here.'

'I'm goin' to get me one them dang blasted varmints. They're takin' over the whole place.'

The old man grabbed a scratched and filthy .45-calibre pistol from underneath old receipts and greasy socks. He flipped open the cylinder, spun it, and clicked it back in place. Then he blew into the barrel and rubbed the gun against his shirt as he opened the door of the truck and bolted onto the deserted road.

'For Christ sake!' called Raymond. 'Get back in here!'

Raymond saw the old man run partway down the road and then lost him in the darkness. A moment later he heard one shot. Grandfather Racket reappeared, grasping a plump woodchuck by the neck. He leaned into the cab of the truck and dangled the bloodied animal in Raymond's face.

'So you think they're too quick for me, huh?' He flung the limp creature into the back of the pick-up, jumped into the driver's seat, and stuffed the gun back among the junk in the glove compartment.

He engaged the gears and the truck flew down the road.

'You're crazy!' said Raymond. 'What did you go and do that for?'

'What's the matter with you, Raymond? Goddamn rodents. And another thing, we got to clean up this dump for Lucy, look how you been keepin' it.'

'Me? It's not *my* problem, it's *your* goddamn truck.'

The cab of the vehicle was littered with rags, empty oil cans, wrenches and rusty screws. The speedometer read zero, the needle on the fuel gauge pointed to empty, and the knob on the heater was missing. The floor of the passenger side had rusted through, leaving a jagged hole which Lucy had taped over with part of a paper bag labelled 'hol'. The ripped leatherette seat had disgorged bits of kapok stuffing that dotted the floor. The faded flowery bedspread Babs had used to cover the seat was still in place, stained with grease and dirt.

Raymond gripped the dashboard. 'You're going to get us killed!'

'I can't see a blasted thing out here tonight,' replied Grandfather Racket. He jammed in the clutch, shifted to fourth, and accelerated.

'Someday this thing will just grind to a halt,' said Raymond, thrown against the door as the old man rounded a curve.

'Can't afford a new one now, can we? Ain't much we *can* afford by the look of that dang bank book. What time is it?'

'How the hell would *I* know?'

'So what's our plan, Raymond? We got to have a plan of attack. You're the one was in the war, let's hear all them tricks you boys learned against the Krauts.'

'I didn't learn any tricks,' replied Raymond.

'How are you feeling?' asked Grandfather Racket.

'What do you mean by that? Watch the road for Christ sake.'

'You know what I mean.'

'I'm all right,' said Raymond. 'There's nothing wrong with me.'

'When we get there we both go to the door. We act like we're surprised they didn't bring her back like they said they would, even though we ain't one bit surprised, and we make like maybe we thought we were supposed to come to Little Hoosick for Lucy, so here we are. How's that sound?'

Raymond shrugged.

'I ain't goin' to be nice about it, Raymond, don't get me wrong. I just mean for when they open the door.'

'Look,' said Raymond, 'they never intended to bring her back. You heard what Tyler Hughes said. They're filing for temporary custody and then adoption. Face reality. We don't stand a chance. I don't even know why we're bothering. And let me tell you something else: *I'll* make my own decisions about drinking from now on. Tonight's the last time you decide. Do you hear me?'

Raymond glared in the darkness at Grandfather Racket. The young farmer was beginning to feel edgy, irritated. His hands shook when he released the dashboard to wipe his forehead.

'I took that bottle out of the glove compartment for your

own good,' said Grandfather Racket. 'You want Lucy back here, you stay sober.'

'Who says I want her?' snapped Raymond. 'Maybe I've changed my mind, maybe I don't like the whole idea. And you know what else? I think she's better off with them. They can have her.'

The old man jammed on the brakes. Raymond suddenly made himself into a ball, covered his head, and was thrown into the narrow space between the seat and the dashboard, wedged in at his shoulders.

'What did you say?'

'You heard me,' cried Raymond. 'Don't push me around.'

He lifted his face and spat at Grandfather Racket. 'Go to hell. I don't want her. I don't care about her. It's a wild goose chase. And you know what I think? I think you took your own money out of the goddamn bank. You're trying to turn me against Babs, aren't you, the only thing I ever loved!'

Raymond banged his head repeatedly on the dashboard as the ringing inside his head began.

'You were a fool!' shouted Grandfather Racket. 'She never cared about anybody. Get over it. And get up out of there. You think you're in a foxhole? Don't look for my sympathy, I can tell you that – some people weren't so lucky to survive that dang blasted war. Grow up. Babs stole my money.'

'*You* took it out!' screamed Raymond. '*You* took it out and hid it because you were afraid she'd give it to *me*. And she would have. We had plans. You probably can't even remember where you put it, you broken-down old man. Look at you. Look at everything you own. Broken. A pile of shit!'

Raymond wrenched himself free and hit the dashboard with his fist. 'She loved me' he cried. 'She didn't want your stinking money.'

Willard leaned across the seat and slapped Raymond's face.

'This is *my* truck,' he snarled, 'and that was *my* money. You just sit up here and behave yourself.'

He whacked Raymond again, engaged the gears, and sped off towards Little Hoosick.

Raymond sobbed bitterly in the seat beside him.

32

We've got to talk, said Raymond, slamming the door.

Barbara Jean did not look up from the sink. She continued to wash the plates, holding each one up and flicking it gently to drain off the soapsuds.

Raymond. Please. Take your boots off. How many times do I have to say it? I just did the floor.

That's what we have to talk about, he replied: how you've been speaking to me lately. And what Pops just told me in the barnyard.

What was he doing in the barnyard?

Taking Lucy for a picnic. I am trying to say something to you, Babs. Leave down those dishes.

Take your hands off me, Raymond. I'll talk when I'm ready.

No. You'll talk now. What does he mean, you agree this ends when he says so? And boys in Akron, boys here. What's he getting at? Is Lucy my child?

Babs dashed a plate into the sink where it exploded, leaving shards and chunks of worn pottery.

You tell me, Raymond Smith, she said, turning on him. I'm the one who wrote to you. Did you even read it? *I* remember every word. Do *you*? 'My Dearest Raymond, We are going to have a baby, my dearest Raymond, you are going to be a father.' But nobody wrote back. So maybe

I was wrong: maybe it's not you. Maybe I should have written to someone else.

What does a letter matter, Babs? That's over. I'm here now. I couldn't write, I can't explain it. Why can't you let it go? I wanted to write, I wanted to.

But you didn't, did you?

Babs held up one finger after another.

1944, she said: nothing. 1945: nothing. 1946: nothing. Then one day I was standing right here where I am now and you walked through that door as if nothing had happened. As if you were just coming in from the chores for your dinner.

I'm sorry. It's just – I don't know, it's just how it worked out. I didn't want to hurt you. But you've got to give us a chance. I'm back now.

Babs leaned over the sink.

Well, I'm not, she wept. I'm not back.

But you will be, said Raymond, we just need time. I'm the same person and so are you. The war is over. Finished. Just like we always said it would be.

Barbara Jean looked at him sorrowfully, regret welling in her eyes.

No, she replied. No.

Look, said Raymond. Let me move in, once and for all. Then we'll be able to work it out. We're getting nowhere like this.

That's not how I see it, for you to move in.

Is that what Pops meant? demanded Raymond. I'm good enough to work for him but not good enough to marry his daughter? And even that – even the work – he was talking like I should find another job.

You know that's just how he is, Raymond. You don't need to find another job. Don't be ridiculous.

But do I need to find another girlfriend? Is that what you're saying? Is that what the two of you have worked out behind my back? I can have the job and once in a while do what you need in bed? I'm a servant, is that it?

You don't have to stay, Raymond. No one is forcing you.

I don't call that much of an invitation, Babs. 'You don't have to stay.'

Well, you don't.

So it's *your* place, *your* life, *your* child?

She whipped her arm through the air.

That's right! she cried. Pops and I have done everything. Everything. Where were you?

Oh, I get it now. It was my fault I got drafted.

Things are different, Raymond. You're not facing reality.

You can't treat me like this, he shouted.

What should I do? You're not the same person. I'm not the same person.

How am I not the same?

Barbara Jean looked at him.

You're edgy. I don't know. Something is wrong. Like now, Raymond.

She paused.

And you drink too much. I don't like it.

She turned back to the sink.

There: I said it.

That's crazy, replied Raymond. You drink as much as me, you don't know what you're saying.

Everyone notices what I'm talking about except you, Raymond. Nobody we know would say I drink like you.

Raymond shook his head.

Look, he said, if that's all you're upset about, I'll drink less. I don't care, it doesn't matter that much.

Well, said Babs, that would help.

Okay.

Because when you drink you're in another world.

Completely. Lately it happens all the time, something snaps and you're another person in another place. I can't describe it.

What do you mean? I raise my voice?

Sometimes. But that's not really it. I don't know. And you forget what's happened. As if you were here but not here.

I don't understand what you mean, Babs, I'm trying, please.

I know. Oh, Raymond, I'm sorry, maybe it's not that important, I just want it to stop.

Okay, it'll stop. I'll make sure. And I want you and Pops to treat me like I'm a human being, it's got to be you and *me*, not you and him.

Barbara Jean did not reply.

Do you think I was on a vacation in Belgium? Do you think I *wanted* to go over there? It wasn't fun, Babs.

I don't know what it was, Raymond, you never say. But no, nobody here thought it was a holiday.

Well, I'd appreciate a little thought in that direction once in a while.

Babs nodded.

So? asked Raymond.

Barbara Jean faced him again and put her hands on her hips.

For God's sake, Raymond, what are you trying to say?

You *know* what I'm trying to say, he replied. It's time to get married. You need it, I need it.

This is what I mean! You're not listening, you're not facing reality: it's not that simple any more. Not for me, not for Pops. I don't know what I need. And a lot depends on you.

Well, isn't that just great.

Raymond stormed out of the kitchen.

Babs went back to the sink, stared at the broken pieces of china, and finally turned and walked out of the door.

33

Go, go! Run! They're all over us.

My gun is jammed, Dom. The clip won't go in right, I can't see.

Never mind. *Run! Follow me. Over this way. Oh, God, oh, God, they're attacking.*

Where's Raymond? Where's Raymond?

I'm here, Johnny. Here. Get down. Both of you. Now.

I just fell on something. Oh, Raymond, oh, it's Stephanopoulos, look at him, what happened to him, oh, God. Stop, Raymond. Wait! We've got to help him. He's bleeding.

Leave him, Johnny, leave him. He's dead. Run!

Oh, Jesus, it's on my hands, Raymond. Stephanopoulos! He's alive, Raymond. He said something.

Dom, hold him down if you have to, hold him. Johnny, quiet.

I'm telling you, he's alive, I heard him.

Leave him, *Johnny. Get down. Dom, lie on him if you have to. I'll crawl this way, I think they've gone around.*

Raymond, they're on both sides, they've surrounded the plateau. They're closing in on us from both sides. *Listen. Listen. Do you hear them? The tanks are on both sides, the shelling is* north and south.

Yes, yes, you're right Are you okay, Johnny?

What's happening, Raymond? What are they doing? It's so loud. What's that sound?

Quiet, Johnny. They're all around us, in tanks, on foot. Stay down. Not a move. Not a sound.

Raymond, he's hearing Panzers. Listen. That's what Johnny is hearing – you can tell the difference, the Panzerfausts, the Schmeissers, the heavy artillery. But what he's hearing right now are the Panzers. They're almost on top of us, Raymond! Jesus! Run!

Out, out! Dom's right, Johnny, it's Panzers. They're coming at us, we'll be crushed. Go! Go!

Raymond, a shell's coming. I can hear the scream.

Move, Johnny! Move! Push him, Dom. Follow me, I'll go ahead. They're firing the big ones. Go!

Oh, my head, Raymond, the blast, my ears.

Keep your head down, *Johnny.* Down. *The flash will blind you. Dom. Dom!*

I'm here, Raymond, just behind you. I – I think my eardrums have burst, I – I'm very dizzy.

Don't stop, Dom, we can't stop, please, grab Johnny, the tanks will crush us. Are you there? Do you hear me? I can't see *you.*

I'm coming, Raymond, I'm coming, I'm all right, I've got Johnny, I'm okay now.

That's it, that's it, crawl. Hold my ankles. Faster! Keep down. The woods ahead, remember? From yesterday, I'm going that way. Johnny!

I'm following you, Raymond, I – I, the explosions, my head is splitting.

Yes, I know, Johnny, just come. Are you there, Dom?

Yes, yes, the woods we scouted yesterday, we can't be in the open, the tanks are getting louder, Raymond, they'll run us over, how far is it, how far is it?

When I say, you must stand up. You must run *when I say. Okay? We'll have to run now, it's not far, I don't think it's far, we have to run from the tanks. Okay, okay, are you ready?*

No. No. They'll shoot us, Raymond!

We'll run fast, Johnny. Zig-zag, like I showed you, zig-zag, it's dark, they can't see us. We'll be all right. You've got to.

Oh, God, the shells, Raymond.

Listen, Raymond. They've gone right over the foxholes, listen, oh, my God.

We can't wait. Crouch and run, zig-zags, Johnny, as fast as we can, we're not far, we've got to do it, we've got to, now get up. Now! Go! That's it, run, *Johnny.*

I'm stuck, Raymond, it's all muddy and wet, my boots are too heavy.

Push him, Dom, grab him, they're almost on top of us.

I'm down, Raymond, wait, wait, Johnny and I are down.

Get up, get up, run.

What's that? Raymond! Are you all right?

I'm not hit, I'm not hit, I – I can't see where it came from, I – my eyes, wait, I can't hear – now, okay, we've got to run, I – I twisted my ankle.

I'm here, Raymond, here, get up, that's it, hold his other arm, Johnny, now, fast, *like you told us, Raymond, don't stop, we're nearly there.*

Yes, yes, okay, we're okay, we're here, get down.

Oh, God, Raymond, do you hear them? They've just gone right over our foxholes, they've just driven across our positions, everything, nothing stopping them. Don't listen, it's our boys, don't listen.

But we're out, we're out, it's all right, they didn't get us. Lay low now.

It's so cold, Raymond, I'm all wet, I'm shaking.

Here, Johnny, come to me, yes, yes, that's it, you're freezing.

You're shivering, Raymond.

Cold, Johnny, cold. Dom, take off his pack, take them all off, we've got to dig in, we've got to dig in as deep as we can before daylight.

I can't, Raymond, I can't do it, I'm too weak, I – I can't move my hands.

Yes, yes, you can do it, Johnny, we have to, now listen to me, they'll see us in a couple of hours, we'll dig in and we'll hide until we can move out, do you hear me? Dom, Dom?

I've got the shovels, Raymond, they're unpacked.

Can't risk a light now, let me just feel along the ground, between some trees, that's what we need. We can dig in, cover ourselves with bark and branches, snow – Johnny, dig! You've got to stay warm, keep moving. Here, Dom, come here, what do you think? How about this, right here?

Yes, yes, fine, Raymond. Push away the snow, that's it, oh, Jesus, the ground is frozen.

No, no, I've got a pick, I stole a long, sharp pick, handle in two parts, in my pack, it's not frozen deep, too much rain, it's all mud just below, see? Just cold mud, we're okay. Dig now, Johnny, dig. You can do it.

My hands won't move, Raymond, my fingers.

Take these dry gloves, here, take them. Give me the wet ones, don't get rid of them, we'll dry them somehow, now dig, only two hours 'til daybreak.

34

By the time Grandfather Racket and Raymond arrived at the Racket Funeral Home, the fog was so dense that the lampposts were invisible. The bulbs, tucked under egg-shaped wrought-iron shades, emitted a fuzzy glow that hovered above the still neighbourhood like rows of shimmering planets.

Grandfather Racket stopped the truck and turned off the engine.

'Why is it dark?' he asked, leaning across Raymond to peer out the passenger window.

'Maybe they went out,' sighed Raymond. 'Or to bed.'

He slid down, folded his arms across his chest, and rested his head on the back of the seat.

'Sit up,' said the old man. 'Do you hear me? I said for you to sit up.'

Raymond rolled his head and looked at Grandfather Racket.

'What are you lookin' at?'

'You,' replied Raymond. 'Wondering what you did with all that money.'

'Go ahead, you 'ornery drunk. It's all you can handle right now, isn't it? To blame me, after what Babs done to you. But I don't know how you can face yourself if you don't walk up that path to save your own daughter, for Christ sake.'

'I know what I have to do.'

'I hope so, Raymond, because if they're at home, we take her. We tell them she stays with us 'til it's all settled.'

Raymond sat up. 'You go first,' he said. 'Then I'll come.'

Grandfather Racket left the cab of the truck and slammed the rickety door.

Raymond could feel that he had stepped over a brink. His body shuddered in protest, registering its nakedness on arriving at the cold place of no return. It grieved the familiar, soft terrain of decisions not taken and thresholds left uncrossed.

Raymond watched Grandfather Racket march up the path to the entrance of the house. He moved to the edge of the seat, lifted the cushion, and took a bottle of whiskey from beneath the springs. He drank without pleasure, a whore doing business.

When the bottle was back in place, Raymond looked out of the window and saw Grandfather Racket at Howard and Shirley's door. He was banging, ringing the bell, and shouting. He dashed back and forth across the porch, trying to see past the curtained windows.

All of a sudden a light in the reception area went on, then the porch light.

Raymond shot up in his seat and bolted from the cab of the truck.

Grandfather Racket called, 'Open up! We're takin' the child!'

As Raymond reached the porch, the door was being unlocked. Vernon stood facing them in his pyjamas, robe and slippers.

'Good evenin', Willard,' he said. 'Raymond.'

'Don't pull your nigger stunt with me, Verne,' snapped Grandfather Racket. 'We know each other a long time. Get the girl.'

Vernon sighed and put his hands in the pockets of his robe.

'You know I can't do that, Willard.'

'Where are they?' asked Grandfather Racket.

'They all asleep.'

'Lucy don't go to bed at this hour.'

Vernon shrugged.

'She do when she get a pill. Eight o'clock is when Mis' Racket says, eight o'clock is when she goes.'

'We'll come in and wait 'til morning then,' replied Grandfather Racket. He started to push his way past Vernon. 'We'll just sit ourselves right in here on them nice sofas and then come morning we'll have us a little chat with her majesty.'

'You can't come in here, Willard,' said Vernon. 'You going to get me in a lot of trouble, you come in this house.'

'Verne,' said Raymond, 'wake them up. I'm Lucy's father, they're breaking the law. You told me to look after my responsibilities and now I'm doing it.'

'You don't want to be part of nothin' illegal, Verne,' said Grandfather Racket. 'Do like Raymond says.'

'I can't let you in this house, Willard. Lord knows I want to, Lord knows I wish there was a way to work this out. But there ain't. I overheard a lot since this morning.'

At the far end of the reception room, Lillian nudged open the door to her quarters and peered out.

'Who's that, Verne?' she called.

'Willard and Raymond,' he replied. 'They come to get Lucy.'

Lillian, also in a robe and slippers, with a towel around her head, padded to the front door. She fumbled with her glasses and put them on.

'Hello, Willard,' she nodded. 'Hello, Raymond.'

'Lucy's goin' back home, Lillian,' said Raymond. 'Don't try to stop us.'

Lillian shook her head.

'No, she ain't. You know what I'm tryin' to say.'

'Lillian,' said Raymond. 'Please. I'm not going to let her stay here. I thought you wanted to help. It's not right and you know it.'

'Any fool can see it's wrong,' the woman replied. 'But you think they ask my opinion? If they knew you two was here right now they have you arrested. We heard her tellin' Tyler Hughes. The police already know they be called if you come. I should be on the phone this minute, the orders I got.'

'Well, I never—' said Grandfather Racket.

'If you want to help that poor child, you go right back to the farm this minute. You make trouble, you know what will happen. You know how they get.'

'I know how Lucy gets, Lillian,' shouted Grandfather Racket. 'She needs to come home!'

'Shut your mouth, Willard Racket!' demanded Lillian in a harsh whisper, pointing upstairs. 'That child's got no *mother*. How you goin' to raise her, you two? Just look at the pair of you. I know this ain't a life here, but what's wrong is the whole situation, the mother dyin' is what's wrong. How you going to change that? There ain't no solution going to bring Barbara Jean back to Lucy, that's finished for this child.'

'I won't stand for it, Lillian,' pleaded Grandfather Racket.

'Lillian, let me just go up quickly and get her,' said Raymond. 'We'll be gone in a few minutes and then we can hire a lawyer to talk to Howard and Shirley tomorrow.'

Lillian shook her head. 'Oh, Raymond, honey, you can't do that. Don't you understand what's happenin' here? They gon' arrest you for kidnapping, you do that. How will that help Lucy? Just give me time. Verne and me know how to deal with Shirley Racket by now.'

'She be okay with us,' said Vernon. 'I'll watch out for her.'

'I don't like it,' said Raymond.

'You're dang right,' said Grandfather Racket. 'I won't put up with it.'

'We'll get word to you soon's we can,' said Lillian. 'Verne is always runnin' their errands and he'll bring her over to you. But don't you come here again. Do you hear me? It will go a lot worse for her.'

'How? How could it be worse?' wept the old man. 'Answer me that. I ain't waitin' and neither is Lucy. You two know it ain't right and look at you just stand there.'

'Let me handle it, Willard,' said Lillian. 'The way you talk to Shirley Racket she never let you see that girl again.'

'I don't care! I'm comin' in. Move out of my way, Verne – both of you. Don't block this door. She's my granddaughter, she needs me!'

Raymond held the old man back. 'Don't,' he said. 'They're right, now isn't the time. She'll be okay for a few days 'til we figure things out.'

Grandfather Racket shook his finger at Vernon.

'You bring that girl down to her home in Halfmoon, Verne. I'm telling you. You do it or you'll answer to me. I'm only goin' away this one time. Next time, you don't keep your promise, I take her, I don't care about police. I'll come right in here and take her.'

Raymond took Grandfather Racket's arm as he turned and stumbled down the porch steps. The two men disappeared into the fog which now surrounded the house.

35

Thursday, 21 December, 1944. Almost 11:00 p.m.
Dear Johnny,

The reports are getting worse, if only I had a letter from you. Yes, it was your Division in the surprise attack, we know that much but we can't seem to find out exactly where you and Raymond were in the attack or if you were attacked direct. Billy has been studying a map – he and Lizzie went right down to the Five And Dime at the first report but they were all sold out, everyone has the same thing on their mind – they had to walk four miles to Defreetsville and back and the man in the general store there had one left. The bus service is so unreliable now due to the strict rules about gas and tyres. He felt so sorry for the two of them, he gave them the map free. Right now there isn't a map of Europe or the Pacific to be had. Billy and Lizzie have it all marked, different places circled, and they've made up a chart of what has been happening each day as far as we can tell. Billy says there were five infantry divisions in the Ardennes and we as yet have no idea where the 108th was, or is now, that is the main thing on our minds. We do know the weather is bad and Billy says you would not have got air support because of this. I am not sure I understand what he means but he and Lizzie are explaining everything to Dad and me. Dad hardly has any energy for the cows and I had to remind him Christmas is in four days. He doesn't take an interest in anything, hardly touches his food. Bert and Sadie and Carl and Mildred and Willard and Barbara Jean were all here last night with us for all the news reports, hours and hours by the radio, we were in and out of the kitchen with soup and tea and crackers all night. It was the first time in all these years I have seen Barbara Jean cry. Dad went to bed at eight o'clock and missed the main news. After he left the room Willard asked Bert and Carl could they manage all our work, or did they need him to help out – wasn't that sweet, and he has more than enough of his own to handle, he and Barbara Jean look like they are on their last breath and her carrying a child. Willard thinks no one knows, but he has sold a lot of his best land to keep going. I know he is stubborn but there is nothing he loves more than that farm and this must be eating away at him, to have to sell anything. I told Bert and Carl not to hold back saying anything on my account or the children's, we can hear what they have to say – I could tell they wanted to say something – and Carl said Dad just goes down to the barn with them and sits while they do the milking and feeding. He said they try to talk to him but he won't answer and doesn't seem to hear them. Bert and Carl have both sold cattle now and they've told Dad to sell off the hogs but he just shrugged his shoulders. Johnny, we're all of us down to the minimum animals, and Carl said, Hazel, we can't keep it up, I'm sorry, Bert and I want your permission to tell Avery we'll sell the hogs for him, we're sure you can use the money. (No land gone yet, thank goodness). Poor Carl, he broke down then, he was ashamed to say he couldn't keep up the pace, and of course I said, Carl, you have my permission to tell Dad whatever you think is best, and then Mildred helped him up and they went home. Bert just held his head, saying over and over, I'm sorry, Hazel, I'm sorry, Hazel, we're so tired. The doctor says Dad is very upset still over our Joseph, and now you, not having exact information where you are, and he says Dad doesn't know how to put it into words. Last night I had a dream it was Christmas morning, you and Joe were little again, wearing those matching red robes Dad and I gave you one year. Raymond was holding you on his lap, he was explaining how to fire a gun and I was saying *Pay attention, Johnny, Raymond will tell you what to do*. This morning I am full of confidence. Isn't that strange.

Everyone is due here in another few minutes, the main news will be on and I think President Roosevelt may be speaking, too. Sadie and Mildred and I are working on sweaters to send you and Raymond – we should have done this *much* sooner, if only the authorities hadn't been so strict about how much you were allowed to pack. Sometimes I think I follow the rules more than I need to. We have only had light snow twice since November, the second time yesterday. There was a peace and a softness in it that made tears come to my eyes. Dad walked through it without a jacket, just overalls and shirtsleeves, down to the barn, and he seemed not to notice or feel the flakes turning to drops of water on his arms when I ran after him with the jacket. He turned to me and he was crying, the tears on his face, without a sound, they were just falling. I said, Avery, come up to the house with me, you need to cry it out, but he just shook his head slowly and went down by himself without the jacket and I thought he looked so lonely, but he won't let anyone help. I didn't mean to tell you all this, Johnny, I'll never send a letter like this because I've never told you personal business between

Dad and me and I shouldn't do it now. Of course, he always had Joe to talk to, they went over things while they did the chores. God watch over you, Johnny. I'll write tomorrow.

Mom

36

Vernon bent down and carefully lowered Lucy so her head rested on Lillian's lap in the back seat of the Chrysler. The child opened her eyes groggily and closed them again as Lillian smoothed her hair.

The rows of lights on Main Street, 3 September, gave off a crisp brilliance that pierced the chilly autumn air with the clarity of bells. Stars shimmied in the sky, lighting Vernon's way as he guided the car out of Little Hoosick towards Halfmoon. There was no one else on Route 18. The Chrysler glided over the road, passing swiftly by the silent outlines of the Mohawks' trees as if they were ghosts, swaying Lucy into a deep sleep.

Back in Little Hoosick, Jungle finally discovered an open window – in the basement – and fled.

* * *

Grandfather Racket sat in his daughter's armchair, head back and legs extended. A thick white mug containing the dregs of his coffee lay tipped over on the floor next to a plate of cold toast. His arms hung over the sides of the chair, discarded. He watched the drawn curtains intently, as if they had something to say.

Raymond was on the couch, flat on his back, staring at

the ceiling. With his left hand he fingered the cap of a full jug of red wine which stood on the floor beside the sofa. He rolled his head and looked at Grandfather Racket's toast.

'You've got to eat something,' he said.

The old man did not reply, and Raymond returned to the ceiling.

In a moment, Grandfather Racket said, 'It's four days now.'

Raymond shrugged. He let go of the wine, closed his eyes, and massaged his neck and unshaven face with his hands.

'I ain't going to wait much longer, I can tell you that,' said Grandfather Racket.

'You better get used to it,' answered Raymond.

Grandfather Racket sat up slowly and peered around the side of his chair at Raymond.

'Over my dead body.'

'Looks to me like that's the way you're going,' said Raymond. 'You're nothing but skin and bones.'

Grandfather Racket leaned back in the chair again and coughed.

'I can't keep anything down. Something with my chest. My stomach. One or the other.'

'Maybe we should go to a restaurant,' said Raymond.

'I don't care about a restaurant.'

'Fine.'

The two men did not speak for fifteen minutes.

At nine-thirty Grandfather Racket said, 'What's that?'

'What's what?'

'I heard a car comin' down our road.'

'I didn't hear anything.'

'There it is again,' said Grandfather Racket.

Suddenly there was a banging on the door and the two men shot up.

'Who's there?' shouted Grandfather Racket. 'What's going on?'

He stumbled, disorientated, away from the chair. Raymond tripped and kicked over the wine, which leaked onto the floor from the loosened cap.

'Who is it, who is it?' he called.

The two men fell against each other as they rushed to the hall and flung open the door.

'Stand aside, Willard,' said Vernon. 'The child will get cold and there ain't much time.'

'In here,' directed Raymond. 'Set her down on the sofa.'

He and Vernon moved quickly into the living room.

Grandfather Racket clutched the door and stared at Lillian who stood like a statue, vaguely illuminated by the bulb in the hall.

'I thought you'd never come,' said the old man. 'I'm right near sick with waiting, I'm not too well, Lillian.'

Lillian stepped into the house.

'My Lord, Willard, look at you,' she said.

She led the stooped man towards the living room.

'I don't know what happened,' he said. 'Just lately. Something came over me, sudden-like.'

'You got to take it easy, Willard,' said Lillian.

'It's a weakness. My legs is gone all weak.'

'I know,' replied Lillian. 'I can see what's goin' on.'

'Raymond's doin' all the work, Lillian, you know that's not like me, that's not how I am. But he's gettin' jumpy lately, we're both not right.'

'It's time to slow down, Willard, way past time. When will you ever learn to listen?'

In the living room, Raymond sat on the edge of the sofa. Lucy lay behind him, snoring gently. Vernon stood in the middle of the room, his arms at his sides.

'Sit here, Willard,' said Lillian, turning his chair until it faced the sofa. She eased the old man down. Then she opened a folding metal chair left behind from the funeral and sat beside him.

'Well, now, I got somethin' to say,' she sighed. 'Listen good to me, we ain't got no time at all, they went out at seven and they be back at 11:30 sharp. So we got to leave here by 10:30. One hour. We waited 'til it got dark.'

'Where the hell you been?' complained Grandfather Racket. 'I'm waitin' four days, Lillian. And then I thought she'd be able to stay awhile, do some of the chores, the things she's used to, and now here it is 9:30 at night. What good is all this? She's sound asleep.'

'Just wait a minute,' said Raymond. 'We're not talking about a few chores or a few hours. She's here now, she's staying.'

Vernon shook his head.

'No, Raymond,' he said. 'I'm tellin' you, they will *arrest* you. There's no end to the trouble they like to cause. That child goes back with us. It's gone too far now, that's what we came to tell you.'

'She won't even get to look around the place,' said Grandfather Racket. 'And here I went and fixed it all up.'

Vernon and Lillian exchanged glances.

'I did!' said Grandfather Racket. 'Don't you go givin' each other a look. I swept the floor. I put them maple branches in a jar over there. The leaves is already changin' and she loves 'em red like that.'

'Vernon,' said Lillian, 'go in that kitchen and see have they got anything I can cook up quick. Willard is near starved. We got to get some food in him. And then I got to lay the situation straight out to them.'

'We're leaving at 10:30,' replied her brother. He turned and went out of the room.

Lillian looked at Raymond.

'Hello, Raymond.'

'Hello, Lillian.'

'Get rid of that wine 'fore that child wakes up,' she

said. 'Get it out of my sight. How many times you have to be told?'

Raymond reached down and picked up the leaking jug as Vernon came back in from the kitchen. He was trembling only slightly in response to his attempt, in the last four days, to stop drinking. Raymond was feeling pleasantly surprised at the gentleness of the symptoms, and although he was monitoring his body carefully for signs of the violent realities he was used to, he believed he had somehow eluded them.

'And wipe that spill,' said the woman. 'Just look around this place. Look at Willard, all worn out. What it going to take, make you a grown man, Raymond?'

Holding the bottle of wine with one hand, Raymond knelt on the floor and rubbed the pool of red liquid with the shirtsleeve on his other arm.

'There,' he said. 'Satisfied?'

'Lord have mercy,' said Lillian. 'There is no way to put reason in you.'

'Don't insult me, Lillian,' said Raymond. 'I'm as upset as you, and I'm trying just as hard as you. I'm not putting up with you talking like that.'

'Good,' said Lillian. 'Because I see you wander off someplace, then I don't have confidence where this all is goin'.

'They got eggs,' said Vernon. 'Bit of bread and soup. Milk.'

'Well, that's something, anyway,' said Lillian.

'I got in chicken noodle soup for Lucy,' said Grandfather Racket. 'Campbell's. She loves Campbell's. With saltines.'

'We'll wake her up and maybe she'll eat,' said Lillian. 'She got no interest in food lately.'

'So what are you feedin' her over there?' snapped Grandfather Racket. 'She's a damn good eater her whole life.'

'We're feedin' her everything she loves,' said Lillian. 'She tells us, we make it, she don't eat it. Poor Shirley get her whatever she say, but the child lost her appetite.'

'Poor Shirley,' repeated Grandfather Racket.

'She's tryin' her best, Willard. It ain't her fault. You think she want a child to starve?'

Grandfather Racket thrust his arm out at the kitchen door. 'Go in that kitchen, Raymond, and show them where we keep the soup. Can't anybody open a can around here? And put cut-up carrots on a plate next to it. She grew the goddamn carrots herself. We done enough sittin' around.'

Lillian nodded to Vernon.

'Come and help me, Raymond,' he said.

He held out his hand. Raymond pushed it away.

'I don't need your help,' he said.

Vernon stood aside and Raymond led the way into the kitchen.

'He drinks too goddamn much,' said Grandfather Racket, flicking his hand after Raymond. 'I tell him and he don't listen. And now he's gettin' the shakes again, I can see it comin' on.'

'He can't stop himself, Willard,' said Lillian. 'You know that.'

'He dang well better,' said the old man. 'I won't put up with it.'

He looked at Lucy. 'Did you try hamburgers?'

'I'm tellin' you, Willard, there ain't nothin' she didn't get. Doctor Blake put her on some kind of vitamin liquid. She drinks okay.'

'School started yesterday.'

'Me and Mis' Racket took her.'

'She likes school,' said Grandfather Racket.

'Not yesterday she didn't. Wouldn't colour, wouldn't sing, wouldn't bring her little chair into the circle. Shirley spoke to the teacher, she's real nice.'

'She should be speakin' to *me*, Lillian. The teacher doesn't know a thing about what that girl needs. She needs to come home!'

He twisted himself out of his chair and went to the sofa. He sat on the edge beside Lucy and clasped her tiny hands.

Vernon and Raymond came through the kitchen door, Vernon carrying a tray with two bowls of soup, saltines, a plate of carrot sticks, and two glasses of milk. Raymond sank into Babsie's chair and began tapping the sides with his agitated hands.

'Put that down here on the floor beside me, Vernon,' said Grandfather Racket. 'I'll wake her up. She get one of them pills tonight, Lillian?'

'I switched it,' replied the woman. 'She got chopped-up candy.'

Grandfather Racket sighed and shook his head at Lillian. 'You're somethin', ain't you.'

She shrugged. 'It ain't much. Every day I try to think of something.'

'I'll feed her the soup,' said Raymond, springing suddenly from his chair.

'Lillian,' said Vernon, 'it's ten o'clock.'

'Take it easy, Verne,' she said, 'we ain't going' to be late.'

'I'm just tellin' you,' replied her brother.

'Willard, before you wake up the child,' said Lillian, 'I was saying I got to talk to you and you interrupted me.'

'I did not,' said the old man.

'You act like he's the only one in the room,' said Raymond. 'If you have something to say, you say it to me, too, Lillian. You heard what I said before.'

'Jesus Christ the Lord, Raymond,' said Grandfather Racket. 'Will you never shut up with your garbage?'

'Shut up yourself!' yelled Raymond. 'I'm her father!'

'A lot of good it's doin' her.

'Okay, Raymond,' interrupted Lillian.

Raymond retrieved the jug from the floor near the sofa and exited to the kitchen.

'He's throwin' it down the sink,' said Grandfather Racket. 'You know how many times he's done that?'

'It don't matter,' said Vernon. 'Let him. Let him be hisself and maybe he'll be all right.'

He turned to his sister.

'I'm not sayin' it again, Lillian. In fifteen minutes I go out and warm up the car.'

'Get in here, Raymond!' shouted Grandfather Racket. 'Do you hear me?'

The sound of crashing glass came from the kitchen as Raymond threw the empty bottle in the trash bin. Then he came through the door and sat in Babsie's chair.

'Now talk,' he said.

'I'll say it quick,' replied Lillian.

Vernon folded his arms across his chest and continued to stand.

Lillian leaned forward.

'They got the custody.'

Grandfather Racket stared at Lillian.

'That's impossible,' snapped Raymond.

'Oh, no it ain't,' said Vernon. 'Tyler brought papers to the house yesterday. I took them at the door.'

'They managed that pretty fast,' said Raymond. 'What happened?'

'Tyler Hughes got connections,' said Vernon. 'Best interest of the child, I heard him say, due to circumstances and so on.'

'What circumstances?' said Grandfather Racket. 'We won't stand for it. We're going to do something about it.' The old man doubled over in a fit of coughing.

'You ain't goin' to do nothin',' said Lillian. 'You must

be livin' on another planet someplace. Why, Verne and me overheard Tyler say you went and threw the social worker out of here! Of all things, Willard Racket. What in the name of the good Lord got into you to do a thing like that?'

'She was trespassin'.'

'Trespassin' nothin',' said Lillian. 'She is the County social worker. She's the lady in charge of movin' children around. You're a bigger fool than I thought.'

Raymond sat forward, his elbows on his knees and his head lowered. He tapped his fingers against each other. He intertwined and unwound them, one set of hypotheses testing another.

'How long do you figure before the adoption order comes through?' he asked.

'It could be any time,' shrugged Lillian. 'What I'm tellin' you, Raymond, is they don't intend for her ever to come back here or ever to see you two again. I listen to every call and every conversation. As of now it's just a matter of procedure, and like Verne says, Mr Hughes gets things the way he wants.'

Raymond said nothing. He continued to weave an invisible garment between his fingers.

Vernon moved to the sofa and sat beside Grandfather Racket. He reached for the bowl of soup on the floor and ladled out a spoonful.

'You take this, Willard,' he said, lifting the spoon. 'You gon' need your strength.'

'Why, thank you, Vernon,' said Grandfather Racket. 'Lucy and me love Campbell's chicken noodle, don't we, honey?'

The old man strained forward. He sucked the hot liquid and slippery noodles through his puckered lips like a scrawny bird.

'Isn't that nice?' he said. His shrunken face reached out

again, and again Vernon placed a full spoon against his mouth and waited for him to draw in the food.

Raymond lifted his head and looked at Lucy. He got up and knelt beside her at the sofa.

'Wake up, Lucy,' he said, placing his hand on her forehead. 'We've got chicken noodle soup for you.'

Lucy opened her eyes slowly, lifted her head, and looked around the room.

'Have some soup now,' said Raymond.

The child smiled sleepily at the young man.

'Good girl,' she said.

Her head fell back and she was sound asleep.

Grandfather Racket's eyes filled with tears.

'Let her sleep,' he said. 'She don't know where she is.'

Vernon put the bowl of soup on the floor and stood up. 'We got to go, Lillian.'

'What are you in such a goddamn hurry for?' asked Raymond. 'You haven't stopped talking about leaving since you got here and we haven't figured out what we're doing.'

'I have,' replied Vernon. 'That child is going back to Little Hoosick, Raymond. This is serious business and I don't think you see it.'

Vernon went out of the house to the car.

The Chrysler started with a roar and purred heavily as Vernon yanked out the handbrake. He returned to the living room and stood at a distance near the front hall.

'Raymond,' he said, 'bring her out to that car now.'

Raymond collected Lucy in his arms. 'This is the last time,' he said to Lillian. 'Next visit she stays no matter what, and you better be prepared for that.'

'Watch how you hold her,' said Grandfather Racket. 'You don't look so steady to me.'

'I don't need to be told how to hold my own child,' said Raymond.

Lillian stood up.

'Okay, Raymond. Maybe you're right. But I can't promise nothin' and I won't. The only idea I had is they supposed to go to a undertakers' convention in Albany next week. Friday, Saturday, and Sunday. Overnight. Mis' Racket won't leave the girl but one night, and she and Mr Racket agreed they got to go at least one day and one night, so we be bringin' her back here one of those times and I'll keep Lucy awake. If it ain't Friday it be Saturday. So don't go upsettin' yourselves if we ain't here on Friday. And another thing: you start eatin', Willard Racket. I mean it, or I'll have to phone Doctor Blake and you'll end up in the hospital. You be no use to that child in a hospital but I ain't goin' to let you get sick on me neither.'

As she and Raymond turned and walked silently to the car with Lucy, Grandfather Racket leaned down and lifted the tray of food carefully on to his lap.

37

Can you see anything, Raymond?

No, no, it's snowing again, Dom, heavy snow, can't see any Krauts, no. Trees. I don't dare lift the cover of this thing much more.

I never saw anybody weave branches together like that in my life.

That's because you live in Brooklyn, Dom. Isn't that right, Johnny? Just a city boy.

Yeah. All you guys think us farmers are so dumb. Raymond and me used to make rafts, let me tell you. Rafts for carrying junk down our stream, you name it, we sent it down, one place to another, secret clubs. The Indians used to do it like that, you just lash the branches together like me and Raymond did just now, rope, twine, whatever, bark, and there you are. What we got over our heads in this mud hole right now, Dom, is a raft, courtesy of RFD #2, Halfmoon, New York. When we move out we'll take it with us in case we hit a river. We'll show you a little fun.

Do you think anyone can see us, Raymond?

No. The only way they'll know we're here, Dom, is if they step on us and fall in – and we're so covered with mud they might even think we're Krauts. But don't worry – we'll shoot them before they see us. We just poke our guns up and under the roof, just a little like I'm doing now, and we'll have all sides covered.

Bring your gun in now, Raymond, there's nothing there, crouch down and get warm in this nice Belgian mud.

Ah. That's better. My neck is stiff.

What I wouldn't do for a cup of coffee.

The fighting's far away now, isn't it, Raymond?

Yes and no, Johnny. I still hear it. I hear it off to the west now, too. If this compass is working. The Panzers just pushed right through and kept going. What do you think, Dom?

Yeah, they levelled everything. I – I wouldn't want to see what happened. It was so sudden. Was I sleeping?

Yes, you and Johnny had dozed off. I couldn't figure it out right away – I just kept hearing things, I wasn't sure, at first I thought I'd been having a dream, I couldn't put it together. I actually crawled out of the foxhole to listen, and finally I heard it through the ground. I cleared the snow and put my ear against the ground and I heard rumbling and that's when I shook you, when I started screaming at the top of my lungs and woke everyone down the line.

They told you to go back to sleep, said it was just the usual movement we'd been hearing. Even now I don't want to believe you. And look at us!

But that's it, Dom, that explains what we were hearing all along. It wasn't just a little defence, they were going for an all-out attack. Suddenly it hit me. I knew. I just knew what was coming.

Doesn't say much for Ike and his boys. What's the date today, Raymond? I've lost track. I want to remember so if I ever have kids I can tell them I was in one of the biggest hoaxes of World War II.

Saturday, 16 December.

Christmas in the mud.

Hey, listen!

What is it, Johnny?

I thought I heard something. Maybe not.

Wait, Raymond. Listen. He's right.

Yes, yes. Not a word. I'll poke my gun up under the roof again, just a peek. Don't move.

See anything?

No. Hold on. Over here maybe. Nothing. Wait. Jesus! Kraut patrol! Four of them. Six of them. Yes, yes, Dom! That's what you heard, Johnny.

What do I do, Raymond? What do I do first?

Whisper now, just whisper, I can hear them, I can see them, they're coming in this direction, they're talking. Now listen to me: we are going to kill them, they don't know we're here, they won't know where to look, they won't look down, that's the last place they'll look.

My gun jammed before, Raymond. What if my gun jams?

It won't jam, Johnny, I fixed it, I fixed it. Here's what we do, I want you both, very, very slowly, to put the tip of your gun up under the roof, don't do anything else, that's it, we have a couple of minutes I think, just let the guns poke out from the hole, move your eyes up to the slit of daylight and take a look at them. Do you see them? You see them coming?

Yes, Raymond, yes, I see them, I – I can't do it, Raymond.

You can do it, Johnny, here's what you're going to do, just keep firing when I say and you'll get off enough rounds to kill them all but the angle is hard, so wait, wait 'til I say, *don't think about anything else, just steady, steady, and not a word. Dom?*

Okay, Raymond, I see them, I'm ready. They've stopped. Lighting a cigarette.

Raymond, they're coming right for us, what do I do first? Raymond, I'm scared. What do I do?

Watch, Johnny, watch, that's it, nothing yet. Do you see? Dom, look. You see what I mean? The angle. Let them in close, very close, then fire up. *We have to fire* up. *They're staying together, they're not paying attention. Here's what we do, I fire left to right, Johnny, you fire at the men in the middle, Dom, you fire right to left – we'll take the ends, Johnny takes the middle, they're walking close together in a line, we can do it.*

I'm shaking, my gun is shaking, Raymond, I can't aim, I can't see good.

Hold steady, Johnny, you're going to do it, you can do it, they're coming to us, they're coming right to us, are you ready, Dom?

Quiet. They're walking. It's going to be now. Get ready. Get ready, Johnny.

I'm ready, I – I, they're coming so close, Raymond.

That's it, that's it, here they come, just another second, angle up, angle up, steady, steady. Okay, NOW! NOW! Fire! Shoot. Shoot, Johnny!

I missed, Raymond!

No, No! They're hit, Johnny, they're hit. They're all down.

One of them's seen us. Get out! Run! He's got a grenade. Raymond, Raymond!

Go, Johnny! Out! Jump out shooting. Push up the roof, Dom. Zig-zag, Johnny. Move, move! He's going to throw a grenade!

I got him, Raymond, I got him.

Look out! That one moved. Look out. Your bayonet, Dom. Stab him!

Oh, Raymond, oh, God, look. Look. They're dead, the blood, all the blood.

Johnny, stab him! He moved. Stab him, stab him!

I can't! No! I can't do it!

There, I got him, it's okay, it's okay, he's done.

I did it, Raymond, I did it, I stabbed him. Is he dead?

He's dead, Johnny, yes, yes, I think so. Dom. Dom!

I'm sick, Raymond. I can't move, I can't get up.

Are you hit, are you hit?

No, I'm sick, I – I have to throw up. I'm dizzy.

They're dead, Raymond, I think they're dead. Oh, God, oh, God, I shot his face, Raymond, he saw me do it, he saw me, he held up his hand. He spoke to me. I shouldn't have done it.

Come here, Johnny, you had to do it.

I'm so cold, Raymond, I'm shaking, oh, take my gun, get it away from me. Look at his face. There's blood on my bayonet, Raymond, take it away.

It's okay now, Johnnny, they're dead, we did it. Dom?

I'm sick, Raymond.

Wait, we'll all wait now. We'll eat, we need to eat.

I can't eat, I'm sick.

Eat the snow, Dom, it's cool, it's fresh, we need water.

I can't get air, Raymond, I can't breathe.

You're all right now, Johnny, you did it, that's it, take my jacket, stay warm.

What are we going to do, Raymond? We've got to run somewhere. What if there's more coming?

Let's wait now, wait, Dom is sick. The map – let me look at my map and work out somewhere we can go.

I'm freezing, Raymond.

Here's where we are, Johnny, do you see where I'm pointing?

I can't look. I can't take any more.

I think it's only four kilometres to Meyerode, I think we can make it there by nightfall. Rest now, we'll be all right.

38

22 December, 1944. Midnight.

Dear Johnny,

I hardly slept last night, I am exhausted. All day news is pouring in about the Ardennes, they are calling it the Battle of the Bulge, something about the way your front line is shaped. If only a letter would come, telling me you are all right. We know now that the 108th was attacked in the first few days, probably the first hours. Billy and Lizzie have your position as far as we know it starred on the map. The news said many were killed right away due to it being a surprise attack, and on 17 December the Germans massacred unarmed American soldiers held prisoner in a little town called Malmedy which the Germans are taking over along with all the other small villages around. Everyone here is disgusted. Do you remember a family over in Defreetsville named Hartman? Well, people were throwing things at their house a few days ago, claiming they have German ancestors, which they might, and they have moved down to Albany (her sister) on the advice of the police. Then on the 19th over 7,000 of our troops surrendered *in the exact place where you probably were*. Where are you, Johnny? I know you won't read this until it is all over but all of us have discussed you and Raymond being prisoners and we agree *you must cooperate*. Don't do anything to upset the Germans, just go along with whatever they say, we feel the war will be over soon. *They can't win*, they are just trying anything, and eventually *they will have to let all the prisoners go*. We pray to God they will come to their senses and not kill any more of our boys. Now, we can't see how you and Raymond could have been in Malmedy by the 17th, already captured, to be among those shot. Writing to you helps me feel you are still there somewhere, which all of us are *absolutely convinced of*. I spoke to the Army people and they said I was right to hold on to any mail for now, they can't guarantee you getting it with a battle still going on. He told me they are getting reports by the hour on the situation. Lizzie and Billy have the living room like Army headquarters what with their map and chart and summaries of the news. I will now be calling the Army every day, I don't care what they think of me. Today I gave the man both your names and all the particulars, the numbers, etc., and he said he will try to find out what he can. I told him I know how busy he must be but please to get any information he could. I don't honestly know how the news goes back and forth, but he was very kind. I told him I was sure you and Raymond were alive, we'd lost one son already, our good friends had each lost a daughter, plus another family a son as well, so if he could let me know. He was very patient and said he too felt you and Raymond were alive. The news seems very bad, Johnny, no one can explain how such a big attack could have happened without our side knowing, so accusations are going all over about who is responsible, why we didn't know ahead of time, why were they telling us the war was almost won, etc. I don't know what to think. I even wonder if I may be going mentally ill, what with wanting to tell you everything, feeling I am talking to you and Raymond. I don't know what they call it, pretending someone is there when they are not. I haven't mentioned this to anyone, not even Mildred and Sadie, they seem to manage so well, I don't know what is wrong with me.

Billy and Lizzie are writing things up every day, they say Bastogne is the centre of fighting now, that the Germans have not yet been stopped. They seem to be moving forward all the time, and yet I thought we were supposed to be winning? Now the doctor has given me sleeping pills, too, he says I must get some rest and eat better, but I can't settle my mind down, I worry all the time. I know I shouldn't but I go over everything. Now, I *know* you are all right, Johnny, I just feel it, but still I can only imagine the horrors you must have seen and the pain and fear you have suffered along the way, and that is really the thing that is on my mind, that because of how I worry, the way I have of fretting over things, that I babied you. After the rheumatic fever you were so weak, the other boys teased you but the doctor said you just could *not* undergo any strain, that the heart had been affected and you could not play rough games and so the farm was all Dad and I would allow, making sure Raymond was doing all the real work. I am sorry, son, that I lied to you when I said Raymond was told to give you equal work to do. What I really told him was to take all the hardest jobs, and when you came to me in a fury saying you could handle as much as him and had I told him to go easy, I lied and said no, I never said any such thing, Raymond just feels because he's older he should do the heavy work, he needs to prove himself and so on. I was especially worried because of the pneumonia, the winter you were eight and I let Raymond take you on the Indian hike with that teacher, the one who led you out into the woods to re-create a Mohawk camp, and there you were building lean-tos and sleeping out in the cold, making fires all night and eating God knows what. I should *not* have let you go. I could never make up my mind what to say yes to, and what to say no to, and the doctor just said to use my judgement but be careful. Now what kind of advice was that? As a result of that Indian hike you missed months of school and at one point the doctor said we might lose you, pleurisy and then pneumonia. I never told you, Johnny, because I didn't want you to be like me: *I didn't want you to be afraid*. Raymond helped me nurse you, he stayed up with you all night so many nights, he blamed himself, I know. But you had to try things! You had to break away from me! You came to me for everything, or to Raymond. I am sorry to say all this to you, I am just so upset, but I am trying to get all the facts down. I want to face both of us with things as they are so when you come back I will realise you are grown up now. I should have done things this way before, seeing them the way they are because now I am afraid it is my fault you weren't strong enough. So last year when you wanted to join the Army and there you were, eating like a horse, lifting and hauling anything to build yourself up, I encouraged you. Then you were drafted. Everyone said you would never pass the physical, not with your history. Was I wrong to let you lie about your health in all the papers? Was I wrong to plead with the doctor to leave the rheumatic fever off the forms? I'm not supposed to do this, Mrs Martin, he said, I could get in a lot of trouble for this, but *I begged him*. He's a strong young man, I said, please, he wants to go and fight for his country like the other boys, and he said, well, I suppose he is in good health now, I suppose there's no harm to let him have his chance. Was I wrong? Can anyone tell me now? Dad never knew, I never breathed a word of it, you wanted to go so badly.

And when you passed the physical I was so proud, just like everyone else. Oh, Ma, you said, I never wanted anything so much in my whole life, I'll thank you for the rest of my life! I felt it was your right to *try*, Johnny, I felt for once I had to stop worrying and *let you try*.

We made our decision and now this. May the Lord forgive me if I have put you in harm's way.

39

By the time Raymond returned to the living room from Vernon's car and saw Grandfather Racket gulping down a glass of milk, the tremors had begun.

He knew from many attempts to stop drinking abruptly that after two or three days he had to take more alcohol or his tension and irritation would turn to uncontrollable shaking, sweating and vomiting. Tentacles of panic would seize him and his skin would crawl with the ice-pick legs of hallucinated spiders. He would see them scurrying up the walls and across the floor, hear their steel feet, be blinded by their shiny helmets and traumatised by their jagged teeth gouging out chunks of his flesh. He would have to chase and pound them with his fists, his feet, heavy objects. His heart would race and slam against the inside of his chest. By tomorrow, without alcohol now, he might also be curled up in a corner of his shack or underneath a sympathetic cow in the barn, holding his head and banging it against a wall as shells screamed down at him, blasting his eardrums, splitting apart his skull. Gunfire would lace through his body. The smell of cordite would choke him, he would gag for air, run in circles. He would see Johnny's corpse beside him, the boy's feet and ankles gangrenous from frostbite, and he would grab him, lie on him, shout at him to get down. Then he would begin to shiver, his teeth would chatter, he would scream for blankets and jump up and empty his illusory pistol into German soldiers who were stabbing Johnny who could no longer run, who had become a red stain criss-crossing the beautiful snow like fingerpaint. And then Raymond would feel himself being stabbed, shoulders, chest, legs, crying out as he rolled over and over, crawling, rolling, somehow pulling himself up, zig-zagging across a soft, downy blanket of snow, kicking up snow, the incessant whiteness blinding him, dodging, ducking, the Germans' ammunition gone but knives and bayonets drawn and cutting, and secretly, gasping, fumbling, Raymond would grope for his two camouflaged pistols and fire, fire, kill the Germans, and fall again across Johnny, sheltering him again with his own punctured body which he would watch in horror seep into the snow and melt away until, after perhaps three days in this delirium, a silence like a bolt, a steel door, thudded in on him, a dead weight, and then he would sleep for eighteen hours or more. He would awake lucid, calm, and free of alcohol, without conscious memory. But on each occasion, within days, dread would mount again, anxiety would tighten its grip, a barrage of machine-gun fire would rattle his skull, the smells and sounds and sight of Johnny's suffering and his own mutilation would reappear, and again he would gorge himself on alcohol and repeat the cycle. He had tried to stop, with the same results, at least two dozen times in three years. He had heard about but never mastered the task of self-detoxification: drinking, but drinking less and less over time so his battered mind and body might be cushioned on impact with sobriety. There was regular talk at the Roadside Rest about the details of home-detoxification, but Raymond boasted that he could stop cold whenever he liked.

He walked past Grandfather Racket into the kitchen. He gripped the Kelvinator in his arms, twisted it left, right, and left again, until it was out from the wall. Then he knelt on the floor and reached behind the machine into a crude hole in the floor for one of two bottles of whiskey which he kept there.

Still on his knees, he opened the bottle, held it up, and measured two inches on the neck with his thumb and index finger. He took a gulp. He re-measured. He took another gulp, measured again, re-capped the bottle, and put it back in the hole. After wiping his hands on his trousers, he stood up and jockeyed the refrigerator into place.

When Raymond returned to the living room, Grandfather Racket was asleep on the couch. The soup, milk, carrots, and crackers had been eaten.

Raymond dozed in Babsie's chair and returned twice in the night to the whiskey, each time drinking no more than his two-inch measure.

By dawn the next day, when he went to the kitchen to make coffee and ready himself for the day's chores, he was only slightly tremulous and not drunk. He gulped a quart of orange juice and a quart of milk, the regimen prescribed at the Roadside Rest.

It was 4 September: each blade of grass was dotted at the tip with a touch of frost. A thin layer of ice glistened on the road encircling the house. This was the third day in a row of morning frost, and as Raymond opened the back door and stepped into the startling daylight, he saw that a cluster of birch and maple trees, autumn's heralds, were already proclaiming the new season: a brassy symphony of the maples' red, orange, and purple plumage was backed by shimmering gold and yellow leaves which had burst like a clash of cymbals from every branch of a dozen sleek birch trees.

This panorama of fire against the cool touch of frost stunned Raymond, and for the first time in years he felt a radiant tingling on his face.

[illegible]

[illegible]

[illegible]

[illegible]

[illegible]

[illegible]

[illegible]

40

Qui est là?

The bird has taken flight. Trois Oiseaux.

Entrez, entrez. Ne parlez pas, *no speaking.*

Marie-Claire! Viens ici. Des soldats Americains!

My daughter she speaks English, she will come now. Marie-Claire!

Everyone, speak quietly, please, The Germans are everywhere, they are searching house to house.

Thank you, we are exhausted.

I apologise for my father, we are all frightened. Sit down by the fire, you must dry your clothes. Put the belts and helmets and the guns, please, under here. They must not be visible. I am sorry but we must to put out the lights now. I will bring food. Papa, reste-là avec les soldats. Monsieur, *your friends? Are they wounded? You are all limping.*

No. Sick. Cold. Our hands and feet.

Is she getting food, Raymond?

Yes, Johnny, yes, let me just tell her what happened. We were attacked, we were attacked early on the 16th. Do you understand? We have been trying to reach Meyerode for two days – three? It must be three. We were lost, we met one German patrol the first day, another yesterday.

You have killed them all?

Yes.

That is very good. There are thousands of Germans, they are pushing towards Bastogne, no one is stopping them. They want to reach Antwerp and then they will win the war. We will all be dead.

When they move out from Meyerode we will go back to our unit at the front line.

Mais non. C'est impossible! Il n'y a plus de *front line!*

My father says it is impossible, monsieur, *and he is right. The front line is gone, there is nothing between here and the Schnee Eifel now but German soldiers. They have killed many hundreds of your men and taken thousands more prisoner. This is what we hear. You cannot hope to return. You may stay here tonight. Tomorrow we will see what is possible. If they find you here we will all be shot. I will get the food now. Stay by the fire.*

I am Raymond, sir. My name is Raymond. This is Johnny, and Dom.

Je m'appelle *Jacques. Jacques Marais.*

This is good, Raymond. Can you feel the heat?

Take off your boots too, Dom. All of us, hands and feet by the fire. Can we hang these socks? Do you understand? Everything is wet.

Ah, oui, oui *– here. All your clothings on the chairs. Now I get something for you.*

Move your feet slowly, Dom. Come here, I'll rub them.

Not hard, Raymond, not hard.

We have to get your circulation going. That's it. What about you, Johnny?

I can't feel my feet, Raymond, I don't know, and my fingers.

Voilà.

Sweaters! Socks!

Take, please. What is it the matter with your friends?

Their feet. Mostly their feet.

And you?

The same, hands and feet.

Je comprend. *I come back again. Ah, Marie-Claire.* Je

cherche une pleine cuvette de l'eau chaude pour ses pieds.

Here. Please eat. My father is getting a basin of hot water for your friends' feet. We must try to bring the circulation back quickly, there is not much time for you and to do it slowly will cause much damage. Do not touch the feet please. Now eat. There is plenty more soup and bread and cheese. I am sorry but we have no meat. There is no meat.

Oh, this is good! What do they call this, Raymond?

I don't know. Johnny. This is delicious, thank you.

I will help your friends, Monsieur Raymond, while you eat. Then we will do your feet also. All of you must be very careful with your hands and fingers, move them slowly at first. I will feed you if necessary. I call this my everything soup, I do not know how you say in English. It is a joke.

It's the best soup I've ever had.

Marie-Claire, assistes-moi.

Je viens, Papa. *Now. Here.*

What should they do?

They must to put their feet in.

But it's hot, Raymond. No. It will hurt.

Hold on, Johnny, listen to her.

Raymond, I don't know if she's right. The water's too hot.

Dom, she knows what she's doing.

Please, all of you listen to me. It must be rapid, the thawing. Thirty-eight to forty degrees Centigrade is the correct temperature. The feet are not frozen through yet, I think they will be better by morning.

Go ahead, Dom, Johnny. Put your feet in there.

Dom, you do it first, I can't do it.

Okay, okay. I—

How is it, how is it?

Take it easy, Johnny, let him get used to it.

I – I'm going to faint, Raymond, my feet are burning, I can't say – burning ice. I can't take it.

You'll be all right, Dom. You have to do it.

Papa. Du vin. *You must drink some wine for the pain. I am sorry that it hurts, it is the only way. Here, Monsieur Johnny, drink this beautiful red wine, keep drinking, and now put your feet in the pan.*

I – should I do it, Raymond?

Yes, Johnny, you have to. Drink some more and I'll help you. I'll lift your feet. There.

No, Raymond, no. Don't make me. It hurts.

You have to, Johnny. Keep them in. Get more wine, Miss Marais, please. Please.

Your feet are not so bad, Monsieur Raymond.

I guess not.

Would you like some more soup?

Dom? How about you?

I can't, Raymond. I – I need more wine.

There. Drink this. I will have more soup if you don't mind, Miss Marais.

Yes. Papa – du pain et du fromage aussi. *He will get more for you. I must watch now for patrols. We are one of the few French-speaking families in our village, the rest speak German although they are not German sympathisers – so we are often watched. I am sorry, but you must finish eating now. It is not safe for you down here. We will move your things upstairs now, clear the plates away. Can your friends walk? It is better that they walk, for the circulation.*

Can you manage, Dom?

Yes, yes, I'll manage, but you better help Johnny, he's not doing too well. Johnny!

I hear you, I hear you, Dom.

Yes, Monsieur Johnny is drunk and in pain, he is only a young boy. I am so sorry. We see it all the time.

Raymond. Raymond.

I'm here, Johnny, I'm right here, now put your arm around

me, I'll help you upstairs. Your feet will be fine, you're going to sleep well tonight.

Come upstairs now. You must hide. I will bring a fresh pan of water. Monsieur Raymond must put in his feet in the night. My father and I will remain downstairs eating as we do each evening. They will become suspicious when there is no light. Come with me. Be careful of the stairs, they are narrow. I will put your things in this trunk for now.

Marie-Claire! Vite! Vite! Ils arrivent!

Quickly! Two of you here, under this bed. You, in this room, under the bed! Do not move! The cover will shield you. No sound please, I must go down now.

Qu'est-ce que tu vois, Papa?

Ils ont passè devant la maison, ils n'arrêtent pas, merci à Dieu.

* * *

Saturday, 23 December, 1944.

Dear Johnny,

Apparently the 108th suffered a lot of casualties. I haven't been able to reach the man at the Army, he has been taken ill, and the other one I spoke to was very impatient, said I knew as much as he did, but I said, I beg your pardon, *You are the Army*. Then of course I apologised for losing my temper, and he apologised for not being more polite, he had been on duty seventy-two hours, but he could understand my concern. He took down your names and said he would check. Willard is bringing a ham for all of us on the 25th. We will all be here in the 'war room' as Lizzie calls it for Christmas day. She says Bastogne will decide the battle and she feels we will know nothing until that is over. Billy agrees. Dad screamed at Billy, why don't you tell us something new, we've been hearing the same thing for days, *where are Johnny and Raymond*? Billy burst into tears and ran to his room, Dad left the house and was gone a long time. Everyone's nerves are on edge. Willard and Barbara Jean were down last night as usual. Willard can't sit still during the newscasts, he paces up and down, saying things like, Is that where they are, Lizzie?, What's the name of that place again?, What's the matter with the damn government?, and so on. Billy and Lizzie won't utter a word during the news, they just concentrate on writing everything down. Barbara Jean sits on the edge of a chair, elbows propped on her knees, holding her head. Every night she sits this way during the news. She is almost three months pregnant now. She isn't eating properly at all so every night I feed her a huge meal and she – and Willard, too – just pick at it. I think they have stopped cooking altogether. She is starting to show ever so slightly and soon I'd say she will have to stop the farm work. Willard told her, A fine state you've got yourself in, and him disappeared out of sight in some goddamn war. Barbara Jean told him to shut up (you can see they haven't changed), that it wasn't his life, but of course he said it is so my goddamn life if you have no place else to go. Thousands of boys are coming home every week now, Johnny. If only we knew where you were, we could celebrate, too. We think of you both every minute, we are convinced you are safe. Sadie and I have finished the sweaters and I will ask the man at the Army where he thinks I should send them. Mildred is down with the flu, I took her soup today.

41

Avery Martin sat in his rocking chair close to a blazing fire, Saturday night, 10 September, 1949. Bold swatches of amber light hung on the walls, lining and containing the Martins' living room like tapestries. Billy sat behind him on the sofa; Lizzie had left for college in Boston. Hazel would soon be in with hot chocolate.

Avery rested his lifeless head against the high back of the Lincoln rocker. Oak logs snapped and spat in the flames, releasing the wood's unmistakable dark aroma, which wafted about the room like memories.

In 1947, Raymond, Billy, and Bert Stilman had cut these logs for Avery, from massive branches pulled off bur oaks in an ice storm, and from the trunks of entire trees uprooted by the winds. He had been too tired to help.

Much of the finely seasoned timber had shrunk in two years of drying, and now it shed casings of rough, furrowed bark which littered the hearth. Avery stared into the fire. He and Joe used to cut the trees.

The mantelpiece held a jumble of photographs, some in sturdy frames, others propped loosely against the wall. Avery tracked the figures in the largest picture as if they had come to life: a snapshot of himself with Joe, Johnny, Raymond, and Billy, all in red- and black-checked winter hunting hats, flaps down over ears and eyebrows. They were toasting Barbara Jean Racket, the photographer, with mugs of cocoa held up against a grey, brooding sky. It was Christmas Day, 1940. They were thanking her for the caps. Great Britain, a far-away land of kings and queens, was fighting a war that no one thought of in Albany-Rennsalaer, a war that had no meaning to the Martins or the Rackets.

Dusted with snow, arms linked, the men in the photograph formed a sheltering arc around the top of a fluffy canvas: on the down at their feet rested a tiny regiment of five flattened angels, imprinted only moments earlier by their splayed, swishing arms and legs as they lay on their backs in the snow.

Hazel entered the room. She carried a tray to the table and went to her husband. She placed her arm around his shoulders. Billy pushed himself awkwardly off the sofa, cradling his right leg, and left the room.

Hazel brought the hot chocolate and sat beside the rocking chair on a footstool, her knees propping the drink.

When she finished, she set her mug on the floor and stood up.

She kissed Avery on the forehead and felt the intense heat from the fire merge with her lips. This heat clung to her until she closed the door of the house and started down the stone path to Grandfather Racket's farm.

* * *

Sunday, 24 December, 1944. Christmas Eve.

Dear Johnny,

All of us went to church tonight, a lovely service of carols and candlelight. I don't know when the last time was Willard and Barbara Jean set foot in the place, but they went along without a peep and held candles like everyone else. There wasn't an empty seat or a dry eye to be seen, including Willard and Barbara Jean who held hands the whole time. I stood beside Dad of course, and everyone came up to us, put their arms around us, and said, Hazel, Avery, quietly, knowing our situation. Well, goodness, Johnny, most are in it the same themselves, most coming up to us have smaller families now and no more than half the spirit of only a few years ago, so much drained away. But I must not burden you. Billy and Lizzie were at home by that infernal radio. Not on Christmas Eve! I said to them, can't we have one normal night, but they wouldn't come and of course I am only trying to fool myself: life is not normal. There is still no news of you and Raymond, I am numb from the waiting, most of the time I feel nothing, I hope you will forgive me, it is just that day in and day out everything stays the same, no news, no hope, nothing definite. When we left church tonight, Dad looked at me with such hopeless empty eyes. I had thought maybe you and Joe and Raymond would be home for Christmas but now I see that was just a dream. Wherever you are, Johnny, our love be with you.

42

Raymond stood in the doorway of the living room. Grandfather Racket was on the sofa, Hazel in Babs' chair.

'There's no sign of them,' he said. 'They're not coming.'

'They dang well *better* come,' said Grandfather Racket, slamming his fork down on the chair cradled between his legs. On it was a plate of eggs, ham, toast, and potatoes prepared by Hazel. It was two o'clock in the morning.

'I'm telling you, Raymond!'

'For Christ sake, don't tell *me*,' said Raymond.

'We're sittin' here the three of us like fools, second night in a row since six o'clock, after waitin' all week, keepin' our promise to lay low. What does that child think now? Huh? She thinks we've gone and forgot her, that's what, us just sittin' here.'

He pushed the chair away and started to get up.

'You stay right where you are, Willard Racket,' said Hazel, 'until every bite of that food is gone. You can talk just as good from the sofa as you can pacing up and down.'

'Leave me alone, I've got my strength back just fine.'

'No, you haven't. You heard me. Sit down there this minute.'

Grandfather Racket yanked the chair back into place and began wolfing down forkloads of food.

'So *now* what are we goin' to do?' he asked, chewing angrily. '*Now* what's our bright idea?'

Raymond leaned against the door jamb and folded his arms across his chest.

'Ha! Dead silence. Not a word out of ya, neither of ya.'

'Give me a minute,' said Raymond. He furrowed his brow and stared across the living room at the darkened window. Hazel looked at him; he averted his eyes. When he turned back she was still watching him.

'What are you looking at?' he asked. 'You don't know what to do either.'

'That's true,' replied Hazel. 'I don't. I can hardly begin to puzzle it out. I was wondering about you.'

'Well, you can stop wondering,' he said. 'Whatever that means. I don't need it.'

'I'll be danged if I can figure out what you two think the big mystery is,' said Grandfather Racket, wiping his mouth with the back of his hand. 'They've stolen *my* granddaughter, *your* daughter, and they don't intend givin' her back to where she belongs. Question is, we let them get away with it, or we take charge. Which is it goin' to be?'

'And?' said Raymond.

'I'm just sayin' what the situation is,' replied the old man.

Raymond looked at him.

Grandfather Racket paused.

Finally he replied, 'I say take charge.'

Raymond nodded. 'I'm just trying to figure out how,' he said, and began to tap his fingers again.

Hazel stood up and took Grandfather Racket's empty plate into the kitchen. In a moment she returned with a tray of coffee and handed mugs to the two men.

The only sound in the room was a blowing and cautious sucking at hot coffee.

Finally Hazel spoke. 'I'm afraid it's too late,' she said. 'I'm afraid it's gone too far.'

'Jesus Christ, Hazel,' said Grandfather Racket. 'What kind of a thing are you sayin'?'

'I'm saying I think the time has passed, Willard. That we won't be able to save Lucy now.' She sighed. 'And maybe Howard and Shirley aren't the worst. She'll make her way, she's strong. It's some kind of a life anyway.'

'Have I gone deaf?' asked Grandfather Racket. 'Are we talkin' about the same people over there in Little Hoosick?'

'Hazel, I'm sorry,' said Raymond, 'but that's just not good enough.'

'Oh, Raymond, what can we possibly do?' pleaded Hazel. 'What possible plan would bring Lucy back? Nothing will get things back any more.' She covered her face.

'She needs us,' replied Raymond. 'That's what you've been saying all along. And you're right.'

'It's too late,' the woman said again.

Raymond drained his mug of coffee, plunked the cup on the floor, and marched out of the house, slamming the door behind him.

'Now look what you did, Hazel Martin!' cried Grandfather Racket, shooting up from the couch. 'Answer me why you had to go and do that. Whose side you on anyway? Make up your mind.'

'I'm trying to think of the child, Willard. I'm desperate trying to think what she needs, I'm doing my best. Maybe I'm wrong, I don't know, but who's going to tell me? Who's going to say what's right? Nobody. I can't pray for any more children. I can't survive, clutching at them, watching them drown again and again. Maybe I just want to get rid of Lucy before I start to have hope. God forgive me if I've come to such selfishness.'

Hazel wept.

The front door opened and Raymond re-entered. He had started the pick-up truck; the engine rattled in the driveway.

'I'm going to get her,' he said.

Hazel lifted her head.

'What are you talking about?' said Grandfather Racket.

'Do you know which one is her room?' asked Raymond.

'Well, I – let's see now – that would be the big window on the right, second floor. Yup, Babsie been in the house once, that was the guest room. Howard and Shirley is on the other side.'

'I'm sorry, Hazel,' said Raymond, 'but I can't let her go, not like that.'

Hazel did not reply. She nodded in silence to Raymond, lost in her own grief.

Grandfather Racket was wide-eyed and excited. 'Where we takin' her?' he asked.

'There's a cabin and a shed up in the woods beyond Bennett's Gorge.'

'The county place?'

'Where they keep the road equipment. Sometimes the men stay over. There's a good road up to it but it's way off Route 18, nobody can see it. There's no more work until spring. It'll be abandoned now.'

Grandfather Racket nodded.

'I know the place,' he said, 'I know it. And I heard the same thing, no roadwork or nothin' 'til at least March or April. I think you got an idea, Raymond.'

'We'll need food and blankets. There's logs already there. A few other supplies. I'll meet you in the truck.'

'Put in the ladder, Raymond. We got to get up to her dang room some way.'

'I'll need your help, we have to take the big one. And the flashlight. I couldn't find it.'

'Under the seat.'

Raymond nodded.

'What do we do with her after that?' asked Grandfather Racket.

'We'll see,' replied the young man.

'Well, then. I'll pack up some things,' said the old man.

Hazel and Raymond stared at each other. He turned and walked out of the door.

He took the flashlight and a burlap sack from under the seat of the truck and stepped carefully off the dirt road into the flower bed, tiptoeing through the petunias. He shone the light across the ground, then knelt, and began digging with his hands. He retrieved three bottles of whiskey from the soil and stuffed them into the bag. Returning to the truck, he hid the bag under the seat behind a bundle of rags and put the flashlight on the dashboard.

Inside, Hazel followed Grandfather Racket into the kitchen.

'You better go home, Hazel,' said the old man. 'This is no place for you to be right now.'

Without answering, Hazel took paper bags from a cupboard, stuck her hand inside one after another and whacked them open. Then she began methodically packing them. Grandfather Racket watched, hypnotised. Suddenly he grabbed a bag himself and stuffed it with cans, jars, bread, eggs, slabs of ham and bacon.

'How much you figure we need?' he asked breathlessly.

'Take everything you can,' replied Hazel.

'Hazel,' said Grandfather Racket, 'Avery and Bert and Billy will have to do them animals, you hear me? Leave the rest. Leave the corn.'

'We'll do what's needed.'

'Don't do the heavy work, Hazel. Leave it be. The hell with it.'

'We'll do it, Willard.'

'Hazel, I—'

'I know what you're trying to say, Willard. And you know what I am saying. That's just the way it has always been. Whatever there is, we both do it. I'll go up to her room now and get some books. Paper and crayons. I suppose she'll need clothes.'

Grandfather Racket struggled through the living room and out of the front door with two sacks. Raymond had the bonnet of the pick-up truck lifted and was adding oil.

'There's a few more bags,' said Grandfather Racket. 'Hazel's gettin' stuff from her room.'

Raymond slammed the bonnet and wiped his hands on a greasy cloth hanging from the pocket of his overalls. He re-entered the house and climbed the stairs to Lucy's old room.

Hazel was sitting on the edge of the bed.

'If you show me how,' she said, 'I'll drive you away from the house. It'll take two of you to put up the ladder and get her down. I'll keep the truck going and it'll be quicker getting away. I'm sure I can manage.'

'We'll drop you home on the way to Bennett's Gorge,' said Raymond. 'I can't let you go there.'

The only light was a haze from the bulb in the hall. Lucy's birthday poster emerged and faded in the flickering shadows as Hazel and Raymond moved through the innocence of the room like spirits, collecting toys, books, and clothes. They tied these inside the child's bedspread. They gathered up sheets and blankets.

Hazel paused. 'Raymond, they keep the snowploughs up there. All the emergency equipment. You'll be found if there's a storm. I'm worried.'

'We'll be long gone before that,' he replied.

He walked into the hall and dragged the bundles down the stairs.

As Hazel was about to descend, she turned and stepped one last time across the threshold of Lucy's room before she finally drew back and closed the door.

43

Monday, 25 December, 1944. Christmas Day.

Dear Johnny,

Merry Christmas, son. Today I am not going to *mention* the war or Bastogne or any of it. I have given myself a good talking to and I will not worry any more, there is nothing we can do but pray and keep our confidence up for your sake. Billy and Lizzie are saying that the situation in Belgium is desperate. Well, I *feel* you and Raymond are alive and any other thoughts are of no use to anybody. I sent a parcel way back in November and I hope you got it somehow. Willard and Barbara Jean have had no letters at all from Raymond, I am so worried that he will just sink into himself over there and when I write to him I do my best to keep his spirits up. *Please* tell him to write, Johnny. I know it is not the kind of thing he likes to do but Barbara Jean is very upset. She talks to me now, and she admits to loving Raymond very much, but still Willard will not hear of marriage, he didn't even want Barbara Jean to tell Raymond she was pregnant, he is always worried about someone taking his precious farm away and he is worse now since he had to sell off land even though he is bragging to everyone that thank God he hasn't had to. Barbara Jean told me she has written three or four letters to Raymond which Willard doesn't know about and wants desperately to hear from him, to know he feels the same way about her as she feels about him, and that he is safe. I believe he does care but only he can say it, Johnny. I have never seen her need anything like this in her life – maybe being at home alone with Willard makes her realise she needs a life of her own, but he is not easy to stand up to although I know she tries hard and talks back plenty. But as far as this business with Raymond, for once she is not fighting herself, I believe she truly loves him. The problem is how Raymond feels, and how to deal with Willard. She said if necessary she'll find a way she and Raymond can get a place of their own. But I'm not sure. I think it would just about kill her to give up that farm, although she never says that. Anyway, Johnny, I said a prayer in church last night for a *White Christmas*. I don't know why, and it is the only one of my prayers to be answered these days. Let me tell you what happened. I slept very badly last night after we came home from church. Dad tossed and turned, too, so at four a.m. we just gave up and I said I would make some cocoa, so I took Dad's hand and we padded down to the sitting room in our robes and slippers, and who do we find there by just one candle lit in the room but Barbara Jean. There she was, sitting all by herself, her hands on her tummy which is beginning to show, and despite Raymond being away and all the confusion she is more and more pleased to be having a baby and even talks to it about everyday little things, pats it and so on. Why, Barbara Jean, I said, what are you doing here. You weren't supposed to wake up yet, she laughed, you'll spoil the surprise, don't you know nobody is allowed to see Santa. Even Dad smiled, Barbara Jean can be so clever, and he said, Barbara Jean, if I see Santa this year I must be God. It is the first joke Dad has made in months – wasn't it a good one? Perhaps he is getting back to himself after our beloved Joseph. Then he took Barbara Jean's head in his hands and kissed her face. She looked up at him and I thought she might cry and he said: Merry Christmas, Barbara Jean Racket, and he patted her tummy and said, Merry Christmas to you, too, in there, you're our only hope, the grown-ups have made a mess of the world. Barbara Jean and I sat, we didn't speak, just sat together watching the candle flicker while Dad went for the cocoa. When he came back in carrying the tray, Barbara Jean got up and said, Now Avery, you just sit right there next to your old girlfriend Hazel and I want to show you something amazing. First she put on the outside light, then she slowly opened the drapes and what did we see but the most delicate snowfall, like a lace curtain dancing at the window, innocent flakes playing in the darkness, and do you know what I thought of immediately? – isn't it a miracle how the mind works – I thought of you and Joe and Raymond playing Indians around the campfires at the end of summer when you were boys. Do you remember? The sun would already be going down early, the air was so chilly, and there you were dancing around the fire with those feathers in your hair, the glow of the flames lit and warmed everything, and you would chant Oh Brave Spirit Hawenio Banish The Darkness With This Your Eternal Fire. I never knew if you made that up or if it came from a book. Imagine seeing snowflakes in the middle of winter and remembering summer! A calm feeling came over me, and Dad and Barbara Jean and I watched until dawn. Not a word passed between us, the cocoa was lovely and hot. It was the only peace we have had in years.

Johnny, Johnny, may the Lord give you that peace, too, wherever you are.

44

Wake up please, monsieur. *It is four o'clock. We must talk before daylight.*

I'm awake, Miss Marais.

Did you and your friends sleep?

No.

You must try to sleep, you cannot think without sleep.

Where are we going today, Raymond?

I don't know yet, Johnny. Can you move your feet?

A little. Boy! It's good to feel warm! I think I'll stop drinking red wine, though – no offence, Miss Marais.

Dom?

I'm all right, Raymond.

All of you must be extremely careful. There is fresh snow on the ground this morning. Your socks and your boots are dry now but you must take special care with the hands and feet. The temperature is very cold.

Marie-Claire! Est-ce qu'ils voudraient du café?

Would you like to drink some coffee?

Coffee? Coffee?

We have it for special occasions. You may come downstairs for the coffee. My father will prepare it for you. Put back on your sweaters. You may keep them. No loud sounds please, and no lights. I will light this candle only.

Thank you.

You will need the sweaters. You were not carrying much.

We left our packs behind yesterday. We couldn't carry them any more.

And the heavy coats? The American soldiers have long heavy coats.

We couldn't run in them so we just kept the jackets.

Your friends do not say much.

They're tired. I'm sorry if we've been any trouble.

You are no trouble. I notice that your jacket is quite, how do you say, quite full compared to the others?

Yes, well, I suppose so.

It is a special one?

You should see what he's carrying in it, Miss Marais! Special is right!

Johnny—

No, really, go ahead, Raymond, show her! He's carrying around a general store in there. Isn't he, Dom?

Open it up, Raymond. She won't believe it. We could all use a laugh.

Mon Dieu! *What is this? More ammunition, food, bandages, pockets and more pockets! What is in all these pockets? You are amazing. I never saw even a woman to sew this way.*

If you think this is good, Miss Marais, you should have seen our raft! Saved our lives twice in the last three days, didn't it, guys?

Raft? What is raft?

Us city folk wouldn't understand, Miss Marais. It's something Raymond and Johnny learned on the farm.

Darn right!

So, Monsieur Raymond: you are prepared. This I can see.

Yes, I guess I am.

That is good. We do not know what the future holds.

Marie-Claire! Le café est prêt.

Come. I will descend the stairs first. Follow me. We will discuss the plans while we eat.

Bonjour, bonjour.

Bonjour, *Mr Marais. Hey, I'm learning French, you guys! Wait til Mom hears me spouting off this stuff.*

Come by the fire, please.

Coffee. I can't believe it.

Here is bread and cheese also.

I've never tasted anything like it, Miss Marais. And I thought we made good coffee in Brooklyn.

Be quiet please.

What is it? What do you hear?

Shelling. Gunfire. Listen.

Where is it coming from?

They are advancing on St Vith, also Bastogne. I got information in the night.

What is the date today, Miss Marais?

The 20th, Monsieur. *I am told in the night that the remainder of your division has been completely isolated and surrounded on the Schnee Eifel. There is no hope for you to return. They will all be taken prisoner or killed, or both. Vielselm has fallen, Schonberg has fallen. St Vith will fall soon, in the next few days, and I am sorry to tell you that unarmed American prisoners have been executed in Malmedy. Meyerode is completely surrounded, occupied. Soon they will take over this house, they already have seized many. We will be lucky now to get you out alive. We must move quickly and you must listen carefully.*

What do you suggest?

Behind this house is a very dense woods. Not the forest you came through from the Schnee Eifel, but another, which has many paths crossing through it, very large and away from the direction now to be taken by the German army. Do you understand?

Yes, yes. Go on.

You can hear that the shelling is now moving away from us, n'est-ce pas? *Therefore my father and I think you and your friends can remain in these woods – he has been there himself for logs and to cut Christmas trees for the Germans. There are no patrols going there now. Anyway, it would be difficult for them to find you in these woods if you go far in.*

Miss Marais, I appreciate your help, but we won't have enough to eat. The food I have in my jacket will run out in just a few days. Is there no way we can stay here, or at least come back at night?

No, absolutely not, it is impossible, I am sorry. Within days, perhaps hours, our house will be occupied by Germans, I have no doubt of this. Let me tell you the plan: my father will every two days leave you a parcel of food in a designated place. If he can. When he comes to cut logs, he will bury this parcel. I will write to you of news in the war. If my father cannot get away, or if a German soldier accompanies him, there will be no parcel and you must do your best. It is safe now but you must be ready for any change. I cannot promise. You must make no fires, you must never show yourselves in the daylight. If you dig deeply in and line the sides of the hole I think you will not freeze – my father will give you canvas for this purpose – but do not make the hole too large, you must remain close together for the warmth. At night you must come out and move around cautiously, always listening, but move your limbs for circulation. Am I clear?

Yes.

How long will we be in hiding, Miss Marais? What do you think? I know you can't really say, but—

Monsieur Dominick, I think you must be prepared for at least one month, at least. In one month's time we will know if the Germans have reached Antwerp. If Bastogne falls, it will be very bad for all of us. I will inform you. If the Germans succeed, and if my father and I are still alive, we will contact you and make a new plan. If the weather breaks, the Allies will come with planes and the Germans will have great difficulty. So my answer is: if, if, if. That is all I can say to you. And now we must prepare to go. My father will accompany you.

Where is he now?

He is getting your food. It was made for you in the night. He will come to you in two days. You will agree on a place to collect the parcels. He will bring them in the morning, you will collect only at night. Now you must put on all your clothes and equipment and follow my father. When he leaves you, you must go much further into the forest and dig in before daylight. I see that you each have a pistol as well as an M-1. That is good. Monsieur Raymond, you will kindly stay back with me for one moment, your friends will go out the back way to meet my father and wait for you. Thank you.

What's this, Miss Marais?

This packet contains three capsules of cyanide, Monsieur Raymond. I will not describe to you your fate if you are captured. I have seen events in Meyerode. And if you and your friends succeed in killing more Germans but are yourselves wounded, I am afraid there will be no help for you in such a circumstance, no hope of survival, and I would beg you please to spare yourselves the pain of a slow death.

I don't want to take this, I can't take this.

The other problem is your two friends. I examined their feet and they are very swollen this morning, they have the oedema, which I do not like to see, and the limbs are still cold despite the hot water. Do you follow me?

No, what do you mean?

And you saw the violet colour?

Yes, but we all fell, we were running, those are bruises.

No, I am afraid not, Monsieur Raymond, this colour and this oedema is frostbite. Very bad frostbite. Profound damage to the tissue.

But you said it was better!

I am sorry. I lied, I did not want them to face it, it is already too much, they must have hope as long as possible. The boy has small dark spots under his skin. These are blood vessels which have ruptured, they are beyond repair. Your friends will not improve under these conditions. It is impossible when they must go again out into the cold. They will develop gangrene.

No! We have plenty of socks now, I will make them move, we will move constantly.

I am telling you how it will be, Monsieur Raymond. I am only trying to prepare you. Please do not let your friends suffer. Your own feet are not so bad, you will have permanent nerve damage, I think, but your other symptoms will improve if help comes soon, but your friends, no. The difference is that you do not yet have the oedema or the violaceous colour.

Miss Marais, I—

My father and I will listen for gunfire from the woods. If we hear any fighting, we will try to come when it finishes. If we can, if the way is clear. If we are still here. Or, if you are able, you may leave a message for my father in the place where you find the food to tell us of your condition. We will do our best. I am always saying if. Do you have any questions?

No.

Put these capsules in one of your many pockets, Monsieur Raymond. And if we survive this war, you will return to Meyerode as a seamstress and become a very rich man. I am sorry, there will be no more talking now please. I say good-bye here.

* * *

Wednesday, 10 January, 1945.

Dear Johnny,

Two letters from you! Oh, how I wept! It was as if you had walked in the door. I just know you're alive, son. Now, I do realise (Billy and Lizzie reminded me after they saw the dates) that those letters were written before the battle, but still there is no doubt in my mind that you are alive, that you and Raymond have survived. You must know by now what Billy and Lizzie have told us: that Bastogne has been saved, the Germans have retreated again, and there is no hope of their winning now, what with the Russians coming in from the east – our army will meet them and end the war. But the Germans came so close, Johnny. Nobody high up had any idea. Willard said, Those Krauts were two steps away from taking over Albany, you know how he is, and he hates Billy when he laughs at these things. We believe you and Raymond are together since both of you are unaccounted for and we know Raymond would look after you if there was trouble, we all agree about this. The way you describe things I even wonder if you were at the scene of the battle, it all sounds so calm and easy-going. Billy and Lizzie have checked and double-checked, and they say yes, you were right there, both of you, it's just that your letters were written before the attack and of course the attack was a complete surprise so you wouldn't have been worried when you wrote the letters. I phoned the authorities again to tell them about the letters, but they too said they were written before the attack, when I gave them the dates, and no definite information has come through on you and Raymond. I told Billy and Lizzie if you and Raymond were dead, they would probably know that, a lot of names of dead are available. Now we just pray for a letter dated after 16 December. If there is one, it should come soon. I wait up at the road by the mailbox every morning starting at eight. I know that sounds ridiculous, but sometimes Homer does come early, it all depends.

I've got a cold. I am out of bed only a few minutes and then I am too weak to stand, I get so dizzy. Mildred comes to cook for Billy and Lizzie even though they hardly touch a thing. I'll go and lie down now. Thank you for those letters, Johnny. They really brought us a ray of hope.

45

Raymond opened the door and jumped down from the driver's side of the Ford pick-up, four a.m., Sunday, 11 September. Hazel slid over to take his place behind the wheel.

'You'll be able to see us,' he said. 'Watch the flashlight. When we've got her down on the lawn, put the clutch all the way in, shift straight up into first the way I showed you, and turn on the engine. Hold it there until we're in.'

He walked quickly around to the other side of the cab and opened the door for Grandfather Racket. The old man put a finger to his lips. Sitting with his legs dangling outside, he scrutinised the Racket Funeral Home.

He jerked his finger at a large window upstairs on the right side of the house.

'It'll be that one right there,' he said.

'Are you sure?' said Raymond.

'Yep. Give me a hand, Raymond, these dang-blasted legs is givin' out again.'

Raymond put one hand on the old man's shoulder and held his arm with the other as he pulled him up.

'Hurry,' said Raymond.

The two men moved quickly to the back of the truck. Raymond jumped up and lifted the far end of a long wooden ladder which was lying the length of the flatbed.

'Get the other end,' he whispered. 'Onto your shoulder.'

Grandfather Racket winced and his legs buckled as his body took the weight of ladder. With his back to Raymond he raised his free arm and signalled.

Holding up his end of the ladder Raymond took a short bottle of whiskey from his back pocket and gulped it hungrily. During the week he had kept to a regime of alternating one day on small amounts of alcohol with one day off it altogether. Each moment was fraught with a tense, wilful determination, but he had managed to avoid convulsions and the DTs. Now, however, the vice was tightening. He panicked at the thought that the three bottles he had hidden under the seat might not be enough.

'Raymond!' whispered Grandfather Racket. 'Move!'

'I'm getting a grip.'

Grandfather Racket walked gingerly, one step at a time, as Raymond worked his way to the edge of the truck and jumped down. The ladder, held above his head, slammed on to his skull with a force that resonated through his jaw.

Grandfather Racket craned his neck but could not turn enough to see Raymond.

'You okay?'

'Go!' said Raymond.

The two men walked steadily to the house. When they were under Lucy's window, Raymond motioned for Grandfather Racket to rest his end of the ladder on the grass. The old man produced a flashlight which he shone onto the window as Raymond manoeuvred the ladder into place. Then he followed Raymond with the light as he ascended.

The window was locked. Raymond took a long screwdriver from his pocket, inserted it under the bottom half of the window, and pushed down on the handle. He repeated this effort around the sides of the window, and again, using full force, at the bottom. The screwdriver snapped, wedged underneath the frame of the window, leaving Raymond with the handle.

'Hurry up!' called Grandfather Racket in a coarse whisper.

Raymond tapped the window with the handle. He opened his hand and pressed the pane of glass with his fingers. Then he turned slightly and in the beam from Grandfather Racket's flashlight held up the handle of the screwdriver for the old man to see. Grandfather Racket stamped his foot and shook his fist at Raymond.

Raymond turned back to the window and with a powerful flick of his wrist put the handle of the screwdriver through the glass with a loud pop. He waited in complete stillness until the crash ended. He did not look down at Grandfather Racket who was frantically bobbing the flashlight around the neighbourhood for signs that anyone had heard the noise. Raymond was left in darkness. He gestured aggressively at the window without turning around and in a moment the band of light returned.

He reached up through the hole and undid the catch on the inside of the window. Then he slowly and silently pushed it up at the sash and, one leg at a time, climbed on to the cushioned window seat which was strewn with shards of glass.

Now he was guided by Lucy's nightlight. The door of the room was already closed, so Raymond tiptoed straight to the bed where Lucy lay curled and sleeping deeply. He pulled the covers aside, placed his arms underneath the child, and rolled her up against his chest as if he had scooped her into a basket.

He backed out of the window with his left foot, which slipped as it searched for the top rung of the ladder. Grandfather Racket trained the light straight at Raymond and Lucy without wavering.

Raymond pressed Lucy against his body with one arm as he found the rung and got his balance, and held her this way, his other hand gripping the ladder, until he reached the ground.

He heard Hazel start the truck. Grandfather Racket stumbled ahead, opened the passenger door, and got in. Raymond followed.

'Let up slowly on the clutch as you accelerate,' he said to Hazel.

The woman sat rigid in the seat, clutching the steering wheel and staring blankly ahead at the deserted street. All of a sudden the rickety vehicle chugged and lurched forward, making its way in fits and starts out of Little Hoosick.

The ladder stood eerily abandoned in the faint glow of the streetlights as a cool breeze blew through Lucy's empty room.

* * *

Friday, 12 January, 1945.

Dear Johnny,

Only two days have passed since your letters which brought such high hopes and now just as quickly the hope is dashed. I am writing because suddenly there is so little to hold on to – perhaps a letter will make you come back, a letter is always to *someone* who is *somewhere*. And this is because we got official word today that you and Raymond are listed as 'Missing In Action'. The nice Army man I often speak with said it is too soon to presume either of you is dead, he told me that many of the missing in the Ardennes are just separated from their units, a lot of the boys escaped into the small villages and forests after the fighting broke out – apparently it was not very coordinated, nobody in one part knew what was going on in another part, and I don't understand this at all, I thought everybody got training. He explained it would be difficult to keep track of everything and it was just the usual procedure after a certain length of time to refer to someone as missing. We think the two of you are hiding out somewhere and if so this is very good because the Germans have abandoned the Ardennes, we have officially won the battle! I am very concerned about the weather. The man told me it is very, very bad but said that all our men are very fit and well-trained and well-equipped for any conditions. He thought you would probably have extra food and clothes.

I will hold this letter for you.

46

The Albany-Rennsalaer Road Maintenance Department kept three depots throughout the county for supplies and equipment. Like the others, the one in Bennett's Gorge was the gathering place for that region's work crews.

Each morning at eight a.m. from April to September, the foreman reviewed with his men the status of county timetables for maintenance and repair, or for the building of new roads. The depot at Bennett's Gorge housed two bulldozers, two diggers, two Ford pick-ups, one large, heavy truck for hauling rocks and trees, and three snow-ploughs.

Detailed surveyors' maps lined one wall of the small cabin, stuck into the roughly planed oak with rusted thumbtacks. The maps were starred and dated at key points with red ink, and underneath each map was a handwritten list of jobs in order of priority. Smaller equipment and supplies were stored in a shed to the left of the cabin. The large machinery and trucks stood outdoors, covered with tarpaulins.

The cabin consisted of one room. There were two long pine tables, a dozen chairs, and six folding canvas cots with thin pillows. Because Road Maintenance was responsible for emergency storm damage, and for ploughing and sanding roads in winter, crews often worked late at night far from home. In severe conditions they might be required to stay at the depot for several days.

The only heat in the cabin came from a mammoth square stove. This burned logs which were fed into it through a heavy door on the front of the stove. To poke the logs and adjust the location of the flames for cooking, four circular discs on top could be levered up with a detachable steel handle.

Pots and pans hung from hooks on a metal bar attached to the wall beside the stove, above a large wooden box which held the logs. On the other side of the stove was a warped bookcase. Its shelves held a scattering of knives, forks, spoons, metal plates and cups, a coffee pot, sugar, salt and matches. Three kerosene lanterns, the cabin's only source of light, were lined up on the bottom shelf of the bookcase beside a tin fuel can.

Water came from the upper end of Grandfather Racket's stream which ran through the woods surrounding the clearing, about half a mile away.

The outside of the rustic building was made of unfinished oak logs with their tough, corrugated bark. The logs were stacked on top of each other and fitted together at the corners in a series of intricate grooves. The spaces between the logs had been filled with a crude mixture of cement, sand and gravel. The door to the cabin was made of stained pine planks; there were two small windows on either side.

In the early hours of 11 September, the sun began to rise slowly on Bennett's Gorge. A delicate mist hung in the trees and over the cabin. The road equipment, draped with heavy, water-logged tarpaulins, resembled a muster of stolid prehistoric beasts sunk beneath the weight of their own hides.

Grandfather Racket's truck, skewed and abandoned too close to the small dwelling, had been cleaned out, and the back panel of the pick-up left hanging down. During the night, in the intermittent breezes which rolled through the forest and into the clearing where the cabin stood, this panel swung carelessly on its hinges, banging against the back fenders of the truck.

As the Indian summer sun dispersed the dewy shroud spread across the clearing, it revealed the pine door, standing ajar and splintered at its handle. A crowbar was discarded at the threshold.

Inside, on one of the pine tables, lay an empty bottle of whiskey which, to Raymond's astonishment, Grandfather Racket had produced on the drive to Bennett's Gorge. Holding Lucy on his lap, Raymond had drunk nearly half after Hazel was dropped off in Halfmoon.

Bags and bundles, hastily thrown down in the scant light of Grandfather Racket's torch, littered the floor and tables.

On one of the cots, the old man dozed restlessly underneath a pink blanket, wracked by snores and coughing.

On another cot, close to the cold stove, Raymond slept on his left side. With his right arm, in the cul-de-sac of his curled body, he gripped Lucy. Their blanket had slipped onto the floor.

The journey had not roused the child from a drugged sleep, and, without awareness, she tucked herself against Raymond's chest.

47

Contradictions in weather were not unusual in Albany-Rennsalaer during Indian summer.

The synergy of bold autumn light and daring, uncompromising colour often yielded an invigorating warmth: a clarity and optimism beyond the reach of July's lethargic heat.

At the same time, in late September or early October, blank Arctic skies might begin to travel south: through Canada, across Lake Ontario, and thence into New York State.

The body of air carried along this path was always below atmospheric pressure, and was therefore known as a 'depression'. It was frequently accompanied by rain.

If this cold air mass reached Albany-Rennsalaer during a spell of autumn warmth, the resulting clash of temperatures would create a condition known to weathermen as 'an occluded front': the cold front of the depression would overtake and block out the opposing warm front. Sharp rain, high winds, and gusting snow would follow.

Farmers in Niskayuna, Cohoes, and Halfmoon referred to this battle of climates as 'The French are coming', because the French had timed their ultimate destruction of the Caughnawaga settlement in Halfmoon in 1669 to coincide with the probable occurrence of an occluded front in the region. They caught the Mohawks – women, children, braves and animals – completely by surprise. Penetrating a dense camouflage of rain and sleet, they came upon the Indian families worshipping, celebrating and storing a fine autumn harvest, and attacked without mercy.

On 20 September, Raymond was splitting logs in front of the Bennett's Gorge depot when he saw the first signs – the sky clouding over, unaggressively at first, like a sheet being pulled across the deceased or the eyelids being smoothed shut; the sudden bite in the air; the encroaching darkness.

Raymond released the axe from his shoulder. He rested its head on the ground and held the top of the handle. He looked at the sky, he heard the limbs of the pine trees creak. The gathering wind passed through the trees like an owl. Blond and ruddy leaves trembled. He was wearing only a tee shirt and overalls, and the skin on his arms began to shiver. His skull ached, his heart was racing. He rubbed his chest. He had drunk the last of his whiskey two days ago in a binge: he had not, after all, been able to pace himself, and now, as the critical third day without alcohol loomed, his body was beginning to sound the ominous notes of withdrawal.

Grandfather Racket emerged from the cabin. He propped himself against the doorway like a gnarled stick. He took one step forward, still holding on. He coughed and doubled over. Then he raised himself to survey the sky and take in the movement of the trees.

'Raymond!' he croaked, pointing up.

Raymond nodded.

By now he was rigid from the cold, and yet beads of sweat kept springing from his forehead. His muscles wobbled. He quickly gathered up the logs, his arms like a forklift, and stumbled past Grandfather Racket into the cabin. He dropped the logs and did not lay the fire. He walked in circles massaging his head.

The old man twisted himself, not releasing his tenuous

hold on the door, and re-entered the cabin just as the storm began.

A few moments later, hail slammed at the cabin with the crack of gunfire. Raymond collapsed in a corner, holding his face. Grandfather Racket, burning with fever, huddled under his pink blanket.

As the winds and rain grew to full force, and snow squalls closed in, emergency crews had begun to arrive at Road Maintenance Headquarters in Defreetsville for their deployment to local depots.

The only sight in the cabin visible from outside was the face of a child pressed against a rain-streaked window.

48

Did you kill them, Raymond?

Yes, yes, they're all dead, I think, they're all down, Johnny, I – Oh, God, they're dead, they—

I'm very cold, Raymond, the ground is so wet. I'm just getting colder and colder.

I'm coming to you now, Johnny, stay right there, I'm trying to get over to you, this one is on top of me, I – I don't know – he – oh, oh, he's dead, right on me, oh Jesus God—

I can't get my breath, I'm short of air, I think I'm hit. I have a pain, Raymond, I have a terrible pain in my stomach.

You'll be all right, you'll be all right, now, I'm coming, I'm coming.

Raymond, is that my blood? Do you see that? Raymond? Where are you? Raymond? Hurry. My blood. My blood is coming out, it's all coming out of me on the snow!

No, Johnny! It isn't. I'm here now. I – it's so hard to move, there, you're all right, I've got you now, Johnny. Oh, God. Oh, God, no.

Am I going to die? Make it stop, Raymond. Make it stop, I don't want to die. Mama! Mama!

You're all right. I'm here, Johnny. Wake up. Wake up! Don't sleep, you can't sleep, we've got to move, we'll freeze.

Am I dying, Raymond? Oh, Raymond, I—

No. No. Stay awake, Johnny! It's not a bad wound, it's not bad, we'll do something.

It hurts, Raymond, it just keeps hurting so much. There isn't any air in here, open the door.

Lie back on my arm, Johnny, lie back. No. Don't try to get up. You'll be all right.

I need something for my stomach, I have a stomach ache.

Raymond? Johnny? I – are you hit? Are you hit?

Dom! Where are you? Are you there, are you all right?

Yes, I'm here, I'm down – my legs, I can't tell.

Dom, come here, he's hurt, Johnny's hurt. Wake up, Johnny. Don't sleep.

I'll crawl over to you, I'm trying, there's something wrong with my legs, they just won't—

Oh, Dom, he's out again. He – the snow, the snow is all blood.

Johnny? Johnny? It's Dom! Can you hear me? Wake up.

Oh, yes, I hear you, Dad. We've got to dig in for the night in case the Krauts come.

Okay, Johnny, okay, that's it, let me look at you. Just lift him up a little, Raymond. Let Raymond turn you, Johnny, that's it.

No, no. I can't turn. I'm too cold. Don't make me turn.

Raymond, I – I can't look. Look at him, it's impossible, it's – oh, God.

What are you saying? What's he saying, Raymond? What happened to me?

It's all right, Johnny! Just stay quiet now, he's not saying anything, it's not bad, it's not bad, he's not saying anything.

What is it, Raymond? What? It's so cold in here. Put a blanket on me. It's on the chair by the fire. Tell Mama to bring it. Close the door.

Okay, Johnny, okay, lie back now.

I didn't aim good, Raymond.

You were fine, Johnny. They're all dead. You killed them. You did it.

I'm scared, Raymond, I'm shaking, I can't stop shaking, I need that blanket.

It's all right, Johnny, it's over, they're dead, you're—

They hit you on the head, Raymond, there's blood on your head. Your shoulder. I saw them coming for you. I tried to stop them, I just couldn't, they stabbed you. I'm sorry, I'm sorry.

No, Johnny, no. I'm fine. They ran out of ammo, we didn't, we had plenty. They're dead, they're all dead. I'm all right, it's just a bump, that's all, nothing.

Raymond, hold him up again, prop him up, he's got to sit up, he's got to breathe. Raymond? Did you hear me? Are you all right?

My head. I – I feel dizzy.

I'll take him, you're tired. Here – I – I'll slide over, pass him to me.

No! Don't touch him, you bastard. Get away from him. He's all right. Johnny? Johnny!

Do you think Miss Marais heard the shots? Maybe she'll come.

They'll come. Johnny. They're coming, they'll be here soon and we'll get you to a hospital. Isn't that right, Dom? We'll get him to a hospital.

What if Miss Marais is dead, Raymond? Maybe she and her father are both dead. Oh, God, what if they're dead. I can't feel my legs, Raymond, I need a doctor, I'm bleeding. Do you hear me? My legs are all black.

Stop it, Dom. Stop it! I told you, they're coming. Johnny! Wake up. Listen to what I tell you.

Stop the pain, Raymond.

I will, Johnny, I will. Miss Marais and her father are on their way. I think he'll be all right, Dom, I think they'll be here soon.

Raymond, he won't make it, he's bad, he – look at him.

Shut up! What are you saying? Who do you think you are? Johnny? Johnny! I'm right here.

Hello, oh, it's you, Raymond. When did you get here? I think we should go in now, Mama doesn't like me to get cold, I might get sick.

Raymond, oh God, I'm sorry, I'm sorry.

No, Dom! No! I won't have you saying these things. We've got to stay alert, we've got to listen for Miss Marais.

The pain, Raymond, it's all over me, make it go away, why aren't you helping me, I told you.

Oh, Jesus, Raymond, look at the snow, look at it, blood all over you, the snow is all red, Raymond, put him out of it, I can't watch, I can't listen to him any more. Stop him screaming, Raymond, for God's sake, I can't stand it.

Johnny, Johnny, Johnny, take it easy, calm down, Dom doesn't know what he's saying, you'll be all right, that's it.

But it hurts, Raymond, why does it hurt so much? I've got to go in, I want you to take me in by the fire.

You've got to do it, Raymond, do you want me to do it? There's no hope, we're all going to die, oh, Jesus, we're all going to die. No one is coming. The screams. Stop him, Raymond, I can't hear any more, please. Miss Marais doesn't know what happened, maybe they've been shot. I'll take him, Raymond, I'll do it, give me the stuff, I know she gave you something, don't lie, they all have it – I – where is it? Tell me. Which pocket? Give it to me, give it to me. You'll be all right, Johnny, we have some medicine for you.

Get away from me, get your hands off me. Don't touch him. Did I tell you you could touch him? I'll do it myself. I'll *do it.* I'll *decide.*

Raymond, I'm cold. I'm cold. I already told you. Take me inside. Mama is waiting!

Don't move, Johnny. I – I – I'm getting something for you now, the pain, I just have to get it—

Give it to him, Raymond. Go to God, Johnny, go, you won't suffer any more, you've got to do it, Raymond, it's not our fault, he won't make it, put him out of his misery, you're a good boy, Johnny, Hail Mary full of grace pray for us sinners now and at the hour of our death Hail Mary full of grace pray for us sinners now and at the hour—

There! Are you satisfied now, Dom? Are you happy? Is that

what you wanted? Look at him. Oh, Johnny, just look at Johnny now, look what you made me do.

No! I didn't want it, I didn't want it – I just thought—

Johnny, Johnny. Don't worry now. It's all your fault, Dom. He was going to make it. He was going to be fine and now look what you've done. You made me do it and now they'll come. Hazel. Hazel.

You had to. You had to do it, Raymond, there was nothing else to do. I didn't do it. It wasn't my fault. He was going to hold on and suffer, that's what was going to happen.

Now Miss Marais will come and she would have taken him to a hospital. He could have waited.

No, Raymond, no, he couldn't make it, it was impossible.

Johnny.

I'm sorry, Raymond, you had to, he wanted you to.

Nobody came in time, they didn't come in time, that's what happened, they just didn't come, and now this.

49

The drab Army car wound its way through Halfmoon on newly-ploughed back roads under an ashen sky, 18 February, 1945.

As it passed the Butlers', Mildred held the living room curtain to one side, watched the vehicle until it was out of sight, and released the drape. Even after she had buttoned her coat and left the house to meet Sadie, the fabric continued to sway back and forth behind the window like the pendulum of a clock.

Sadie, too, had seen the official drive by. She was already waiting in her car. The two women made the short drive down the hill in silence.

They pulled up in front of the Martins' just as the young sergeant adjusted his cap and began to walk wearily up the path to the house.

50

The six men dispatched to the Bennett's Gorge Depot in the early hours of 21 September had to walk up the long road to the hidden cabin. Nine inches of snow had fallen in four hours, and the dilapidated school bus ferrying work crews to each location was unable to negotiate the hill.

With extraordinary speed and density, snow continued to fall in endless reams, covering and yet clarifying the lines and contours of the landscape. In the vehicle's headlights, one patch of streaming flakes danced like an apparition, teasing and throwing back the yellow rays.

The workmen disembarked from the bus holding torches and long-handled shovels. Four of the crew would provide two two-man teams for the snowploughs. The remaining pair, in a large truck, would clear fallen trees and branches from roads and power lines.

Within moments, the visors of the men's lined canvas hats were each piled with a square of fluffy snow resembling white cake. The flaps covering their ears soon stiffened and froze. The school bus rumbled away and faded to an echo.

The workmen punched their thick gloves onto their hands, tightened the clips on their rubber boots, and began to trudge forward. They could see no more than twelve inches ahead. They followed the convoluted road by painstaking discovery of the edges with the tapered ends of the shovels.

Within an hour, a bleak dawn was struggling to enter the unrelenting snow, and the men calculated that the depot must be a quarter of a mile farther on. They turned off the torches as their eyes grew accustomed to the eerie pallor of the morning. Their bulky tan leggings and matching jackets were soaked through and rigid from the melted, freezing snow. They approached the final turn in the road. Five hundred yards beyond this point, the cabin would be visible.

As they began to round the bend, still out of sight of the depot, they were startled by a roar in the distance. They tried to look past the snow; they stopped and listened carefully. The sound seemed to be coming nearer. Then they realised it was the urgent speeding of an engine.

In a flash, a worn and rusty Ford pick-up truck appeared out of nowhere, racing, sliding, careering, smashing through powdery hurdles of snow, in the direction of the stunned workmen.

The driver seemed startled, too, at the sight of anyone else on the tortuous path. He braked suddenly, spun, braked again, and swerved abruptly. The truck shot off the road, twisted over onto its side, and crashed against a tree.

The workmen shuffled ahead as fast as they could, shouting and waving their shovels in the air.

Suddenly the free door of the overturned truck opened into the air and a lanky young man wearing a tee shirt and overalls struggled out. He jumped swiftly to the ground, rolled, crouched, got up, darted in zig-zags through the trees and back onto the road towards the workmen.

As the truck driver neared the work crew, they realised that he was limping and that his forehead was gashed and bleeding. They moved forward, thrust their shovels in the air, and called out to him. Then, to their horror, they also saw that at the end of his swaying, dancing arm, he was holding a gun which he had levelled at them.

The young man continued to make his way cunningly towards the small group by dashing left and right, falling to the ground and rolling, pumping himself forward on his knees and elbows, ducking and bobbing and faking. The workmen dropped their shovels and ran. Their pursuer shouted commands they could not make out as he kicked bursts of snow from his way and kept coming.

Without warning, the gun went off and one of the crew fell dead onto the snowy road. A second shot wounded another man, who was fired on again and killed. The remaining four, howling at the silent snow, stumbled down the road they had just come up.

The truck driver chased them, and hit a third workman in the back.

The others kept going. When they realised the shooting had stopped, they clutched at each other, and panting and whimpering, turned around.

In the distance, they saw the man fling the empty gun away and disappear on his hands and knees back into the forest.

[illegible] dancing [illegible]
[illegible] which he had developed [illegible]

[illegible]

51

Homer DeWitt slept in his clothes and set his alarm to ring every two hours after eleven p.m., 19 December, 1949. The only way his 1946 Dodge would start the next morning at eight for his mail rounds was by being run at regular intervals all night and into the dawn. By seven o'clock the roads were well-ploughed but snow was still falling and temperatures remained below freezing. At 7:15 Homer left the car idling.

He turned down his kerosene lamp. He pushed aside the curtain of his room at the back of the Cohoes General Store And Post Office and put on the overhead light. His mottled grey mongrel did not stir from a dusty blanket in the corner of the shop. Homer took a packet of coffee from a shelf behind the counter and returned to his room.

He filled the coffee pot with cold water, inserted the thin cylinder with its basket on top, and tapped in a generous helping of coffee. He turned on the hotplate and sat down to clip up his rubber boots. In a few moments, murky liquid began to pop into the pointed glass knob on top of the coffee pot.

Homer went to the sink and splashed water on his face. The coffee began to gurgle rapidly. He dried his eyes, turned off his small electric heater, and watched the liquid in the clear dome turn jet black. He stretched and breathed deeply of the invigorating cold and rich coffee aroma. When he returned from the outhouse, he poured his thick drink into a chipped tea cup and carried it into the shop.

With his free hand he hoisted a fat canvas bag onto the counter. He yanked at a rope which was woven through a series of metal eyelets around the top of the bag as he sipped his coffee. Stencilled in large red letters on the bag was the label 'US MAIL.'

Homer placed his coffee on the far end of the counter. Gripping the bottom of the mail bag with both hands, he whipped it upside down and hundreds of Christmas cards, letters, parcels and magazines poured out.

His practised eyes and fingers darted through the random collection, rapidly skimming one piece of mail off another and on to discrete piles. Homer's arms, and the rest of his body, stood still as he performed this sleight-of-hand in which the mail appeared to move without his help.

In a few moments all the items were at rest in orderly stacks. Homer reached for his cup and contentedly drank the remaining coffee. When he finished, he wound a thin rubber band twice around each packet of mail.

Then he walked to the door and took his jacket and hat from a hook. He slapped his thigh twice and the dog rose instantly, stretched, and waited patiently as Homer removed a pair of gloves from his pocket.

When he opened the door, the bell above it clanged. A sudden gust of windswept snow nearly pulled the handle away from him, and left a scattering of snowflakes inside the shop. Covering his face against the cutting breezes, Homer forced the door of the chugging Dodge to open against the wind, and the dog jumped in.

The animal organised himself in his usual position in the centre of the back seat, where he sat with his head erect and his eyes fixed like beacons on the road ahead.

Homer made several trips between the store and the car

until the stacks of mail were settled in rows beside him on the front seat. He arranged the empty mail bag on the floor of the passenger side. He adjusted the chains on his tyres, slipped behind the steering wheel, and turned on the windscreen wipers. Then he guided the car carefully away from his store and on to Route 18.

His first stop would be the surrounding farms and shops in Cohoes, then Watervliet, Groom, Defreetsville, Niskayuna, and finally Halfmoon.

Visibility was poor. Bustles of snow flounced across the countryside, bumping Homer's car. As he approached each stop on his route, he slowed, slid towards the middle of the seat, and lifted his right leg over the transmission hump on the floor as his left foot glided on to the accelerator. He began to steer deftly with his left knee and the fingers of his left hand, while his right hand, like radar, searched out and unbound the correct packet of mail and rolled down the passenger-side window.

His eyes scanned the side of the road through the white haze for the long metal mail boxes, flat on the bottom with rounded sides and top, like miniature caves standing on poles. If the red flag on the side was tipped up, there would be mail inside for collection, whether or not Homer had a delivery. He would pull down the small arched door of the box at its clip, remove any waiting cards or letters from inside, place these in the mail sack on the floor, and deposit incoming mail in the box.

Today there was mail for nearly every home and, as Homer had expected, nearly every box had its flag up. At this time of year he collected and passed on hundreds of Christmas cards, letters and packages.

At each stop, Homer was able to open the mail box while holding mail to be delivered, lodge and remove mail, push down the flag, and toss outgoing letters into the sack at his feet, all, apparently, in one swift motion of his hand, and without bringing the car to a full stop.

By the time he entered the community of Halfmoon, and had turned on to Route 18a, the mail bag was stuffed.

Now fully behind the steering wheel, he had to slow down on the hill leading up to the Martins', five hundred yards beyond the junction of 18 and 18a. It was nine a.m. The ploughs had swept through the area once, but three inches of new snow had fallen since, and even with chains on its wheels, the Dodge slipped and twisted across the restless surface of the road. Near the crest of the hill, the tyres spun and the car slid backwards, but Homer accelerated suddenly and turned aggressively to the left, jackknifing the car out of the rut and forward.

The countryside swirled in a blur of white wind which dashed and floated over the road like a ghost. Huge tumbleweed gusts rolled into Homer's car with sudden *poofs*, and then just as suddenly rolled away, rocking the chassis of the lumbering vehicle. Homer and the dog remained firmly in place, their critical gaze never straying from the task at hand.

As Homer neared the Martins' farm, he saw their mail box and saw that the red flag was up. Then, suddenly, he was puzzled. He squinted his eyes and stretched forward, his face almost touching the windscreen. The dog did the same, until his head reached across the front seat and he was peering over Homer's shoulder.

In the midst of the blowing snow, a figure sat on a kitchen chair beside the Martins' mail box. This figure was bundled in a large wool hat, coat, gloves and boots. The straight-back chair was stunned by the wind and cold, but the person in it did not stir.

Homer brought the car to a stop beside the mail box, slid over in his seat, and rolled down the passenger window.

'Why, my Lord,' he called through the wind, 'is that you, Hazel?'

Hazel moved to the edge of her chair and stood. She reached into her coat and removed a letter. She held it out to the car and it flapped in the wind.

Homer leaned out of the window.

'Speak up, Hazel,' he called, 'I can't hear you in this howling.'

Hazel stepped closer to the Dodge. Behind her the chair smacked over onto the snow.

The dog sat back in his place immediately and scrutinised Hazel gravely.

She handed her letter to Homer.

He stared at the envelope.

'You want me to mail this, Hazel?' he said gently. 'Is that what you're saying?'

She did not respond. He looked at the envelope again.

'I'd be glad to do that, Hazel,' he said. 'Now go on back in the house, you'll catch your death of cold out here.'

Homer started to roll up his window. 'Please, Hazel,' he said. 'I hate to see you out here like this.'

Hazel moved back to the mail box. She eased the red flag down. Then she righted the frozen chair, pulled her coat tightly around herself, and sat down.

As the Dodge began to roll away, the dog placed his paws on the top of the front seat and supervised Homer as he lodged Hazel's letter among the others in the sack.

Just before he and Homer descended the hill that would take them out of sight of the Martins', the animal turned his head and watched, until the woman on the chair had disappeared behind a burst of snow.

'Why [illegible]' he called through the window [illegible]

Hazel moved to the edge of her seat [illegible] to the car [illegible] in the wind.

Brooke leaned out of the window.

[illegible]

[illegible] the garden.

[illegible]

[illegible]

[illegible]

52

20 December, 1949. 3:00 a.m.

Dear Johnny,

It seems strange, writing to you again after so long. I'm sorry, but I had to give it up. It was when we got word that you were gone and like with Joe we had no money to bring you home. As I am writing this now I seem to be speaking of a time that happened to someone else. And yet if I feel nothing, why do I want to beg your forgiveness for leaving you in Belgium? President Roosevelt died that same year, in April, and I could hardly go on, the grief over this man consumed us all, oh, we understood what had happened to him.

I stopped writing because I couldn't take any more thinking about you. Please don't misunderstand, I don't really mean that the way it sounds, of course I wanted to think about you and I wanted with all my heart to have you back. It's just that I would go days and days accomplishing nothing, failing everyone around me, going over and over what went wrong, the bad decisions I made, how young you were. My mind had become a racing engine that wouldn't stop, there were days I was out of control of my own mind, Johnny. I was unable to meet my responsibilities, and that is not right, that is not my way – I hope you understand. Once in a while I would get a break, I would find myself wondering about the bake sale at church, or the blouse I was sewing for Lizzie, and then suddenly I would say to myself, Hazel, there you go now, you weren't thinking about Johnny! Why, the worst must be over, you'll get on with living now! I can tell you I had to give myself a good talking to many times. But to think this is what I had come to, trying to will my own child out of my life, the nights and mornings I wept. The knowledge that you would never come back to us was like a vice tightening and crushing me. I was ashamed of shedding those tears when I knew that in the end I would have to turn my back on you and get on with what little life we had left. God forgive me.

So I would go along and begin to think I was past you, and then a bit of news would come along and I'd want to tell you – Bert and Sadie's new calf – and I'd sit down again to write, saying oh, I know he's gone, for goodness sake, it's just a letter, it doesn't mean anything, and before long I'd be fighting the truth again, getting nowhere, my mind so mad at the Army, the Germans, the bad weather in Belgium, my own careless, unforgiveable judgement to have let you go when my duty was to protect you. Even now, right this minute I ask myself: Hazel, *what were you thinking*? A child in a war? What was the matter with you? And when my mind goes this way I am right back where I started, I read and re-read your last letters, the early letters, trying to turn back the clock – I even smashed the clock Granddad gave you. What a thing to do, to blame a clock! I'm sorry, Johnny, I know it meant a lot to you. But there it is, I did it, the incessant ticking was a torture, a knife stabbing me, my rational mind could not overcome it. But of course afterwards I was nowhere nearer to accepting things, nowhere nearer my own life. What is my own life? The girls who came back from their war jobs, they would laugh at me, they seem to laugh at everyone now. They wore men's overalls in the factories, did men's jobs, went against everything their Christian upbringing taught them, pretending all the while they cared only for you boys, but we saw the pictures of them in *Life* Magazine, smiling, their hair in a bob. Well, now they're back and they want 'rights', freedom, I don't know what they're talking about. The world is all changed, Johnny, you wouldn't recognise it yourself, and I don't even know what I mean by all the things I try to say to myself. Like: go on living, Hazel. The past is over, you had a certain life before, now that's done and you'll have a different life, you could be happy in a different way. But in my letters, in my mind, I tell you about the *old* life – it's the only one that seems to make sense to me. But certain events have happened and so I have to stop that life, I must do it once and for all and that is why I am writing to you today. So early in the morning and I cannot sleep. I see that it will snow soon, it has been a bitter winter. I must keep to my determination to write this letter. I am sorry to have to tell you what I have become.

A terrible thing has happened. Not just one thing, really, but many. I can't make out where it started.

Babs has died, Johnny. Yes, in August, very suddenly. As I say it I feel you are here: no, Ma! No! But it is true, it cannot be denied. And from there, well, I will say what I can, it must be said.

Howard and Shirley have taken our precious Lucy. You never saw her, did you? No. Probably you never even knew she was coming, poor Raymond was never one to say such things. You would have loved her, Johnny. Why, you were practically her uncle – I just thought of it! I am enclosing a snapshot taken last Christmas – do you see? Babs, Raymond and Willard are with her. I want you to see them all, I want you to see for yourself. Because not one of them is left to us now.

I don't understand how it happened. Howard and Shirley are not evil people, I suppose it is the whole situation that accounts for what I am saying. Willard and Raymond tried to keep Lucy, the details aren't important, they run together in my mind and blur, but there was no way it would work out and finally one night in September they decided to take her. I was there. What they did was a criminal act, I realise it now, and I went along. It just happened, one small step at a time, and at each step whatever was going on seemed the way it should be, right in its own way – and yet this was a crime, this was kidnapping, but such a word was not what we thought of. Did we even think at all? Do you see what I mean when I say that nothing makes sense any more, Johnny?

They took her to the Bennett's Gorge depot. You'll remember where it is, you used to know the men. I never understood what they planned to do next. I should have asked, I should have made them puzzle it out. But I didn't, I must have taken leave of my mind, and the next morning Howard, Tyler Hughes, the County Sheriff, and the State police arrived here, Howard shouting, where is she, where did they take her, I'll have all of you put in jail, you've given my wife a nervous breakdown, and Tyler kept saying quietly, do not say a word, Howard, do not say another word. They had already been to Willard's and found no one there, the truck gone. Avery and Billy looked straight at them, blank faces, refusing to speak, and finally they just walked past Howard and Tyler and the Sheriff and the State trooper, out of the house and down to the barn. Howard was shouting and shaking after them, you'll see, you won't get away with it, you'll pay, you're all in on it, I'll get you for every crime in the book, with Tyler Hughes trying to calm him. Then something came over me and I just stood with my hands folded in front of my apron, feeling nothing, thinking nothing. I wasn't afraid, I wasn't confident, I was just nothing. After a moment the Sheriff said: Mrs Martin, we have a breaking and entering situation here, followed by a kidnapping. These are very serious crimes and I must advise you to tell us anything you know or I will have to arrest you as an accessory to two felonies. At first I said Willard and Raymond didn't tell me anything, I had no idea they were missing, I was surprised to hear it and so on. Howard yelled, tell the truth, Hazel! Do you hear me! Quit your lying, we all know you're lying! The State trooper put his hand on Howard's shoulder. He spoke quietly to me: Mrs Martin, he said, we are urging you, for your own good, to come forward and help us. Under the Lindbergh Law kidnapping is a capital crime. I do not want to arrest you. Tell us what you know. Then he had to restrain Howard who tried to grab me, he kept shouting and spitting, but I never moved a muscle, I felt nothing. My mind had left me. I ceased to be a person and perhaps never will be one again. All of a sudden, from what place I cannot be sure, I replied to the policeman: Officer, they took her to North Carolina. North Carolina! exclaimed Tyler. Bastards! shouted Howard, we'll track them through every state in the union, I'll kill them! and again the officer stopped him and said to me: Mrs Martin, what time was this? Very late, I said: I don't remember. Don't lie! screamed Howard, and by now he was crying. Where are they, Hazel, he sobbed, just tell me, what did I ever do to you, I tried my best, and he just cried and Tyler and the Sheriff each took one of his arms and the Sheriff said to Howard, Mr Racket, I will call off my men now, there is no need to search the county, and I will send a bulletin through New Jersey, Pennsylvania, and all the southern states. They won't get far, we'll find them, and

Mr Hughes and I will prepare the necessary papers for the indictments. As they turned to go I said: I don't know whether they told me the truth, it's not for me to say. The officer said, I think they told you the truth, Mrs Martin, and you were right to tell us. Good day.

I do not know what possessed me, Johnny. From a dark place inside myself which I have never known, I lied. I have not set foot in church since and when I have finally been able to tell you everything, you will understand why I deserve no forgiveness.

There was a storm about two weeks later, I can't recall exactly when it was, and of course by then it was clear Willard and Raymond were nowhere to be found in Pennsylvania or North Carolina and the police were baffled and Howard was furious, he kept coming to the house, banging on the doors and windows, shouting that I knew where they had taken Lucy, that the law would deal with me. Each time I just sat inside until he went away. When I saw the storm coming I knew Willard and Raymond would be found – it was one of the big ones, I heard the alert on the radio, I heard them say the emergency crews were on their way to the depots, and I just waited.

I don't know what went wrong, Johnny. I have sat and thought for hours, day and night. Maybe I don't understand the world, maybe I've led too simple a life for the way things are these days, or maybe I don't really know the people I think I know. But dear God, Johnny, Raymond *shot* the road maintenance men. He *shot* them. How could he do such a thing? Can *you* explain it?

Lucy and Willard were found in the cabin, they were both ill and had to go to the hospital. Willard was declared unfit to stand trial, he was making no sense at all, and from the hospital he went to a nursing home. Howard and Shirley have put the farm up for sale.

The trial in the County courthouse finished in early November and the jury found Willard and Raymond both guilty of breaking and entering, and kidnapping, and Raymond guilty of three counts of first degree murder. Raymond testified that he had lied to me about North Carolina to protect me, that I had no part in any of it: one lie to cover up another, this is what I am talking about.

I tried to see him two days ago, they agreed to allow me, but when I got to Albany he refused, told them to send me away, and when the guards told me, I pleaded with them, but they said they cannot admit anyone against a prisoner's wishes and that this prisoner has requested no visitors be admitted, so the last time I saw him was when the judge handed down the sentence. The lawyer assigned to Raymond by the court pleaded for mercy and went on and on about mental breakdown and the war, and when he had finally finished, the judge said, sit down, we've heard enough from you for one day, tell your client to rise so I can pass sentence. Raymond stood and there was no sign of life or guilt or sadness or relief or anything, his face was like wax, like a coating of wax had been sealed tight across his face, all the lines and shapes that would have made us say, there is our Raymond, these were all gone. I have never known anyone to look this way – have *no* look to them – and it made me realise how much a person becomes their face, for when this is taken away they can no longer be seen outside themselves. At that moment Raymond was a person I had never met, he did not take in or give out any quiver of existence, in fact it seemed to me he had no eyes.

Yesterday he was put to death in the electric chair.

I will never mention it again, Johnny, this letter is the final time and place.

And now I will tell you what I did last night, after I

knew Raymond was gone, after I had been unable to see him. Then I will leave you in peace – for I know this is a burden to you, because like me, you had no experience of the world. We thought we did and we thought it was all we needed to know. Please hear me out, I am not proud of myself, but I want it said. After Dad and Billy were asleep and I was alone in the living room, I threw all my old letters to you into the fire. I tore them up like an insane person, my hands were shaking with the grief and fury I was in, I had become someone else – it wasn't me and yet I was the only one there, driven by a force beyond my power to stop, tearing those letters and sobbing, throwing feeble bits of paper at a roaring fire, and even then having the memory – shocking myself at what a sweetness suddenly came to me for I have been incapable of the slightest tenderness – the memory of you and Raymond trying to teach me to throw a baseball! I could never get it right! You were so patient with me, so grown-up. And last night as I stood face to face with that fire, I threw with all my might just the way you always said I should – let go and throw with everything you've got, Ma! you used to say – and I felt I was throwing every dream Dad and I ever had into that blaze and I was crying There! There! Take him! Take all of them! Go ahead! I was not in control of my thoughts, Johnny, something carried me away from all reason and common sense, and then I tore open the letters from you, those bright letters from the Front, when everything was fine. You were full of hope and courage and pride! One at a time I ripped them apart in a frenzy, and I screamed *Lies*! *Lies*! and pushed them at the fire, stuffed them deep into the fire, kicked the logs, the sparks flew up like explosions, and at that moment I did not feel the burns on my hands and feet, but now I feel the pain and I am glad of it, the crimson skin is stiff and raw and throbbing, this torment

is the only thing in me that remains alive, the agony of these burns, and if this goes away, I will do it again, and again and again, such a searing wretchedness is what I have become. The shame of it, to have to reveal the darkness I never knew lurked and crept in my soul. But I see now there is no avoiding the mention of things as they are. Where did I go wrong? Can anyone tell me?

This is the place where time and events have brought us.

This is the trail we have left behind.

I am a cold person now, Johnny. I don't mean to be, it's not what I planned, you must be somewhere in my heart, surely a mother cannot forget her own child, surely a living human being cannot turn to stone and ice.

Perhaps someday I will be able to find us both again.

Good-bye.

Acknowledgements

I am grateful to many people for their tireless assistance during the writing of this book. In particular, my thanks go to Renate Ahrens-Kramer, Julie Parsons, Phil MacCarthy, Cecelia McGovern, Sheila Barrett, and Joan O'Neill; to my dear friend Lucinda Franks; to my agent, Anthony Goff of David Higham Associates; to Carole Welch at Sceptre whose insights gave the book its final shape; and to Maureen Lynott for all her support and encouragement over many years.

I want also to express my deepest gratitude to Ailbhe Alvey for her unending generosity and friendship, and to Rita McCarthy without whom this book could not have been written.

And to my daughter Annie, my love and thanks, always and forever, for such a miracle.